THE WOMAN
IN T

Heid insinck

MUSWELL
PRESS

First published by Muswell Press in 2026

Typeset in Bembo by M Rules
Printed by CPI Group (UK) Ltd, Croydon CR0 4YY
A CIP record for this book is available from the British Library

ISBN: 9781068389351
eISBN: 9781068389368

Our authorised representative in the EU for product safety is
Easy Access System Europe, Mustamäe tee 50, 10621 Tallinn, Estonia
gpsr.requests@easproject.com

Muswell Press, London N6 5HQ
www.muswell-press.co.uk

MIX
Paper | Supporting responsible forestry
FSC® C013604
FSC
www.fsc.org

MUSWELL
PRESS

THE WOMAN IN THE WALL

By the same author

Last Train to Helsingør
My Name is Jensen
The Girl in the Photo
Back From the Dead
Out of the Dark

To Helen

May

Day One

1

The flooding had brought Bredgade – an elegant street lined with art galleries, boutiques and rococo mansions – to a virtual standstill.

Detective Inspector Henrik Jungersen had to toot his car horn several times to shift the evacuated office workers who had spilled into the road like confused sheep.

'Bloody idiots,' he muttered as, finally, he was able to pull up behind the patrol cars and fire engine and get out. Despite his grumbling, he was feeling excited, as he always was when embarking on a new murder investigation. He loved his job; it was the only part of his life where he felt in some kind of control.

A dank smell greeted him inside the stairwell, growing stronger as he climbed upwards.

'All yours,' said the incident commander from the fire service on his way down.

Henrik responded with a thumbs-up.

Water sloshed around his feet as he entered the apartment on the fourth floor – a grand affair with high ceilings, cornicing and chequerboard tiles in the hallway.

The décor was understated and chic, punctuated by ironic modern artwork, the sort of home where no children or pets had ever set foot.

Through the window, the giant verdigris-and-gold dome of Copenhagen's Marble Church was majestic in the sunlight, almost shockingly close.

How the rich live, he thought.

Central Copenhagen had become unaffordable for the cops who kept it safe. He and his wife were lucky to have bought their house in leafy Frederiksberg years ago. Even so, they'd been forced to borrow from Louise's dad, a fact the mean old codger never missed an opportunity to remind him of.

In the kitchen, Detective Sergeant Mark Søndergreen was standing in a small lake, chatting to a couple of uniformed officers.

'What happened?' Henrik asked.

'A burst pipe,' said Mark. 'Rusted through. Not uncommon in old buildings, apparently. The water would have built up over weeks inside the walls.'

Water.

It always found a way out.

Like the secrets people tried to bury.

'Where?' he said.

Mark pointed to a walk-in larder, the contents of which had been distributed across the counters. Inside, the back wall had been partially knocked through, plaster and rubble spilling from it like innards from a split belly. 'The guys had to break through to prevent the ceiling of the law firm downstairs from collapsing under the weight of the water. That's when they saw it,' said Mark.

Henrik took his time to put on gloves and a face mask. The cold and wet soaked through his jeans when he got down on his knees.

He shone his torch inside the jagged hole where he could already see a human foot protruding, brown skin stretched taut over bones.

The smell of damp and decay was terrible as he leaned down further, so he could shine his torch upwards inside the cavity.

He had to use all his power not to recoil violently when the light picked out the legs and pelvis of a partially mummified corpse.

He brushed himself down, trying not to let the revulsion show on his face. He thought of Tutankhamun's Tomb, which he'd read about as a boy. According to myth, several people involved with the discovery of the pharaoh burial site had subsequently met an early death.

Would the exposure of the corpse in the wall unleash a similar curse? Were they all going to regret that this had happened?

He shook off the thought, turning to the uniformed officers. 'Go and get the traffic moving again. It's chaos down there.'

As the officers left, radios crackling, he crossed to the open window and pretended to look at the view while taking a few deep breaths.

The weather was glorious. In a few weeks, summer would arrive, weeds would force their way up through the tarmac and the crime rates would soar.

But for now, Copenhagen was looking its best, and people knew instinctively that they had to make the most of it.

Like a brand-new case, spring offered a chance to start afresh, to do better. Given the number of cockups he'd made in his time, it was a chance that was starting to feel undeserved.

'Who lives here?' he asked Mark.

'Guy called Andreas Lund.'

'Has he been contacted?'

'Left a message on his mobile,' said Mark. 'No one has seen him for a few days. It was the staff downstairs who called the emergency services.'

'Do we know how long he's lived here for?'

'Years, they say.' Mark glanced at the sodden rug under his feet. Like everything else in the kitchen, it looked expensive. 'Let's hope he's got insurance,' he said.

That's the least of his worries, thought Henrik.

He turned his attention to the hole in the wall as the cogs in his brain began to turn.

Had the victim been bricked up after death? The alternative seemed positively medieval, but why put the body in the wall at all? Old Copenhagen properties like this one had back stairs leading to a courtyard. It would have been a relatively simple job to carry the body downstairs to a waiting car. At night, when the offices were closed, there would have been no witnesses.

'Jungersen,' said a familiar voice behind him. Pathologist David Goldschmidt had arrived, followed by lead forensic investigator Pia Øster and her colleagues in full protective gear.

'Good to see you,' said Goldschmidt, his handshake firm and warm.

'Likewise,' said Henrik. He meant it. There were several pathologists at Copenhagen's Forensic Institute, but the tall and moustached Goldschmidt was his favourite. 'This is a first,' he said, pointing to the wall. 'To be honest, I'm not sure whether it calls for a medic or an archaeologist.'

Goldschmidt wasted no time dropping to his knees and poking his head inside the cavity. 'Remarkable,' he said, his voice muffled.

'What is it, do you think?'

'Not *it, she.*'

'A girl?'

'A woman.'

'How long has she been in there?'

'Hard to say. The outer wall is thick and whoever did this took care to seal the space, so the remains have mummified to a certain extent. Though they'll deteriorate rapidly with the water damage and change in temperature.' Goldschmidt ducked out, brushing wet brick dust off his white suit.

Henrik envied his ability to look at dead bodies without wanting to gag. 'More than a hundred years?' he said, trying not to breathe through his nose.

'I wouldn't have thought so.'

'But you can run some tests to get it precise, right? Carbon-14 and all that?'

'Not without a significant margin of error.'

Henrik sighed. They wouldn't get anywhere without determining who the woman was.

With a bit of luck, they might find a match in the missing-persons database, but the task would be easier with some sort of time frame.

'I'll need her height, hair colour, approximate age, notable features. How soon can you do the post-mortem?'

Goldschmidt looked confused. 'Is it urgent?'

'Not as such,' said Henrik, 'but you know what the press is like. If we don't give them *something* to chew on, they'll start to make stuff up.'

Jensen never made stuff up. She was the best crime reporter he knew, but she'd just had a baby, so she wouldn't be covering the story for *Dagbladet*.

More was the pity.

He hated to admit it, but she'd been rather helpful on his past few cases. Annoying as hell, but ultimately helpful.

He'd never thought that she would actually go through with her pregnancy – an unintended consequence of her failed relationship with a homicidal nutjob (he had warned her) – but Jensen never did what you expected.

They hadn't been in touch for weeks, primarily because he hadn't been able to think of a good excuse to contact her. He had three kids and a beautiful, clever wife, and had vowed not to let them down again. Incredibly, Louise seemed willing to give their marriage another chance.

He sighed, forcing his thoughts back to the situation at hand.

Tongues would start to wag as soon as the body was carried downstairs on a stretcher. This meant they had to rush out a press release, which would trigger an avalanche of media interest.

The sooner they could answer the most basic questions, the better. Besides, the news coverage might prompt someone with useful information to step forward. 'Could you do it this afternoon?' he said to Goldschmidt.

The pathologist consulted his diary. 'I should be able to fit you in. Come at three?' He turned to Pia Øster. 'We need to be extremely careful when moving the body.'

'We'll demolish more of the wall first,' said Pia, an energetic and competent woman with beady eyes behind gold-rimmed glasses. 'You should examine *in situ* as far as possible.'

Henrik left them to it, knowing that the job was in the best of hands.

Meanwhile, he and Mark took a good look around the apartment. A master bedroom with a walk-in wardrobe. A guest bedroom with a sofa bed, a cross-trainer and three kettlebells in primary colours. An office with a tidy desk and a vast book collection. One toothbrush in the bathroom, one set of toiletries, paracetamol and a small prescription bottle for statins, made out to *Andreas Lund*. Everything swept, tidy and tasteful, verging on the dull.

Had Lund lived here for years, unaware of the macabre secret behind the wall of his larder, inches from his tinned chickpeas and jars of muesli?

Henrik had never known anything more bizarre.

'Stay here and I'll head back and brief the team,' he said to Mark when he'd seen enough.

Mark responded with a sulky nod. Usually loyal and keen (Henrik, who was fond of dogs, used to think of him as a Labrador), he'd complained recently of always being left with the menial tasks.

'That's because you're so good at them,' Henrik had pointed out. To his mind, Mark had done well to make it this far, but his lack of initiative and imagination made further advancement unlikely.

Of late, Mark had been busy training up Maja Olsen, the team's newest recruit, but with his ward now away on holiday, he was getting restless and discontented again.

Henrik was still trying to work out what to do about it.

Outside in the street, the uniforms had managed to wrest back control and get traffic flowing again. The office workers were being led back in to collect laptops and personal possessions before being sent home. No one would be returning for the foreseeable future.

A group of tourists filed past, oblivious to the drama that had unfolded inside the building. They were following a guide holding up a folded red umbrella and speaking English into a microphone headset. Henrik suspected they were passengers from one of the cruise ships that docked regularly at the nearby Langelinie pier.

Wonderful Copenhagen.

This part of town, a stone's throw from Amalienborg, the official residence of King Frederik X and Queen Mary, had a grandeur that reminded him of Paris. He and Louise had spent their honeymoon in the City of Lights, most of it in a creaky hotel bed under the eaves with a view of the Eiffel Tower that had looked a lot closer in the brochure.

They were young and thought they'd found real love. In time they'd built something resembling it: a home, a family, a shared history.

With Jensen it had been real from the start, the thunderbolt you read about in romantic novels. Should he have divorced Louise when he and Jensen had first met in London sixteen years ago?

Perhaps, but Louise had defied her parents to be with him, the rough lad from Brøndby who had joined the police when he could just as easily have ended up on the wrong side of the law. Leaving her for another woman would have been a poor reward for her loyalty. Worst of all, his children, whom he loved more than life itself, would never have been born.

Staying in his marriage had been the right decision.

The other bit – falling out of love with Jensen – was still a work in progress.

As he donned his shades and got into his car, he did his best to push her from his mind.

2

Jensen was on her way home from the supermarket, munching on a ryebread roll with avocado and falafel, when a yellow 'Breaking news' banner lit up her phone screen.

REMAINS OF A WOMAN FOUND BEHIND WALL IN BREDGADE

Her curiosity was like an itch in an amputated limb. She was on maternity leave, but her many years of earning a wage from the news (she'd joined a local paper in the north of Denmark when she was just sixteen) made the headline irresistible.

'Journalism is not a job, it's a state of mind,' her editor at *Dagbladet*, Margrethe Skov, always said.

There was no mention in the article of the woman's age, nor how old the remains were.

> 'We are working on finding out who the woman was and how she died. Meanwhile, I would like to ask anyone with information on this distressing discovery to contact us.'

Seeing Henrik's name after the quote produced an unwelcome flutter in her abdomen.

Would it ever be fully over between them? Maybe if they'd had a chance to be together properly it would have ended years ago.

She wasn't even sure what 'it' was any more, except a fleeting sensation whenever their paths crossed. Her world was her daughter Ea now, and what Jensen felt for her, asleep in a sling on her chest, trumped anything she'd felt before, even for Henrik. It was a different kind of love: unwavering and tender but haunted by a fear of loss so strong it sometimes kept her awake at night.

To everyone's surprise, not least her own, she was turning out to be a decent mother.

Once, in the days before she and Ea had left hospital, the thought of being left in sole charge of a tiny, defenceless human being had made her panic. But a nurse had reassured her: 'Babies are easy – they basically tell you what they need. Ninety-nine per cent of the time, it's one of three things: milk, a clean nappy or comfort.'

So far, it had held true. Though Jensen knew child rearing would eventually get more complicated, she felt ready to take on whatever might come.

Cramming the rest of the sandwich into her mouth (breastfeeding gave her an insatiable appetite), she headed down the gravel path that led to her flat.

She still couldn't believe that this was now her neighbourhood. The three oblong lakes curving gently around the western edge of the city were sapphire-blue and as smooth as mirrors.

The lakes were lined by graceful old apartment blocks, their windows sparkling with reflected sunlight.

Her building was yellow, fronted by a lush garden. She

owned the entire top floor – far more space than she and Ea needed.

Slowly, as if in a dream, she realised that something was happening a little further along on the path in the shade of the tall chestnut trees.

A woman had appeared from around the corner and was running towards her. 'Help! He's after me!'

'Who?' Jensen shouted.

The woman glanced anxiously over her shoulder, and – on seeing the path behind her empty – sank to her knees, clutching her forehead.

Jensen dropped her shopping and ran. When she got closer, she could see blood trickling between the woman's fingers. It was coming from a cut above her left brow; the eye was red and swollen. 'What happened?'

'My boyfriend,' the woman sobbed. 'We were arguing and then he . . . he just hit me. I ran.'

Jensen got her phone out. 'Right, I'm calling the police.'

'No!' cried the woman. 'Don't do that.'

'Why not?'

'He didn't mean it.' The woman had long reddish-brown hair with a blunt fringe, blue eyes and multiple piercings in both ears. Her nails were purple and sparkly, her collarbone tattooed with a string of illegible words. 'Please? If you want to help me, don't do anything,' she pleaded, wiping her nose and smearing blood over her cheek. Her green T-shirt and faded jeans were stained with it.

After a moment's hesitation, Jensen put her phone away and reached into her bag for a tissue. 'Here, keep this pressed to your forehead,' she said. 'My name is Jensen, by the way.'

'And I'm Karo, as in Karoline, but nobody calls me that,' said the woman. She pointed to Ea, sniffling. 'How old is she?'

'Five months. Her name is Ea.'

'I'm expecting a baby too,' said Karo. 'Ten weeks and four days, so not showing yet.' She attempted a smile that morphed into a wince.

Perhaps, with some time to calm down, she could be persuaded to seek help, Jensen thought. 'You can't go home like that. Let me at least lend you some clean clothes and sort out that cut for you.' She pointed to her flat. 'I live just up there. You can wash and change in my bathroom.'

'Are you sure?'

'Of course. Come.'

Karo smiled with her broken face, and it was obvious that, underneath the damage, she was extraordinarily pretty.

'I feel so much better now,' said Karo when she emerged from the bathroom.

The T-shirt and joggers were small on her, exposing an inch of tanned waist and a pierced belly button.

Jensen gave her a bag of frozen peas and instructed her to keep it pressed to her wounded eye. 'Yes, like that,' she said, bouncing Ea on one hip. 'You've had a shock. Sit down for a minute.'

'I'm all right,' said Karo, smiling at Ea and grabbing her little hand. 'Your daughter is adorable.'

'Not at three o'clock in the morning, she isn't.'

Karo laughed. 'Yeah, I'm not looking forward to that bit.'

Ea stared at her, mesmerised. She hadn't seen many adults other than her mother in her short life and found meeting new people exciting.

Karo craned her neck as she looked around the flat. 'This place is so cool, and it really is just the two of you living here?'

'Yes. And Wolfgang, the cat, though he's hiding at the moment. He isn't used to strangers.'

Despite the circumstances, it felt good having Karo there. The past few weeks had been rather lonely, an endless cycle of feeding, nappy changes and exhausted, dreamless sleep. Gustav, her erstwhile apprentice, dropped by as often as he could, but spent much of his time at work, having finally persuaded his aunt, *Dagbladet*'s editor Margrethe Skov, that he wasn't cut out for school. Grudgingly she'd agreed to him temping as video editor until a replacement could be found (the last one had been sacked after being caught making up fake stories).

Jensen's mother, a painter, seldom left her remote cottage in North Jutland, and there were no other relatives, except for the man who insisted that he was her father.

He'd sent her another text message that morning.

Please, Jensen, I need you. Call me back.

It had been three months since he first got in touch: Valde Brix, the fantasy author who was rarely out of the international bestseller list.

She'd known of him all her life. Everyone knew Brix; he was one of Denmark's biggest cultural exports.

'Your mother doesn't want you to know,' he'd told her.

Marion had denied this. 'He's not your father.'

Not knowing who to believe, Jensen had sent a DNA sample to an ancestry website.

Her birth certificate said, 'Father unknown'.

If not Brix, then who?

To her surprise, there was a match with a man called Erik Lange, a possible first cousin or uncle. She'd messaged him to find out more, but as of this morning there'd been no reply.

Brix being her father was not as improbable as it had first seemed. Marion had always surrounded herself with creative people. She was only four years older than Brix, and they'd both grown up in Copenhagen, so their paths could easily have crossed in the late eighties.

'Why would he lie?' she'd asked her mother.

'That's a good question,' Marion had said. 'What does he want from you, and why is he asking for it now?'

Her refusal to discuss or explain had driven a wedge between them. They hadn't spoken in weeks, though Jensen knew that she would have to call eventually.

Her mother sometimes forgot to eat. Her remote, rundown cottage in North Jutland leaked and was infested with mould.

One day, she would be found starved to death by her easel, paint brush in bony hand.

By contrast, Brix had a house in one of the city's most expensive neighbourhoods, known as the Potato Rows, just twenty minutes' walk from Jensen's flat.

He was well off. His books had been translated into more than fifty languages, there'd been several Netflix series and, most recently, the announcement of a movie project with a major Hollywood studio.

His house was as pretty as a picture: three storeys of charmingly soot-stained brick with white casement windows and a white picket fence. In the small front garden an old-fashioned bicycle with a wicker basket leaned against a gnarled apple tree.

She'd walked past several times with Ea in the sling, trying and failing to glean anything personal about the man who lived there.

'And that view is insane!' exclaimed Karo.

She was standing in front of the big picture window with

her arms outstretched. 'You must be rich,' she said. 'Or have some sort of sugar daddy.'

'I wish,' Jensen laughed. 'An old lady used to live here. When she found out that I was having Ea on my own, she changed her will and left the place to me. We were ... friends, though I didn't know her for very long before she died.'

Saying it out loud made her feel guilty again. Was she really a worthy recipient of such outlandish charity when there were plenty of others who had nothing?

'You're so lucky,' said Karo.

Jensen nodded. She *was* lucky. No way would she be able to afford a place like this in central Copenhagen on a journalist's salary.

The contents of the flat had been sold to cover the inheritance tax. Ernst Brøgger, who'd been the old lady's lawyer (and a useful source of information for Jensen during her time in Copenhagen), had dealt with it all. She had donated the leftover cash to a cat charity, the original beneficiary of the will. It seemed only fair.

The flat looked half-empty and in need of a coat of paint. Her modest possessions had recently arrived in a container from London, but there were still cardboard boxes and unassembled furniture in most of the rooms.

As she spent the majority of her time moving between the bedroom and kitchen, this was no great inconvenience, and Karo seemed oblivious to the mess.

'What about Ea's dad?' she said.

'He's ... not in the picture.'

The truth – that he'd tried to kill Jensen and was likely to be convicted for several murders when the case against him reached court next month – was too horrific to share.

Her daughter's father was a monster, a man with no conscience. How would Ea react when she learned the truth? How much of him did she carry in her genetic code? Thinking about this made Jensen feel sick.

'Doesn't he want her?' said Karo, then immediately added: 'I'm sorry. That was rude.'

Jensen laughed. She rather liked Karo's directness. 'It's not like that,' she said. 'It's complicated.'

'Isn't it always?' Karo sighed and a heaviness entered the air between them.

Jensen saw her chance. 'You'll have a black eye tomorrow. Your boyfriend did that to you. I still think you should report it.'

'He's not a violent man. He just lost his temper for a second.'

Jensen was about to argue (she once read that victims of domestic abuse suffered an average of thirty-five incidents before they involved the police), but then Karo's phone pinged. She looked at the screen.

'Told you. It's my boyfriend. He's asking when I'm coming home. He feels terrible about what happened,' she said.

A wistful smile crossed her face as she typed back a reply, her long nails clicking on the screen.

There was a spring in her step as she gathered up her things. 'Please forget about this. Promise? For me?' she said when she was ready to go.

Jensen nodded reluctantly, her sense of unease growing as she saw Karo to the front door and into the lift.

Her boyfriend had punched her and now Karo had to make him feel better about it. It was straight out of the abuser's playbook.

She could still call the police, without Karo's consent, but then she hadn't actually witnessed the incident herself, and Karo would only deny that it had happened.

'Thank you, Jensen, I mean it. And don't worry about me,' Karo said, and then she was gone.

3

At Teglholmen – in the anonymous office block that housed the violent crimes unit of the Copenhagen Police – Henrik checked his watch. There was still time to pick up a take-away latte on his way to the Forensic Institute.

Goldschmidt's coffee was famously undrinkable, and he needed something to bolster him for his face-to-face with the mummy from Bredgade.

The sun was baking on the windows, the meeting room stultifyingly hot. Scattered across the beechwood table were coffee cups, water bottles and the remains of hastily eaten sandwiches.

He longed to be outside in the fresh air. Despite drenching his face in cold water half an hour ago, he still felt nauseous. The feral stench of decay at the crime scene clung to him.

Someone had wiped the whiteboard at the end of the room, ready for answers they didn't have yet. Impossible to clean completely, it carried the ghostly bluish veins of case notes past. Likewise, the glass partition between the room and the corridor was dotted with Sellotape marks where maps and photos from previous investigations used to hang.

A fresh start, like the sense of rebirth that came with spring, was an illusion.

In police work, there was no such thing as starting from scratch. Everyone brought to it the sum of their experiences. Assumptions were made, prejudices brought to bear; this was inevitable.

'You all know what you have to do,' he said, looking meaningfully at the faces around the table as he rose to his feet and grabbed his leather jacket.

Though they were dealing with old remains, the drill was the same as always: identify the victim, collect evidence and interview suspects.

They still hadn't managed to reach Andreas Lund, but his cleaner, who also worked for the law firm downstairs, had told them that he liked to take himself off and go sailing on the Sound every now and again.

Apparently, he was an agent, though no one knew exactly what kind. Henrik's knowledge of the profession was limited to football transfers and spy movies.

From a quick internet search, he'd learned that the flooded building was constructed along with its neighbours in the mid-1700s. The street was part of Frederiksstaden, named after King Frederik V.

The King's Copenhagen, he thought, an old phrase his dad sometimes still used.

He was headed for the stairs when a husky voice stopped him in his tracks. 'Can I have a word, Boss?'

The voice belonged to Detective Sergeant Sarah Funder, a woman in her thirties with a pixie haircut and an obstinate face, whose height reached approximately to his chin.

He knew what she wanted.

'Have you read my report yet?' she said.

'Skimmed it.'

'And?'

'Look, we've just opened a new investigation. Now is not a good time.'

'You said that last week, and the week before.'

'Did I?'

Sarah Funder – a Rottweiler to Mark's Labrador – was one of the most experienced investigators of violent sexual offences on Henrik's team.

More than a year ago, when stuck on desk duty after breaking a leg, she'd asked for permission to comb through historical sex crimes that might warrant a further look, given advances in DNA science and police methods.

However, what started as a side hustle had become an obsession. Funder had developed a theory that a string of particularly violent rapes across the country over the past three decades could have been committed by the same person.

She now wanted time and resources to investigate, and a few weeks ago she'd pulled her idea into a formal proposal, amounting to over one hundred pages. Titled 'Operation Polaris', it had been sitting on his desk gathering dust ever since. Whenever he saw it, he felt ashamed. The rate of successful convictions versus reported rapes was low across the country, not to mention that only a fraction of rapes were reported in the first place.

Funder had acted on her own initiative, going through the files methodically for months, often working until late into the night. The least he could do was to give her a hearing.

'OK,' he said. 'Tomorrow morning at eight. My office. We'll talk about it. I promise.'

4

With her nights still broken, Jensen generally tried to nap during the day whenever Ea did, but meeting Karo had left her restless and after tossing and turning for ages, she got up and went into her office.

It was her favourite room in the flat. Her antique writing desk from London fitted perfectly under the window and alongside one wall were the filing cabinets she'd inherited from *Dagbladet*'s late obituary writer, Henning Würtzen. It was in there that she'd found Brix's home address in amongst hundreds of clippings from his illustrious career.

She should be making a start on filling her old IKEA bookcases with the contents of the cardboard boxes stacked high by the door, but instead she sat at the desk and looked out at the city.

She was annoyed that she hadn't asked for Karo's phone number. At least she could have checked if she was OK.

Why am I so useless at making friends?

There were only two women among her close acquaintances: Fie, the hacker from Roskilde, who was really more Gustav's friend, and her boss Margrethe.

When she was at school, she'd never brought other kids home to play. Marion's run-down flat in Vesterbro had existed in a permanent state of chaos that she was ashamed of, full of strangers coming and going.

By the time she and Marion had moved to North Jutland, she'd learned to be happy by herself, and for years work had more than satisfied her need for contact with other people.

But now that there was no work, she was yearning for adult company.

How different would her life have been if she'd grown up with Brix? He'd settled down in his thirties, marrying Lis Vendel, a popular actor, and having a son and daughter, now grown-ups. Christmases and birthdays would have been lively affairs, with everyone gathered around a big table, rather than the invariably disappointing ones she'd spent alone with her mother.

She took out her phone and pressed Brix's number quickly before she could change her mind.

If she didn't meet him, she would never know if he was telling the truth.

Last time she'd walked past his house there'd been a pair of tiny red wellies beside the front step. She knew from the gossip magazines that Brix had divorced Lis and married a much younger woman, Astrid, and that the couple had a toddler together.

He picked up her call immediately, as if he'd been waiting by the phone.

'It's me,' she said.

'Hello me.'

They'd only spoken once before, but she recognised his deep, gravelly voice from the dozens of video clips she'd watched of him in the past few weeks.

'OK, let's meet,' she said, cutting dead any prospect of awkward small talk.

'I'm glad.' Thankfully, there was no gloating or saccharine emotion in his voice; she wouldn't have been able to bear that. 'Where?' he said, sounding relieved more than anything.

She didn't want it to be on her turf, not until she was sure about him. 'I'll come to yours.'

'Tomorrow morning at ten?'

It was sooner than she'd imagined. 'Yes, OK.'

She prepared to end the call.

'Wait,' he said. 'Just one thing.'

'What?'

'If you're coming to my house, you're going to be needing my address, aren't you? Or perhaps you already know where I live? I don't think it's in the public domain.'

She blushed.

Had he spotted her walking past his house?

'Go on,' she said, feeling her cheeks grow hot. She pretended to take down the details, then said her goodbyes.

Flustered, she opened the drawer in her bedside table and took out the small cardboard box that had arrived in the post a few days ago.

Paternity Test. 99.999% accuracy.

She'd planned to warn him but reckoned it would be better coming as a surprise. Face-to-face it would be harder for him to turn down her request for a sample of his saliva. And if he'd been telling the truth, why would he?

Soon she would know for sure if he really was her father.

5

'The tissue is hard and dry, so we're having to use a saw rather than a knife,' Goldschmidt explained over the grinding mechanical noise that was drilling into Henrik's brain.

Sweat pearled on his top lip; as ever, he wished the pathologist would be less explicit.

Outside the concrete buildings of the Forensic Institute green shoots of new life were pushing up through the tarmac, but down here in the basement, there was only death and decay.

The post-mortem room, lined with white tiles and furnished with stainless steel, was cold and sharply resonant: metal against metal, saw against mummified flesh.

The condition of the corpse was even worse than he'd feared, barely more than a dried-up husk. It reminded him of the blackened bog man he once saw in a museum in Aarhus, except for the long sand-coloured hair that lay like a halo around the skull. According to Goldschmidt, the woman had been a natural white blonde.

He watched as the pathologist directed his female assistant Layla, a young woman with serious eyes and arched black brows. Their choreography was well-rehearsed and efficient, while somehow still managing to be respectful of the corpse lying prone on the stainless-steel table.

A forensic technician worked unobtrusively around the two medics, taking the photos that would eventually accompany Goldschmidt's written report.

Layla measured the femur, then consulted a laptop to determine the height of the victim. 'One hundred and fifty-eight centimetres,' she said. 'Female of slight build.'

Henrik nodded to himself.

This was useful information. From her teeth, Goldschmidt and Layla had already put the woman somewhere between eighteen and twenty-five years old when she died.

'By the way, the femur showed signs of an old fracture.'

'Meaning?'

'Meaning that she'd broken her leg at some point in her life.'

'Cause of death?'

'She was most likely strangled. Look here,' Goldschmidt points to the back of the throat. 'You can see that the tongue bone is broken which indicates that a great degree of pressure was applied.'

'So she died before she was bricked up?'

'I don't know. She was badly beaten with fractures to her right shoulder and left forearm. There's also a significant injury to the top of her skull, made with a flat object, such as a plank or a brick.'

'Sexually assaulted?' he asked, thinking of Detective Sergeant Sarah Funder.

'Difficult to tell with any certainty.'

It made Henrik shiver: a young woman, brutally used, murdered and disposed of behind a brick wall like so much garbage.

'Any possibility of getting the killer's DNA?' he said.

'If he left any on her, it is unlikely to have survived,' said Goldschmidt, dashing his hopes. 'Hers should be possible.'

'At least that's something.'

'Though I'm less certain about the foetus.'

Henrik stared at him in disbelief. 'Excuse me?'

'She was pregnant, around ten to twelve weeks.'

'My God.'

'Yes,' said Goldschmidt. 'Terribly sad.'

Henrik didn't know why the news about the baby should affect him so; the remains in front of him couldn't possibly get any more wretched. Yet he suddenly felt an overwhelming sadness for the young woman.

Someone must have missed her, wondering why she'd disappeared from their life, perhaps over the years beginning to fantasise about her having invented a new identity and drinking cocktails aboard a yacht in the Caribbean.

Knowing that she'd been dead all along would break them.

It's the hope that kills you, he thought. It occurred to him that the same could be said about him and Jensen.

'How are you?' said Goldschmidt when the post-mortem was over and the two of them were seated in his subterranean office, which was warm and cosy, in contrast to its bleak surroundings.

On the well-ordered shelves, in amongst ring binders and medical textbooks, were knick-knacks from his travels, pictures of his team and holiday snaps of his husband and young son.

'All the better for this,' Henrik said, indicating his mug.

Much to his surprise, Goldschmidt had brewed him a

latte from a gleaming new coffee machine, topped up with plenty of foaming milk.

Goldschmidt laughed. 'I finally caved in to popular demand. Though I never thought the coffee here was that bad.'

'It was revolting,' said Henrik. 'And I'm fine, thanks for asking.'

'Really?' The pathologist leaned forward in his office chair in a tell-me-more pose.

Henrik imagined this was what he did when humouring a medical student's unlikely theory. 'You don't believe me?' he said, vaguely offended.

'No, no, I'm glad to hear it,' Goldschmidt corrected himself. 'I mean, you've been through a lot.'

Henrik knew this wasn't just a reference to the senseless murder of a detective sergeant in his team last summer. Though they'd never discussed it outright, his complicated personal life hadn't escaped the pathologist's attention.

Henrik had long rued the winter night when he'd brought Jensen along to the Forensic Institute for a post-mortem on a young stab victim she'd found buried in the snow in Magstræde. He should have known that the clever medic would see through them immediately.

'So your friend had a baby?' Goldschmidt said.

Henrik, sensing the inverted commas around the word 'friend', feigned confusion. 'Who do you mean?'

'The one you introduced me to, *Dagbladet*'s crime reporter. The one you said was no one.'

'Ah, her,' Henrik said. 'Yes, I gather she got pregnant by a man who's now in jail,' he added, in case Goldschmidt assumed that he was the father.

He couldn't deny that he'd sometimes wished he was.

'I actually saw her a few days ago near my house, with

her baby in a sling,' said Goldschmidt. 'She looked . . . how shall I put it . . .'

Happy? Gorgeous? Glowing? Superlatives crowded on the tip of Henrik's tongue, but Goldschmidt went off in another direction. 'Preoccupied,' he said. 'I waved at her, but she didn't seem to notice me.'

'Recognising people out of context can be tricky.' Henrik had no idea why he felt the need to explain Jensen's odd behaviour. Normally, he was the first to confront her about it.

'No, it's not that. She was looking at a specific house in our street. She walked past it, then turned around and came back to look at it again, lost in deep thought.'

'Which house was that?' said Henrik. He remembered that Goldschmidt had an enviable home in the Potato Rows, which he'd inherited from his late father, also a pathologist at the national hospital.

'That's just the thing. It belongs to our local celebrity, Valde Brix, the author.'

Henrik wasn't a reader, except for case notes and football match reports, but he knew Brix all right. Louise had read several of his books (they invariably had dragons and ancient scripts on the front). She had even dragged him along to see the man talk on stage at the Copenhagen Book Fair once.

Henrik had thought Brix rather smarmy, basking in the adoration of his sycophantic audience. He was perturbed that Jensen might be a fan. She'd never mentioned him.

What was she up to now?

'We're not . . . in touch these days,' he said. 'But I'm sure there's a perfectly good explanation.'

'Yeah, you're right,' said Goldschmidt. 'Anyway, ignore me.'

They small-talked for a while about changes at the

institute and cut-backs in police budgets (as ever, the news was relentlessly bad), but Henrik wasn't paying much attention.

After a few minutes, he got up and mumbled something about needing to get going. As he walked away, he was glad the pathologist couldn't see his face.

Day Two

6

Jensen was woken by the old lift jolting to a halt, then a loud clank as the door was opened. Seconds later, the door was closed again, and the lift descended.

Hers was the only flat on the top floor. No one else came up here, except Gustav, and he had his own key.

Ea was still asleep, having refused to settle during the night.

Jensen felt headachy and spaced out as she put her feet on the floor. Remembering that in just two hours from now she would be meeting Brix sent a wave of anxiety through her. Was she doing the right thing?

When her mother had insisted that Brix wasn't her father, had she meant that he hadn't earned the right to the title?

If so, Jensen agreed. She'd been fine growing up without a father, just like Ea would be fine growing up without hers.

Set to see out his days in prison, Ea's father would never change her nappy, stick a plaster on her knee or take her to school.

Nevertheless, he was a known quantity. One day, Jensen

would tell Ea about him, and there would be answers, albeit difficult ones, to her daughter's inevitable questions.

She wanted only the same for herself. To know. Afterwards, she could decide whether or not to build a relationship with someone who – all through her life to this point – had only been her father in the narrowest biological sense of the word.

Surely, Marion could see that?

She padded barefoot through to the entrance hall, yawning as she opened the front door. Something had been left on the doormat: the clothes she'd lent to Karo, washed, ironed and folded.

Jensen buried her nose in the jumper, inhaling the unfamiliar scent. A note fell to the floor.

Thanks for yesterday and sorry for being such a drama queen! Do you want to go for a walk later?

There was a mobile number followed by a smiley.

Yes, Jensen thought, flooded with relief that Karo was OK, that they would have another chance to make friends. *I'd like that very much.*

7

Henrik had managed to forget all about his promise to Sarah Funder. He was seventeen minutes late by the time he opened the door to his office and saw her sitting in his visitor's chair.

'Bloody traffic,' he said.

Funder stared at the takeaway latte in his hand, silently pointing out that he'd had time enough to stop at Espresso House.

Flustered, he threw the paper cup in the bin. 'Right,' he said, rubbing his hands. 'What's this report of yours all about then?'

'I thought you said you'd skimmed it.'

'Refresh my memory,' he said, taking the report from his in-tray and thumbing through it as she began to speak.

Last night had been a write-off. He'd spent most of it googling Valde Brix and found it hard to sleep afterwards. Not that he'd found anything worthy of Jensen's interest.

Brix had published two literary novels to modest critical acclaim by the time he was thirty, but it wasn't until two years later, when he'd turned his hand to the fantasy genre, that he'd broken through internationally.

Since then, he'd rarely been out of the papers. There were hundreds of photos of him online, more often than not in the company of beautiful women.

Why would Jensen be staking out his property? Curiosity gnawed at him. She wasn't the type to do things without good reason.

'Are you listening?' said Funder.

'Absolutely.'

'I looked at reported rapes by assailants thought to be unknown to the victim then filtered out the most serious cases based on injuries sustained. Since 1992, I've identified a total of eleven cases across Denmark with a number of common denominators – traumatic injuries, no witnesses to the assault itself, no biological traces except for one case, no CCTV evidence or suspicious mobile-phone records in the case of the later assaults. We only have the women's testimonies and the evidence on their bodies. All were found to have been drugged, either through injection or by having their drink spiked. None were able to account precisely for what had happened to them.'

'Without evidence, how can you be sure there's a link?' Henrik said.

'On the contrary, the link *is* the absence of evidence,' said Funder. 'These were meticulously planned attacks, executed by someone who knew exactly what he was doing. He would have worn a face mask, disposable gloves and a condom, and left his mobile at home. The violence had no purpose, given that the victims had already been rendered senseless by drugs. You could argue that there was an almost ritualistic element to it.'

'Where did the assaults take place?'

'No unified picture there. Sometimes in the victims' homes, sometimes outside, in parks and woodland. Wherever he could get them on their own, it seems.'

Henrik thought about it. Funder was right that the complete absence of evidence made the cases unusual. The violence, too.

'Any other patterns? Age of the victims? Appearance? Lifestyle?'

'A slight leaning towards more affluent victims, but not consistently. Otherwise nothing aside from a rise in the age of the victim. In the newer cases, the women are older than the earlier ones.' She pointed to a chart. 'You can see the distribution curve here. The women were aged from twenty-two to fifty-seven when they were assaulted. I think that might reflect that the perpetrator himself has grown older.'

'That's it?'

'No. Interestingly, five of the women reported seeing someone in hi-vis clothing prior to the incident, though they weren't able to describe the person's face.'

'Hi-vis clothing? What, like a builder or a roadworker?'

Funder nodded. 'It might be something or nothing.'

Henrik thought the latter was more likely.

'Maybe the six others weren't asked about it,' Funder continued. 'Or they didn't notice. It's a thing. Look it up. People in hi-vis travel invisibly among us. Put on a hard hat and a neon vest, and people naturally assume you've some sort of legitimate business and stop questioning why you're there. It could have been a deliberate ploy by the attacker.'

Henrik suspected Funder was making the cardinal error of choosing the facts that fitted her theory, rather than the other way around, but he admired her tenacity. She reminded him strongly of Jensen: once she got hold of an idea, she wouldn't let it go.

'What do you want?' said Henrik.

'I want six months initially to speak to as many of the women as I can find, and to interview the investigators who worked on these cases. Were the victims picked by chance or for a particular reason? I also want to see if any evidence was missed, or if items of clothing were kept that could be resubmitted for DNA profiling. I'll need a team. Two constables should be enough to start with.'

'You said earlier that there were no biological traces, except for one instance?'

'Yes, the Agnes Beck case in 2007. DNA but the sample was incomplete, and no match was found in the register. I'd like to have it looked at again. I think the attacker made a mistake. A tiny drop of blood was found on Agnes's clothing, which turned out not to come from her. People in her immediate circle were ruled out. It feels promising.'

Thoughts and feelings. They weren't enough to justify the expense, Henrik reflected. Even the police operated under budget constraints. Each sample, each test, each cold-case investigation cost money they didn't have.

'So eleven cases over more than thirty years,' he said. 'If we assume our man was at least eighteen at the time of the first rape, he would be, what . . . in his fifties now?'

Funder nodded as if she found this perfectly realistic. 'Eleven cases that we know of, but given his preference for drugging his victims, leaving them unable to remember what had happened to them, there could be more. I also think it's fair to assume that some victims chose not to report what had happened to them, perhaps the ones that got off more lightly. In other cases, the rape element might not have been detected, because the violence was so extensive.'

Henrik couldn't see Operation Polaris being greenlit.

They barely had enough detectives as it was. The chances that the top brass would agree to three people spending six months trying to nail fog to a wall were practically non-existent. 'Why did you call it Polaris?' he said.

'You mean aside from the obvious?'

'Which is?'

'True north. People have navigated by Polaris for centuries. Likewise, all these cases seem to point to the same answer, a North Star.'

'I see. And the less obvious?'

'Me,' said Funder. 'I lost my way when I broke my leg. Work became meaningless. I even considered leaving the force, until I found this. It reminded me why I joined in the first place.'

She stared at him, blushing. He'd never heard her say anything so personal before. 'OK. I'll have a word with Liv, but don't get your hopes up,' he said.

Chief Inspector Liv Harder was his new boss. He was still trying to get used to reporting to a woman, let alone calling her by her first name, something she insisted on.

Before Funder could reply, there was a triple knock on the door. Mark entered, looking confused when he saw her in the visitor's chair.

'Come in,' Henrik said. Funder made no move to get up, leaving Mark standing awkwardly in the middle of the floor.

It would be good for them to work together. She had a reputation for being difficult, but Mark could learn a thing or two from her tenacity and resourcefulness, and in return she might be distracted from Operation Polaris.

'Liv wants to send out a new press release,' said Mark as he began to read aloud from a printed sheet. 'Woman aged between eighteen and twenty-five, long blonde hair, about

158 centimetres tall, around three months pregnant at the time of her death. Age of the remains yet to be determined, and tests go on, though the evidence points to murder. Again, we'd like to appeal for any member of the public with information to call us, blah, blah, blah.'

'Fine,' said Henrik. 'Though let's not mention that she was pregnant.'

Holding back information would help them sift through the calls from the public. Most would be the usual attention-seekers working off things they had read in the papers.

Besides, the pregnancy was sensitive personal information.

'Could she have been raped?' asked Funder.

'They can't tell because of the state of the remains,' said Henrik. 'But we can't rule it out. Her injuries were extensive.'

'Can I take a look at the post-mortem report?'

'Be my guest.'

Mark was looking wary. Was he jealous of Funder? Perhaps he was worried that she was muscling in on Henrik's affections?

He should be.

'What else?' Henrik said, a little snappily.

'We're still going through the misper database. Nothing matching in the past twenty years, so we're looking further back now. But on the plus side, I finally heard from the owner late last night,' said Mark.

'How did he seem?'

'Mortified, I'd say, genuinely shocked. He'd been sailing and hadn't checked his phone. He should be back in Copenhagen later today and will be coming straight here. Oh, and Liv wants you to do a press conference with her this afternoon. The media is going nuts, apparently.'

Henrik groaned inwardly. His track record for going in

front of the press was terrible. He invariably lost his temper or got flustered and said the wrong thing.

He was about to send Funder and Mark away when his phone began to buzz, shaking furiously on the table. He looked at the display, feeling a small jolt of adrenaline when he saw that it was a call from the duty officer.

'Jungersen,' he said, and the duty officer wasted no time getting to the point.

When the call ended, he found Funder and Mark staring at him. 'That sounded bad,' she said.

Henrik rose to his feet. 'I need you to go to Frederiksberg Gardens immediately. Assault and possible rape. Victim is being blue-lighted to hospital as we speak. Alert forensics.'

'Who?' said Mark, pointing to Funder, who was already out of her chair and heading for the door. 'Me or her?'

'Both of you,' said Henrik. 'As of now, you're working together. I'll be along as soon as I've given Liv a heads-up.'

8

Jensen almost bottled it, walking straight past Brix's house, before forcing her feet to turn.

In the spring sunlight, the street was achingly pretty, lined with expensive cars, the front gardens exploding in flowers and greenery. Tricycles and cargo bikes had been left across the pavements. Halfway down stood a tree, a wooden playhouse and a picnic table. The inhabitants might be rich, but the neighbourhood wasn't showy; rather it exuded a carefree and bohemian attitude to life. These were people who'd foregone big suburban villas for living minutes from the city centre and everything it had to offer.

Looking over her shoulder, Jensen noticed a blonde woman staring at her from an open doorway across the street and realised that her dithering made her look suspicious.

Brix was a celebrity; his neighbours were probably wary of having their street turned into a destination for adoring fans.

With sweaty hands she rang the doorbell, telling herself not to be such a wimp.

Whatever happens, this changes nothing.

Brix opened the door, tall and striking in dark denims and a white T-shirt that set off his tan. 'Jensen. Finally we meet.'

She looked for a physical likeness to push their familial relationship beyond doubt, but only saw the face she knew from the magazines: grey slicked-back hair, glasses with strong black frames, the bestselling author in his prime.

Except Brix looked nervous, his eyes darting up and down the street as he led her inside.

In the hallway, which was dingy and claustrophobic with the door closed, he kissed her on the forehead in a vaguely papal gesture that made her uncomfortable. He smelled of aftershave and toothpaste.

'And who's this little lady?' he said when, finally, he let her go.

'Her name is Ea.'

'Come,' he said. 'Give Ea to me.'

'I don't think . . .'

'Trust me, I know what I'm doing,' said Brix like a man used to getting what he wanted.

Which was exactly what he was. It had taken him three months, but he'd finally broken her resistance.

Reluctantly, she unbuttoned the sling, and Brix wasted no time pulling Ea out by her armpits. 'Come to Grandad.'

Treacherously, Ea didn't complain. Cooing to her gently, he led the way into a bright open-plan kitchen and dining room with mid-century Danish designer furniture and modern art.

From there, bifold doors led to a small patio with a rattan sofa set and olive trees in big terracotta pots.

The room bore no signs of Brix's young son, apart from a clean highchair and a woven basket with brightly coloured toys.

He saw her looking. 'Oh, Astrid's visiting her sister in Holte with my son August, so I'm home alone.'

He sat down, patting the dining chair next to him. Ea's eyelids were beginning to droop.

Jensen sat and poured herself a glass of water from a carafe on the table. When she lifted it to her mouth, her hand was shaking.

'Does your mother know you're here?' Brix said.

'No,' she said. 'Marion's adamant you're not my dad, so I'm kind of curious why you think you might be.'

Brix smiled. 'Marion was always feisty, the most beautiful woman you ever saw. We were a couple before you were born, even lived together for a short while. Did she tell you that?'

No, she did not.

Jensen shook her head.

'So she's still angry with me. I thought so.'

'Why?'

'I wasn't exactly faithful to her. I was young, it was a different time.'

'That's what *she* keeps saying. She swears she doesn't know who got her pregnant, only that it definitely wasn't you.'

Brix looked bemused rather than hurt. 'Your mother has always been proud. When I learned that you existed, I put two and two together and sent her money, but she returned it immediately. I tried to remonstrate with her, but she was having none of it. The last time I went to her flat in Copenhagen, she refused to even see me. Shortly afterwards she moved to Jutland, and we lost touch.'

Jensen remembered a man shouting up at their balcony, and how the neighbours opened their windows to see what was going on. She'd thought that he was a jilted lover, but now she realised it must have been Brix.

Still, moving to the other end of the country to avoid him seemed like an extreme measure, even for Marion.

'If you've known all my life, why are you only getting in touch now?' she said.

'Because Marion threatened to ruin me if I ever contacted you. My writing career was just taking off at the time. I couldn't risk it.'

'Ruin you how?'

'There are things in my past I'm not proud of. Like I said, today is very different from when Marion and I were young. Marion could do a lot of damage if she wanted to.' He tapered off, looking adoringly at Ea.

Jensen frowned. This didn't sound much like Marion, her helpless, distracted mother who could barely boil an egg.

'How come you're no longer afraid she'll ruin you?'

'Ah,' he said, his expression darkening. 'That's the thing. Someone else got there first.'

'What do you mean?'

'I wasn't going to bring it up. I wanted today to be special. Our first meeting.' He attempted a smile, not quite pulling it off.

'But . . .?'

'I'm in deep shit, Jensen,' he said, his face a grimace of pain.

Sensing the change in mood, Ea began to fuss. Brix looked at her helplessly. 'I think she wants her mother now. Maybe she's hungry?'

'She'll be all right for a minute.' Jensen stood up and put Ea on her shoulder, swaying from side to side. 'You were saying . . .?'

Brix looked at her. 'I have a stalker.'

'So that's why you're keeping the curtains closed?'

'Exactly. A short while ago, I started getting photos of us, taken through the window with a long lens. That's why I sent Astrid and August away. But that's not all. They accused me of . . .' Brix trailed off, swallowed hard, closed his eyes. 'They said they're going to report me for rape.' The last word came out in a whisper.

'Rape?' Jensen instinctively took a step back. The kitchen suddenly felt claustrophobic. Would it be faster to run back to the front door, or could she make it out to the patio and scream for help?

'Of whom?' she said. 'When?'

'God only knows,' said Brix. 'I've been given seven days to own up.'

'Did you respond?'

'Never.'

'And you've no idea who this person is?'

'None. Lots of different aliases, a new social media account every day and lately I've been getting text messages. I change my number, but still the texts come. I mean, how do they even know what my new number is? I thought at first that it was an obsessed fan, but that was before the photos began to appear, and the nonsense about rape.'

Was it nonsense? Really?

Jensen thought carefully before posing the next question. 'I have to ask, have you ever . . .?'

He looked at her angrily. 'Raped someone? For fuck's sake, how can you even ask me that?'

'Maybe you were in a situation that was ambiguous, where you weren't certain that the other person was consenting?'

'Absolutely not. There've been a lot of women in my life, but I have never forced myself on anyone. I know what "No" means. I'm not an animal. Period.'

'OK.'

Brix groaned. 'If they go public with this kind of allegation, I'll be finished. I take it you've heard of the Hollywood film?'

She nodded.

'Well, given the times we're living in, I can't see that going ahead if I'm under a cloud of suspicion. I'll be cancelled.'

'Doesn't sound like there's a lot you can do about it.'

'No, and I *hate* that.' Brix slammed his palms hard into the dining table. Ea, who had drifted off again, woke up with a start and began to cry.

While she was settling her, Jensen found Brix studying her face intensely. 'Could you find out who's doing this to me?'

Marion had been right. Brix *did* want something from her. She avoided his gaze, feeling a little hurt.

They were strangers to each other, yet he was expecting her to back him unquestioningly. 'You should go to the police,' she said.

Brix shook his head. 'The police leaks worse than a sieve. Once they know, everyone will, and some people might start believing the crazy shit. Besides . . .'

'Besides?'

'Like I said, I've been with a lot of women, at times and in situations when I shouldn't have been.'

'Adultery, you mean?'

'Yes. Mine or theirs. Sometimes both. There are people out there who got hurt, people who might take the opportunity to kick me while I'm down.'

'No more than you deserve, I'm sure.'

Brix hung his head. 'I don't claim to be perfect, Jensen. I can't change who I am.'

She thought of Henrik. He could probably do something discreetly, but that would mean telling him how she knew Brix, which was none of his business. He'd told her virtually nothing about his own life. Everything she knew about his wife Louise, their home and their three children, she'd found online. He'd no right to expect an openness from her that he wasn't willing to return.

'Why me?' she said to Brix.

'I trust you. We're family,' he said. 'You wouldn't betray me, my own daughter.'

Some family.

Ea was getting impatient again, her whimpering slowly turning more persistent. Jensen found her a dummy, knowing that the peace would only be temporary. 'So you got in touch because you're in trouble and want me to help you.'

'Not only that. I want to have a relationship with you and with my granddaughter.'

'All those years, when you never contacted me, you really expect me to believe that you were afraid of Marion? She's about as scary as a kitten.'

'You don't know what your mother is capable of,' said Brix sternly. 'But you're right, I should have told you. I'm sorry.'

She felt her anger deflating, despite herself. Tiredness flooded through her body. 'Who told you that I'd had a baby?' she said.

'Ernst Brøgger is an old friend. He knows that you and I are related, but, as you know, he's discretion itself.'

Brøgger? Really? The lawyer who'd helped her when she inherited the flat? The friend to Denmark's rich and powerful who'd been supplying her with stories for more than a year?

This was getting ridiculous. Was she the last person in Denmark to find out who her father was?

'I swear I haven't even told my wife. Only Brøgger knows. And Andreas, of course.'

'Who?'

'My Man Friday. My fixer. My agent. Andreas knows everything. I'll send you his details. If you need anything, anything at all, then Andreas is your man.'

'OK,' she said, curiosity getting the better of her. After all, finding out the truth about Brix's stalker was in her own interest.

If the rape allegation was false, she wanted to know who hated him enough to make it. And if it was true, she wanted nothing more to do with him. 'I'll help you, but it will be on my terms.'

'Whatever you want.'

'You tell me *everything*, no secrets.'

'Of course.'

'I want you to share copies of all correspondence from the stalker. You *have* kept copies?'

'I'm not a total idiot.'

'I'll also need a list of the women you have known intimately since the beginning of time, with approximate dates, and how the relationship ended.

He lowered his voice. 'I can't do that.'

'Then I wish you good luck.'

'If a list like that falls into the wrong hands . . .'

'Encrypt it.'

'I don't remember details.'

'Try. If you don't, then I'm out.'

'OK, I'll do it.' He got up.

'Wait,' she said. 'I haven't finished.' She fumbled with one hand in her shoulder bag, shoving aside nappies, baby wipes and nipple cream to find the slim, white cardboard box.

'I need to know who is telling the truth, you or Marion,' she said. 'Since you don't agree amongst yourselves, there is only one way to settle it. I want you to swab your cheek for me. Right now.'

9

Frederiksberg Gardens had been closed to the public, and uniformed officers were busy turning away runners and dog-walkers. The usual spectators had gathered in front of the gates, loitering in unsavoury curiosity.

As he made his way past them, Henrik struggled to reproduce the excitement he'd felt yesterday in Bredgade. This new case would stretch his team, and the papers – already whipped into a frenzy by the woman in the wall – were bound to reach for their most alarmist headlines.

He and Liv had agreed to include both cases at the press conference this afternoon. To his immense relief, she would be taking the lead, but wanted him there for reassurance, a preference which could only be explained by the fact that she was new in the role.

Henrik had been called many things in his life, but reassuring had never been one of them.

The park was a few minutes' drive from his home. He'd been here hundreds of times, running or kicking a ball around with his kids, but he'd never seen it empty.

He walked up the broad entrance between two old,

ochre-coloured buildings fronted by manicured lawns and flowerbeds, past the statue of King Frederik VI on his plinth.

From here, two paths extended into the park in the shape of a V. A constable pointed to the left. 'Keep going,' he said. 'You can't miss it.'

Soon Henrik's view of the sweeping lawn was blocked by trees and shrubbery. He'd almost reached the point where the park opened up again, inclining past regiments of ornamental trees towards the castle, when he spotted the white-clad forensic technicians working in amongst the dense bushes.

Funder stood on the path a short distance away, gesticulating angrily at Mark, who was scowling back, shoulders hunched.

He walked up to them. 'Good to see you getting on,' he said. 'Talk to me.'

'Jane Dahl-Thomsen,' Funder said, as Mark opened and closed his mouth. He would need to be faster if he wanted to get a word in. 'Fifty-four years old, lives out at Ørestaden. Severe sexual assault and battering. Was found by a dog-walker, crawling out of those bushes over there, covered in blood and mumbling incoherently.'

Henrik frowned. 'She'd been there all night?'

'We believe so. The park is locked at ten p.m. at this time of year. The assailant must have got in beforehand, either attacking her here, or bringing her into the park with him. We're getting as much CCTV as we can lay our hands on.'

'How is she?'

'Barely alive. The paramedics who took her to hospital said they'd never seen anything like it. The doctors have sedated her while they investigate her injuries and prepare her for surgery. Her daughter, whom we spoke to briefly on the phone, said she had a date last night with a man she'd met online.'

'Could it have been him who did this?'

'It's possible. Of course, we'll go through her chat history. We don't yet know where the date took place. There are several bars and restaurants near here. We've sent some uniforms around with a photo.'

'Will she make it?'

Funder spoke again. 'The next few hours are critical, the doctors say. On top of her injuries she suffered hypothermia. The temperature dropped into low single figures last night. If she pulls through, she'll be scarred for life in most ways you can think of. As of now, we're unable to interview her.'

'Anything else?'

Funder pointed to technicians working between the trees. 'They've only just started, but there's nothing obvious in there, aside from Jane Dahl-Thomsen's torn clothing, and her handbag.'

'We think this is where she was attacked?'

'Hard to say at this point, but I don't see why she would have chosen to walk through the park after her date. It's more likely that he brought her. My guess is she was drugged, maybe at the bar. We'll have to wait for the blood tests, of course, but she'd vomited, which could be an indicator.'

Henrik nodded. He'd been wondering how the assailant had got her into the park, but now it made sense. With Rohypnol, or a similar substance, in her blood stream, she would have been confused and defenceless.

'That's as much as we know for now,' said Funder. 'But if you want my opinion?'

Mark made a face. It seemed he'd already heard it.

'This has all the hallmarks of the Polaris cases,' she said, ignoring him.

'Yes, well, let's not begin to theorise yet,' said Henrik.

'See?' said Mark. A sharp glance from Henrik and he stuck his hands in the pockets of his dark denims and skulked off.

'No one is theorising,' said Funder. 'I'm just putting it out there that it could be the same man.'

'Would have been unusually risky for your Polaris perpetrator, wouldn't it?' Henrik said, humouring her. 'Picking up his victim from a bar with loads of witnesses and CCTV around?'

Funder shrugged. 'If it's him, there'll be no witnesses or CCTV. He wouldn't be making such a rookie mistake.'

Henrik scratched his head. Funder was a good detective, and he knew only too well how quickly passion could veer into obsession.

A while back, he'd almost lost his mind, let alone his job, over mysterious photos of a young girl turning up at seemingly unrelated crime scenes, yet his instinct had turned out to be correct.

Was Funder on to something?

'You believe me, don't you?' she said, suddenly.

'I believe you could be right,' said Henrik, choosing his words carefully. 'You're clearly dedicated and conscientious, and your thinking springs from good intentions.'

'I mean, every year, many thousands of people are thought to be subjected to rape or attempted rape, but only a couple of thousand report it and under two hundred are convicted for it. Are we supposed to think that's good enough?'

'Of course not.'

After a tightening of Danish law, rape was now defined as knowingly having sex with someone without their consent, but this was hard to prove, and often the scales tipped in favour of the defendant.

In the case of the Polaris perpetrator – if he even existed – there was no question he'd acted without consent, but without evidence, let alone a single suspect, they hadn't a hope in hell.

'I'm not stupid,' said Funder. 'I know it's just one guy, and if we get him, it will be a drop in the ocean, but I can't stand the thought that he's out there, getting away with it year after year, while we're running around in circles and giving up.'

Henrik reached out to put a reassuring arm around her back, but then remembered the warnings about inappropriate touching in the workplace (he'd recently been on a course) and pulled his hand back.

'I get it,' he said. 'One thing I'm wondering is whether Jane Dahl-Thomsen was picked at random. I mean if her date didn't do it.'

'I don't think so. Pulling a stunt like this without anyone noticing takes careful planning.'

'We'll need to look at her background. Previous boyfriends, an ex-husband, anyone she could have been in contact with. How did the attacker know where she'd be last night? And how did he get her here?'

'Trust me,' she said. 'We'll be going through her life with a fine-tooth comb. I just hate this. That it happened right here in Copenhagen.'

'Yes,' said Henrik. He'd had the same thought. He liked to think of Copenhagen as his responsibility. This was where his family was.

Where Jensen was.

'All we can do is gather the facts, put together a picture, see where it gets us,' he said. 'We can do our job. Let's get started.'

He went in search of Mark, who seemed to have

recovered his composure somewhat as he watched the technicians work. His inability to carry a grudge for too long had always been one of his strongest attributes. Without it, Henrik doubted they would have lasted this long as a double act. 'By the way,' he said. 'Did you find out what kind of agent Andreas Lund is? The guy from Bredgade?'

'Yes, a literary agent, apparently,' Mark said. 'Though I gather he only has one client.'

'And who is that?' said Henrik with a horrible sense of foreboding.

'Valde Brix, the author.'

10

Jensen had barely made it home when she received an email from Brix. The attached encrypted file contained multiple screengrabs of texts and messages from Instagram, WhatsApp and Facebook Messenger.

She would have to look at it later. Right now, she was exhausted and sweaty after the walk back with Ea on her front, and a book the size and weight of a brick in her shoulder bag. Brix had insisted on signing it for her.

To darling Jensen with all my love.

It would make a good doorstop.

On the way back, she'd been convinced that someone was following her, though the path had been empty whenever she'd looked over her shoulder.

You're getting as paranoid as Brix, she thought, but the truth was that she no longer felt as invincible as she once did.

First, there'd been Ea's premature birth and the crushing fear that her tiny daughter wouldn't pull through, and now she was terrified of something happening to herself. If she were to die, who would look after Ea?

The conversation with Brix had left her shaky. Her own mother had been lying to her, or at the very least had withheld information.

What else had she left out of the story?

Brix's warning that she didn't know what her mother was capable of made her wonder if she knew Marion at all.

Her mother's romantic relationships had followed a pattern: she'd failed to attach to her partners, and invariably they'd ended up leaving her.

As a parent, she'd always been kind, but distant and rather passive. Jensen remembered times when she had glanced up from a toy or a book to catch Marion looking at her strangely.

She fed Ea and changed her nappy, then put her in her cot for a nap. Afterwards, resisting the temptation to dive into bed, she dialled Marion's number, launching straight in without a preamble. 'Why didn't you tell me that Brix was your boyfriend before I was born?'

'Not relevant,' Marion responded.

'What does that mean?'

Silence.

She imagined her mother standing in her studio in North Jutland, squeezing her mobile between chin and shoulder as she dabbed paint on a canvas, some new variation on her usual theme of sea, sand and sky.

'You don't even want to know what he said?'

'No.'

'You're still absolutely certain it wasn't him.'

'Yes.'

'But with other men you're less sure?'

'I've said what I wanted to say. You're making a big mistake.'

'Well I got him to do a paternity test.'

'Waste of money.'

'I have to know what I'm made of.'

'You are loved,' Marion said sharply. 'By me. Always have been, always will be. That's what you're made of. Love.'

Jensen was moved by the fervour of her mother's emotion. It was what she might say herself about Ea. She bit her lip. 'I know, but—'

'Do what you feel is right,' said Marion, her voice softening. 'But remember what I told you.'

After the call, Jensen stood resolutely in front of the bathroom mirror and swabbed the inside of her cheek.

Then she packaged up her sample with Brix's and put the parcel in her bag.

She was surprised to find that she was crying. It might not matter to her mother who her father was, but it mattered to her.

Angrily swiping away her tears, she composed a message for Karo.

> *Would love a walk. Meet me outside my place at two?*

11

While Funder drove to the hospital to wait for Jane Dahl-Thomsen to wake up, Henrik returned to the office with Mark, both of them in a glum mood.

'I can't work with that woman. Why do I have to?' Mark said.

'You were asking for more exciting work. Funder has a lot of experience of these sorts of cases. You can learn from her.'

'She keeps telling me what to do, like she's in charge. And that Operation Polaris crap she's always on about, give me a break.'

'She's a dedicated officer,' Henrik said.

'Don't tell me you actually believe in her theory?'

'I don't know,' he said truthfully.

If Funder was right, it would be one of the biggest and most terrifying investigations the force had ever seen.

But what she'd gathered so far was not enough. They needed more evidence, which would take time and cost money.

They passed the rest of the journey in silence.

When they got back, Henrik knocked on the door to Liv's office, a long and narrow room at the end of their floor. It used to belong to his former boss, Chief Inspector Jens Wiese, who had kept it austere and unwelcoming. Henrik had never called Wiese by his first name, nor had Wiese ever encouraged him to do so. If he had, maybe things would have ended differently for the poor sod.

Liv looked up from her papers and waved him inside, as blonde, bright and statuesque as a Norse goddess. There was a mug of tea on the desk, a pot plant, and a picture of Liv shaking hands with the commissioner, but no family photos or children's drawings. No one had worked out yet if she was married or single, though this was a popular topic around the office.

For the first time in living memory, the violent crimes unit had a boss who was properly hot. Henrik would never voice this fact out loud, of course. People's appearances were neither here nor there, and never ever to be commented on (this was another thing they'd taught him on the course).

Liv wasn't, and never tried to be, one of the boys. She preferred smart black trousers and silk shirts to the T-shirts and jeans that most people wore around the office. She was also excellent at her job: warm and empathetic, a good cop and a clever manager.

His former bosses had been either cops or managers, never both.

However, her appointment after a stellar career in Aarhus Police had come as a surprise. She had a reputation for being an outspoken critic of the politics and power games that had so often marred the force in the past.

He'd expected Chief Superintendent Mogens Hansen, AKA Monsen, an old-fashioned copper and dying breed, to pick a candidate more like himself. Was it Monsen's wife Rigmor, an acerbic academic at the University of Copenhagen, who had leaned on the old boy to appoint someone destined to shake things up?

It was now widely expected that Liv would succeed Monsen when he retired in two years, and Henrik for one would support her promotion.

'Just come back from Frederiksberg Gardens,' he said.

'How is the victim doing?' said Liv.

'Touch and go.'

'What do we know?'

'Almost nothing. As the gates are locked between ten p.m. and seven a.m. we believe she'd been there all night. Nothing else to go on yet and she's too poorly to be interviewed.'

'We'll appeal for witnesses,' said Liv.

Henrik nodded. 'There will be questions about public safety at the press conference.'

'Let's get a mobile police station despatched to the main park entrance. It's important we're visible in the community, for reassurance, if nothing else.'

Henrik hadn't planned to mention Operation Polaris but realised that there might not be a better chance.

Liv listened to him without interrupting as he pleaded Funder's case as neutrally as he could.

'You know as well as I do that things are hard right now,' she said when he'd finished. 'With Bredgade and this latest incident in Frederiksberg Gardens, we're at 559 open cases, and money is pretty tight as it is. It would be hard to spare anyone for any length of time.'

'Of course. I thought the same,' he said, wondering why he always became so meek in Liv's company.

Was he getting soft?

She looked at him, and for a moment the corners of her

mouth appeared to curl upwards, as though she was finding him amusing. 'That wasn't a no,' she said. 'I think Sarah should be commended for such diligent work, and on her own initiative. Send me her report. If I think it has merit, I'll talk to her myself.'

There was a triple knock, and Mark opened the door cautiously. 'Andreas Lund has arrived, Boss. He's in the interview room.'

Henrik got up to leave, but Mark wasn't moving. Sometimes, he could be irritatingly ponderous. 'Speak,' Henrik snapped.

'There's something else. We think we might have found out who she is.'

'Who?'

'The woman in the wall. She matches the description of a woman named Mia Steen who was reported missing in August 1988.'

He held up his mobile, showing a grainy photo of a young woman with long, wavy white-blonde hair and a blunt fringe. She was pretty, wearing a white dress and holding a red rose, smiling shyly at the camera. It was her high-school graduation photo, and she had on the customary white hat with the burgundy band and black shade.

Henrik hadn't gone to high school, but there was a similar photo of his wife somewhere in one of the albums at home. In a few weeks' time, Copenhagen would be full of young people wearing those same hats, celebrating their final exams by getting drunk and making a nuisance of themselves.

'She was twenty,' Mark said.

'Let's find her dental records,' Henrik said. 'Once confirmed, contact her next of kin.'

'It was actually her mother who got in touch with us.

She'd read the story in the paper and thought it might be Mia. Incidentally, her daughter once broke her leg in a bobsleigh accident.'

'Get her in,' said Henrik, looking at his watch.

There was less than forty minutes to go before the press conference, and he still had to speak to Lund. They wouldn't be able to confirm in time that the victim was indeed Mia Steen. That meant an opportunity wasted to appeal to the public for information.

'We'll need to keep a lid on it for now,' said Liv, reading his mind. 'We can send a media release once we're sure. Well done, Mark.'

Mark grew taller, his boyish face blushing under Liv's appreciative gaze.

Well done for what? Henrik thought. *For taking a phone call?*

He felt a short, sharp stab of something that, to his horror, he recognised as jealousy. Had Mark been right that he wanted all the glory for himself, preventing his deputy from shining?

Sweet Jesus, he needed to get a grip.

Andreas Lund glanced up anxiously when Henrik entered the interview room, then stood to his full height, an inch or so above his own.

There was something familiar about his face, though Henrik couldn't say why. Lund had intense eyes under black brows, a strong chin and a straight nose, along with an enviable shock of hair falling from a centre parting.

Henrik guessed he'd seen his picture in a magazine or on TV and dismissed the thought.

Lund was tanned and muscular, in good shape for a man around sixty, presumably from all that sailing. He was striking and interesting-looking, rather than handsome.

In his white linen shirt, navy chinos and leather boat shoes, he looked as though he'd come straight from his yacht.

'Detective Inspector Jungersen,' Henrik said, as they shook hands. 'I'm leading the investigation into the remains we found in your apartment.'

'I came as soon as I heard,' said Lund.

'Which wasn't till today, I gather. Surprised you didn't see it on the news. It was all over the front pages yesterday.'

'One of the privileges of being my own boss is that I can take a break when I want to,' Lund said, waving his mobile phone. 'This device rules my life, but every now and again I get to detox by leaving it behind for a few days. When I sail, that's all I think of. The sea, my boat, the direction of the wind. I must say, coming back to all this was a huge shock. I mean it's like something out of a horror story, isn't it?'

'I thought fantasy novels were more your thing? I understand you're Valde Brix's agent.'

Twice in as many days, Brix's name had popped up. Henrik was still trying to get his head around how Jensen came into it. So far, he'd drawn a blank.

'Agent, accountant, PR manager, negotiator, confidant, bad cop to his good. Call it what you like, Brix and I go way back. I've heard it said that he doesn't dare tie his shoelaces without consulting me,' said Lund, laughing with a mouthful of irregular teeth, before checking himself and rearranging his face in sombre folds. 'Do tell me how I can assist you. I'd like to do anything within my power to help.'

'Where are you staying at the moment?'

'Oh, just down the road at D'Angleterre.'

Nice for some, Henrik thought. If Lund could afford one of Copenhagen's most expensive hotels, then Brix had to be doing very well out of his books.

'Of course, I understand that you must search the apartment thoroughly, and they said I'll be allowed back at some point to pick up a few things. Do you know who the poor woman was yet, and how long she's been in there for?'

'Not yet, but we soon will,' said Henrik. 'Meanwhile, what can you tell me about it?'

'Nothing,' said Lund, opening his hands, palms up. 'I've simply no clue. Where exactly was she again?'

'Behind the wall at the back of your larder.'

Henrik watched Lund closely. He was either an excellent actor, or genuinely shocked as his hands flew up to his mouth. 'My God.'

'You ever touched that wall?'

'Never,' said Lund. 'The larder has been there since my parents' time. I took over the flat from them, you see. I simply had no idea.'

'When was that?'

'Let me see now,' said Lund, eyes looking at the ceiling. 'It would have been in 1985.'

Mia Steen had been reported missing in 1988. If it was her, there was no need to go further back into the Lund family history.

'So the flat went to you when they died. No siblings?'

'None.'

'And you were only twenty-one at the time?'

'Yes, but I had a legal guardian until I was twenty-five.'

'What were you doing during those years?'

'Not much. I tried studying law but dropped out. Far too boring for me, and money wasn't an object.'

'So how did you spend your time?'

'Oh, having fun, dabbling in this or that, until Brix had his big breakthrough and needed someone to look after his business interests.'

'Which you were good at?'

'A darn sight better than I am at writing books about wizards and secret scriptures,' said Lund.

'You never married or had kids?'

'No. Never been into all that,' said Lund.

Was he gay, or just not interested? Henrik wondered. His statement was ambiguous.

'How did you two meet?'

'We were at high school together. Like I said, we go way back. Later – it must have been a couple of years after I inherited the apartment – we bumped into each other at a bar and rekindled our friendship.'

'So that must have been what, 1987?' said Henrik.

'Yes, that's about right,' said Lund. 'Anyway, Brix needed a place to stay with his girlfriend for a few months, and I needed the company, so they moved in.'

'What was the girlfriend's name?'

'Marion Jensen, a beautiful woman. Artist. I believe she's still working, though I hear she's become something of a recluse. Alas, it didn't last between them, and she eventually moved out, as did Brix, but the three of us had a summer together if memory serves me right.'

Marion Jensen. The name stirred something in his memory. Where had he heard it before?

'Tell me, were either Brix or Marion, or both of them, ever alone in the apartment?'

'Well, yes. When I was away sailing. They each had their own key,' said Lund. He seemed suddenly to realise the implications of what he'd just said. 'Oh God, you don't think he . . . that they . . .? No, it's too ridiculous, I don't know what possessed me to even think that.'

'I'm not saying anything.' Henrik was developing a headache. Lund seemed sincere but had an oily manner about him – probably to be expected for someone who earned his living talking people into signing on the dotted line.

Henrik threw his business card onto the table. 'Call me if you think of anything else that might be relevant.'

He got up, and Lund rose to his feet, and they shook hands once more. Lund's were dry and leathery. There was no sweat on his brow, no jittery movements.

'We'll need to speak with you again,' Henrik said. 'No more sailing. Stay at your hotel where we can find you. And we'll need a DNA sample from you.'

'Of course,' said Lund. 'Anything at all.'

12

Karo stood on the path wearing a pair of giant sunglasses, and a red summer dress. 'I brought you these as a thank you,' she said, holding up a bouquet of pink roses. 'You should have seen my boyfriend when I got home. He was so remorseful. Made us dinner and everything. Promised never to do it again.'

Why doesn't that make me feel better? Jensen thought as she took the flowers. 'These are lovely,' she said, placing the bouquet on Ea's pram. Like her cot, bouncy chair, changing table and sling – and most of her clothes – it had been bought for her by Margrethe as a gift when Jensen had returned from hospital (Ea had arrived three months early, taking her by surprise).

Jensen was still reeling from her meeting with Brix, and from skimming through the hundreds of messages he'd been sent by his stalker.

It was impossible to read them all, but as far as she could tell, they were loosely divided into three stages.

Starting in December, the first messages had been relatively mild, with no obvious purpose other than annoyance. Typically, they'd consisted of publicly available photos of Brix, on which the stalker had drawn glasses, moustaches and devil horns, like some schoolyard bully. The text amounted to nothing more than lame insults: 'Brix is a randy boar', or 'Brix can't keep his dick in his trousers'.

The second stage had started in February when the stalker had turned harsher and more threatening, calling Brix a hypocrite for pretending to be a family man, and alluding to something he'd done, which would have grave consequences: 'People like you think you can just take whatever you want. You'll soon learn otherwise.'

The third stage had begun just two weeks ago when the threats had become sinister, with a series of photos of Brix and his family, taken in and around his home.

'Own up to what you have done, or I will report you for rape,' read one message.

The stalker had frequently sent more than fifty messages in a day, in two or three separate bursts. The onslaught had been relentless, every single day for five months.

And just now, Brix had texted her the latest missive: a photo of herself and Ea leaving his house this morning. 'You just can't help yourself, can you?' said the message.

She pushed the thought away, smiling at Karo as they started walking towards Østerbro on the lakeside path. 'I meant to ask you about your tattoo. What does it say?'

'This?' said Karo, pointing to her collarbone. 'It says, "Not all those who wander are lost." I saw it somewhere and liked it.'

'What does it mean?' said Jensen.

'It means that we shouldn't be making assumptions about people who make different choices to us. They might still know what they're doing.'

'Do you?' Jensen said.

'I like to think so,' said Karo, looking away.

Jensen reminded herself that she needed to be careful, and not push Karo too hard, if she was going to help her. 'Tell me about yourself,' she said. 'What do you do for work?'

'I'm in marketing,' said Karo. 'Boring, right? But I work freelance from home, which means I can go for a walk in the middle of the day. It'll make things easier once I have the baby. And you?'

'I'm a journalist for *Dagbladet*. When I'm not on maternity leave.'

'Now that sounds glamorous.'

'Try the opposite,' Jensen laughed. 'Newspapers are on their way out. There's no money, everyone's struggling to just stay afloat. I mean, when did you last pay for news?'

'Never,' said Karo. She laughed. 'OK, I see your point.'

'Where did you meet your boyfriend?' Jensen said. 'Have you been together long?'

'Not really. Since just before Christmas last year. We met in a bar. He couldn't take his eyes off me.'

'Sounds romantic. Was it mutual?'

'Very much so. A whirlwind romance. Flowers, expensive restaurants, gifts, tons of texts. We were so happy,' she said. 'I just knew from the off that I wanted his child. Does that sound weird?'

'Not at all,' said Jensen, trying to keep her voice non-judgemental. 'So what's he like?'

'Smart. Really passionate. Works in IT. A good person,' Karo said. 'That's what I was trying to tell you yesterday. He's not some domestic abuser, so please don't think that of him.'

Jensen smiled, careful not to let her complicated emotions show. She'd been laid siege to in much the same way by her last boyfriend. Turned out it was all one big lie.

'How about you and Ea's dad?' Karo said.

'Similar story with the whirlwind romance but we're not together any more,' said Jensen, realising too late that this made it sound as though, cynically, she was condemning Karo's relationship to the same fate. 'It's a bit of a mess, to tell you the truth.'

'I'm sorry.'

'No, no, I'm absolutely fine. It's clearly a very different situation to yours.'

Stop rambling, Jensen commanded herself. *You're making it worse.*

She paused and looked at the swans, wishing she could be more like them, majestic above the water, even when pedalling like fury below. She'd always struggled to hide her emotions.

'Oh, I don't know,' said Karo. 'Sometimes I wonder if he and I will make it.'

'Why do you say that?'

Karo looked wistful all of a sudden. 'Oh, nothing, just . . . love is never straightforward, is it?'

Jensen nodded, thinking of Henrik. Their relationship was definitely complicated. Yet at the heart of things, it was also extremely simple: they loved one another but they couldn't be together.

She had thought of him again earlier as she read the news about the woman who had been raped and beaten in Frederiksberg Gardens. For a moment, she'd wished she was back at the newspaper working on the story.

Instead, she'd texted Gustav, inviting him around for a takeaway this evening, so she could find out more.

'What about your parents?' she said to Karo. 'Do they live nearby? Could they help you when the baby comes?'

'I don't see much of them, to be honest, nor my siblings,'

Karo said. 'They don't like my boyfriend, and the feeling's mutual.'

'Why?'

'They find him odd. He's not, not really . . . We just don't socialise much. We prefer to be together.'

'You used the past tense earlier. You said that the two of you *were* so happy. What changed?'

Karo smiled. 'Wow, I can tell you're a good journalist. Very perceptive. But let's not talk about me. How about your family?'

'My mum lives in North Jutland and hasn't been to Copenhagen in years, so no help there, and I've never met my dad,' said Jensen.

It felt too soon, too personal, to tell Karo about Brix.

'Then we're both on our own,' Karo said. 'Perhaps we can help each other?'

Jensen liked the idea of that. She didn't want to spoil it by pointing out that Karo wasn't really on her own, given that she had a boyfriend, albeit one who had given her a black eye.

They began to walk again, approaching the end of Sortedam Lake. If they turned right and crossed to the other side, they wouldn't be far from the Potato Rows, she realised. The last thing she wanted was to run into Brix.

'I'm famished,' she said. 'I know a really nice café near here. Fancy stopping for a bite to eat? My treat.'

Karo lit up in a big smile. 'Yes, please.'

On the way to the café, they passed a parcel shop and Jensen remembered the cardboard package in her bag.

'What was that?' said Karo when she'd dropped it off.

Realising that Karo might have caught something of the writing on the packaging, Jensen opted for the truth. 'It's a paternity test.'

'So that's what you meant when you said that your

relationship with Ea's dad is messy? He's denying that she's his?'

Jensen made a neutral face. She wasn't lying, she told herself, just failing to correct a misunderstanding.

There would be time enough for the truth when the test result came back. By then, she would be grateful for having someone to talk to about it.

13

Standing a few metres behind Liv under the circular stone colonnade at the old police yard in Copenhagen, Henrik automatically scanned the faces of the assembled reporters, before remembering that Jensen wouldn't be there.

The press conference was packed, the crowd humming with anticipation. As he'd predicted, the attack in Frederiksberg Gardens – announced in a press release an hour ago – had pushed the woman in the wall off the front pages.

He was already hot in his police jacket, his throat constricted by the black tie he kept on the back of his office door for formal occasions.

He'd never cared for wearing uniform. It reminded him of what he was: a mere number in an institution that would carry on long after his death. Liv, on the other hand, looked like she'd been born to represent the force. She stood tall, radiating authority, her blonde hair shining like a crown in the TV lights.

The crowd fell silent when she stepped up to the bouquet of microphones. She had a print-out in her hand but didn't as much as glance at it. 'My name is Liv Harder, and I'm the head of the violent crimes unit of Copenhagen Police. In the past twenty-four hours, we've launched two major investigations. Yesterday morning, during a flooding incident in a property in Bredgade, the remains of a young woman were discovered behind a wall. The identity of the deceased is unknown at this time, and tests into the cause of death are still ongoing, though we hope to have more information shortly.' She stopped for breath as she let her eyes roam over the crowd. You could tell from the silence that she had the journalists wrapped around her little finger. 'Secondly, yesterday morning, a fifty-four-year-old woman was found in Frederiksberg Gardens. She'd sustained a violent sexual assault and is currently undergoing treatment at the national hospital, where her condition remains critical. We're working as hard as we can to solve these two serious crimes and find the perpetrators. Meanwhile, I would like to invite members of the public with information on the two cases to step forward. As of now, we have no further comments. Thank you.'

There was an immediate explosion of noise as the journalists all shouted their questions at once, but Liv had already stepped away and was heading back through the tall black doors of the police building.

Following her, Henrik spotted someone holding up a mobile phone a couple of metres from his face. The lad, barely out of his teens, was familiar to him, although his attire was new. He'd shaved off his lank dark hair and was wearing a bucket hat and khaki utility vest with baggy jeans, like a rapper about to step on stage at the Roskilde music festival.

Jensen's loud-mouthed apprentice.

Gustav Skov.

'Detective Inspector Jungersen,' Gustav shouted in a shrill voice. 'So there's a dangerous rapist on the loose in Copenhagen. Are women safe on our streets?'

The crowd fell silent, and even Liv turned to see what was going on.

Henrik became conscious that everyone was looking at him staring at Gustav, mouth agape, as though the boy had ripped a hole in him.

Liv stepped in. 'People should remain vigilant, as always, and report anything suspicious to us. Otherwise, everyone should carry on as normal, and we'd discourage any panic,' she said, grabbing Henrik's arm.

The shouting resumed, following them inside as the big doors closed behind them.

14

'Kemal sends his regards. He refused to let me pay for the food,' said Gustav, pushing past Jensen with a plastic bag smelling wonderfully of kebabs.

Kemal was the owner of their favourite takeaway in Nørrebro. They'd once helped find a friend of his, and he never let them forget it.

Gustav dumped the bag on the floor and kicked off his trainers. 'Where is she?'

Despite never having shown the remotest interest in babies, he'd formed a strong bond with Ea and now regarded himself as her uncle. Recently, he'd even been babysitting once or twice.

'Asleep, but if you're really quiet, you can go and see her,' she said.

He tiptoed into the bedroom. A few minutes later, he returned with a smile on his face. 'She's got so big.'

'Tell me about it. Never stops feeding.' She opened the boxes of food, salivating at the sight of the kebabs: roasted lamb drenched in garlic sauce, resting on pillowy flatbreads filled with salad. She tucked into hers, letting the sauce run down her hand. 'How are things at the newspaper?' she asked.

'Dismal as per,' said Gustav with his mouth full. 'Even more people have left.'

She'd assumed as much. There'd been no money for a maternity cover for her own role as chief crime reporter (actually, the only crime reporter) and a couple of the other journalists had left or were on long-term sick leave without having been replaced.

'Margrethe is asking when you're coming back. She's drafted in the guys from Christiansborg to cover the crime gig, and they're making a right mess of it.'

Political journalists covering crime? Things must really be getting desperate.

'Anyway, I'm working on this mega cool story,' said Gustav, a smile spreading across his grease-smeared face.

'Oh?'

'Yeah, someone tipped me off.'

'Who?'

'Not Brøgger if that's what you're thinking,' said Gustav.

It was a while since Ernst Brøgger, the ubiquitous solicitor, had passed them anything useful. Jensen reminded herself that she needed a word with him about Brix.

'About what?' she said, wiping sauce off her chin.

'I don't want to say until I've checked it out. But if it comes off, it's going to be epic, a Class A exposé. Prize-winning stuff.' Gustav pretended to busy himself removing bits of lettuce from his multi-pocketed khaki gilet.

She smiled at him. 'I see. You're on a mission to prove to Margrethe that she should hire you permanently.'

'Maybe,' he said.

Jensen couldn't help feeling proud. At Gustav's age, she'd

been just as eager to show her mettle as a reporter, exposing the truths that others tried to hide.

But his dream was unlikely to come true. As he was the editor's nephew, Margrethe would have all manner of trouble if she tried to put him on the permanent payroll, given the number of unemployed union members looking for jobs.

'I saw your boyfriend today,' he said, taking another massive bite of kebab.

'Stop calling him that.'

'He and his fit new boss did a press conference. You know, on the woman in the wall and that rape in Frederiksberg. It was pretty obvious they'd no clue about either.'

'How?'

'They provided zero info. It was a case of, "Can the public please phone in and tell us what's happening?".'

'That's hardly fair, Gustav.'

'See for yourself.' He pulled out his phone, thumbing through his videos before landing on the right one. The camera was shaky at first, panning over the crowd.

She recognised a few competitors from TV and the other papers and felt a painful yearning to be back there. Her turf, her people.

Gustav was right about the statement. It was a holding pattern, even though Liv Harder, blonde and poised, had delivered it with gravitas.

At the end, the video homed in on Henrik, eyes flicking left and right as they did when he was under pressure. He looked uncomfortable in his uniform jacket and kept running a finger around his collar and tie.

Then Gustav shouted a question about safety on the streets, and Henrik stared straight at him, seemingly lost for words, until his boss answered the question and led him inside.

'He hates press conferences. Always has done,' she said, feeling a little sorry for him. 'You could call him, see if he'll give you some background information. We've helped him enough times in the past, you and I.'

'Maybe,' said Gustav, putting away his phone. 'Anyway, have you met your dad yet?'

'I don't know for sure that he's my dad, but yes, I went to see Brix.'

'What's he like?'

She shrugged. 'Bit full of himself.'

'And?'

'And nothing. I got him to take a paternity test, so I'll soon know for sure.' She thought carefully, before continuing. 'He has a stalker and wants me to find out who it is.'

'What, like some nutty fan? Why doesn't he just go to the police?'

'The stalker is threatening to accuse him of rape. He's afraid people will think it's true.'

'Would be a massive scoop if it was.'

'Precisely.'

'But it's definitely not?'

'According to him, no, but to be honest, I don't really know what to think. He's acting very strangely. He sent his wife and child away a few days ago, and has now virtually barricaded himself inside his house, curtains drawn, scared to death of going out.'

'We could ask Fie to look into it,' said Gustav.

'We?'

'Yes. I'll help you, on one condition – I get the exclusive if there's something to it.'

'Wow, that's almost an offer I can't refuse.'

The thought of asking Fie had already crossed her mind. Fie's work on a major investigation before Christmas had brought her exceptional hacking skills to the attention of the police, and she was now employed by the National Cyber Crime Centre, also known as NC3.

Without Fie, the chances of finding Brix's stalker were close to zero.

'I'll call her,' she said.

Having sated his immediate hunger, Gustav began to look around the room, his eyes eventually landing on the long-stemmed pink roses from Karo, which were now in a vase on the windowsill. 'Who gave you those?' he said.

'Oh, just someone I met.'

'What, like a man?' said Gustav.

'No, a woman.'

His eyes widened even further.

'Not in *that* way, for Christ's sake. She's a friend, or I think she might become one.'

Gustav frowned. 'You don't do friends.'

'Thanks.'

'Speaking of which, Liron asked what he's done to offend you, since you never stop by any more.'

This was true, Jensen was embarrassed to admit. She'd gone off coffee in her pregnancy, so her visits to Liron's van in Sankt Peders Stræde, a few minutes' walk from the newspaper, had stopped, and after Ea's arrival she'd never resumed the habit.

Liron had magical powers to brew exactly the kind of coffee she needed at any one time.

She missed their conversations.

Unlike Brix's conundrum, however, this was a problem she could easily solve.

15

In a leafy street in Frederiksberg, Henrik lay awake next to his sleeping wife, worrying about disappointing her.

It was something he excelled at, and normally did without thinking, but he sensed that he and Louise were teetering close to the edge once more.

It was nearly half-past three in the morning, the house was still and dark, and his three kids were safely tucked up in bed. In just three hours, he would be getting up, but sleep continued to evade him.

Yesterday had been difficult, topped by his public humiliation when Liv had to come to his rescue over an inane question from Gustav Skov.

He would have answered it eventually, but the sight of the lad in that stupid bucket hat had reminded him so strongly of Jensen that he'd frozen to the spot.

Liv had been good about it, but the embarrassment still stung, and the feeling that he'd messed up his life wasn't helping.

The day after tomorrow was his wedding anniversary, and Louise had her heart set on lunch at a particular restaurant. Her mother had agreed to having the children, and the table had been booked.

It had seemed easier to agree when she told him over dinner, but he couldn't go.

Four years ago he'd gone to the same restaurant with Jensen, and a member of staff might recognise him. ('Nice to see you again, Mr Jungersen. Same table as last time?')

The chickens are truly coming home to roost, he thought, cringing with shame.

He'd stuck to his promise not to see her but erasing her from his brain had been harder than he thought. It didn't help that he couldn't stop ruminating over what she was doing with Brix.

He'd read somewhere that the author was married to a woman twenty-three years his junior, which put her and Jensen at around the same age.

Had she got herself romantically involved with Brix? After all, she'd proven herself a poor judge of character as far as men were concerned.

He knew that it wasn't fair or realistic to expect Jensen to live as a nun. One day, a good man was bound to enter her life.

But Brix? He was already married, for Christ's sake. Wasn't one woman enough for the bastard? he thought, rather hypocritically.

He forced his mind onto the two new cases.

When it came to it, there wasn't such a big difference between the woman in the wall and Jane Dahl-Thomsen, now fighting for her life in a hospital bed.

Both had been brutally used and tossed aside by a man who regarded it as his right to do as he wanted with their bodies.

What if it had been his wife, snoring gently beside him? Or, God forbid, Jensen?

Violent crime against women, including murder and rape, remained stubbornly frequent, despite Denmark's relatively advanced gender equality. It was a paradox, one on which he had attended many conferences and seminars over the years.

No one seemed to have the answer.

He'd seen first-hand the horror that lay behind the statistics, more times than he wanted to remember, but as he lay blinking into the darkness, he felt a kind of anger rise in him, cold and primitive, a desire to strike back.

Funder was right. It wasn't good enough.

Day Three

16

The coffee van was parked by the old streetlamp in Sankt Peders Stræde, opposite the bakery with the golden pretzel above the door. The man from Jerusalem who'd made it his mission to teach the Danes to drink coffee – or so he had always claimed – was sitting on a folding chair in the sun, looking at his phone.

They'd met shortly after Jensen had returned to Copenhagen, struggling to find her feet after her long stint in London. She'd been drawn to him – one outsider to another – but Liron had turned out to be better connected in the city than she'd first thought. Whether through his network of devoted clients, or by some murkier means, he always seemed able to lay his hands on any information he wanted. She'd benefited from this on more than one occasion.

Liron looked like an old hippie, but she'd been to his flat once, surprised to find it more spartan than a monk's cell. His almost complete lack of personal possessions suggested he was wary of laying down roots – which was fitting for a man who had a habit of disappearing for weeks on end.

He'd always looked out for her, perhaps seeing something reckless in her character that warranted protection, perhaps recognising that she had no one but herself to rely on.

They'd never been out for a drink, didn't even have each other's phone numbers – somehow neither of those things had felt right – but he was a friend, and lately he'd also become friends with Gustav.

'Fuck, Jensen, I thought you were dead!' he shouted with his usual fondness for peppering his broken Danish with swear words.

A flock of pigeons took off in fright as he leapt from his seat, feigning shock that she was carrying a baby, though she was certain Gustav had told him about Ea's arrival.

'Ea,' she said to her daughter. 'Meet Liron.'

Ea opened her eyes and looked at the strange, tall man with the goatee beard and gold tooth. Then she began to cry.

'Right,' he said. 'Pass her to uncle Liron.'

He was having none of Jensen's protests, and for the second time in as many days she handed her daughter over. Gradually, Ea fell quiet, as Liron whispered to her in his foreign tongue, showing her the van, the bakery on the other side of the street and his beaded bangle.

'Sit, Mama,' he commanded, pointing to his folding chair. He poured beans from a blue enamel tin into a grinder, as Ea looked at him adoringly from the crook of his arm.

Jensen didn't ask what he was making her, and he didn't ask what she wanted. That was the way it was between them.

After a few minutes, he handed her a thick-rimmed ceramic mug with a heart drawn in the milk foam. The coffee tasted of hazelnuts and dark chocolate.

'Made from decaffeinated beans, using the Swiss Water Process, so no chemicals. Better for the breast milk,' he said.

She looked at him, astonished. 'How do you know that?'

'My wife taught me.'

'You have a wife?'

'Had. I had many things,' said Liron. He touched his forehead to Ea's, and Jensen sensed that the window that had opened briefly on his past was now firmly closed.

Liron was as good at listening as he was reluctant to talk about his past. One day she would get it out of him.

She sat back, letting the sun and the coffee warm her outside and in.

'Who is her father?' said Liron.

'No one you need to worry about.'

'Is it that bastard cop? Because if it is, I'll smash his face in.'

'It's not Henrik Jungersen, if that's who you mean,' said Jensen. When she'd first taken Henrik to the coffee van, Liron's distinctly frosty reaction had made her regret ever confiding in him about their affair.

'Ea will grow up without a father,' she said. 'I did, and I'm absolutely fine.'

Liron shook his head at Ea, twirling a finger at his temple. Jensen jabbed him with an elbow, and he pretended that she'd hurt him, making Ea chuckle.

'Actually,' she said, 'there's this man who says he's my father, but my mother denies it.'

'She should know.'

'So why won't she tell me the truth?'

Liron shrugged. 'She'll have her reasons. Who is he anyway, this man?'

'That's classified.'

Liron was about to remonstrate with her when they were interrupted by a shout from across the street: 'Jensen?'

It was Karo, standing outside the bakery with a grease-stained paper bag.

'Karo!' Jensen called. 'Come and meet my friend Liron. You won't find better coffee in Copenhagen.'

'Who is *she*?' said Liron under his breath, as Karo crossed the street. In her bright-green dress and big sunglasses, she looked like a film star.

'A woman with a nasty boyfriend.'

'What?'

'There's a big bruise underneath those pretty sunglasses. He hit her, the day before yesterday just outside my flat. That's how we met.'

'What a bastard,' said Liron.

'And she's pregnant, so don't even think about it. Now shush.'

'Pleased to meet you,' said Karo as she walked up to them.

She and Liron shook hands and he held hers a tad too long, studying her face with an intensity that made even Jensen uncomfortable. 'I know you,' he said. 'Now, where have we met before? Take off your glasses and let me see you.'

'Liron, behave!' said Jensen, duffing him on the shoulder. She needed to have a word with him about his dodgy pick-up lines.

Karo laughed, but let her hair fall across her face as she lowered her gaze to the paper bag in her hand. 'I was just thinking that a double espresso would go nicely with these cinnamon swirls.'

Jensen began to salivate. 'Liron,' she said, 'make my friend a coffee, would you? She and I have an appointment with a pair of pastries in the King's Gardens.'

17

Henrik was in the galley kitchen at the office, making his third coffee of the day in a vain attempt to wake himself up. Lack of sleep had put him in a bad mood, and his wife had just reminded him that her parents were coming for dinner. They would be staying over and taking the kids out for the day tomorrow.

He hadn't told Louise yet that their wedding anniversary lunch in the smart restaurant wouldn't be happening. Taking her to a place full of memories of Jensen would be more than he could bear.

'Morning, Boss.' Mark had appeared in the doorway. 'It's been confirmed – the woman in the wall is definitely Mia Steen, reported missing by her mother in August 1988. I've talked to her, and she's on her way over.'

To his embarrassment Henrik felt relieved. The positive identification would make them busy. This meant he no longer had to make up an excuse for tomorrow.

He remembered Andreas Lund talking about the summer of 1987 when Brix and his girlfriend had been living with him for a few months. 'Any luck getting hold of Marion

Jensen?' he said to Mark, sniffing the milk before adding it to his coffee.

'No. A local constable has been out to her property, but it seems she's not there.'

'Where?'

'Somewhere out in the sticks in North Jutland.'

My God.

That was why the name had been so familiar. Jensen's mother was an artist and lived in North Jutland. Her name was Marion. He knew this because Jensen referred to her as Marion rather than 'Mum', which had always struck him as odd.

So Brix had once been her mother's boyfriend, and now Jensen was sniffing around his house. Why?

'Keep trying,' he said, trying not to reveal his thoughts.

In the corridor he bumped into Funder. She looked even worse than he felt. 'That bad?' he said.

'Worse. I only managed a few words with Jane Dahl-Thomsen before the doctors kicked me out, and she doesn't remember anything. Her date didn't do it, though.'

'Oh?'

'A waiter at Aline's Garden, a restaurant near the main park entrance in Frederiksberg, recognised Dahl-Thomsen's photo, so we checked the CCTV. She went to the toilet in the basement just after nine p.m. and never returned. The man she was with joked with the waiter about it. Apparently, it wasn't the first time a woman had left him mid-date, so he thought nothing of it. He stayed at the bar until closing time and got quite drunk. We'll take his statement as soon as we've found him.'

'Now you're going to tell me there's no CCTV from the basement,' said Henrik.

'Well, there's an exit down there, leading up some steps

to a small courtyard at the back where the bins are, but of course the camera facing that area wasn't working.'

'How did Dahl-Thomsen end up inside the park?'

Funder shrugged. 'We don't know that yet. But the perp could have followed her to the toilet and injected her there.'

'Have we been through her devices yet?'

'In progress. Other than her date, she hasn't been in contact with anyone outside her family for months.'

'Is there an ex-husband? Or ex-boyfriend?' From the picture that someone had put up in the incident room, Henrik had noticed that Dahl-Thomsen was a stunning woman with long dark hair and smouldering eyes.

Not that this was relevant, he reminded himself, remembering the course he'd been on.

'No,' said Funder. 'Her daughter told us that she lives alone. Divorced amicably seven years ago. There was someone a while back, a guy she was head over heels with, but it ended. Broke her heart, apparently, and now this. It's so incredibly unfair.'

'Who was it, the big love affair?'

'The daughter didn't know. The guys are going through her work contacts now, to see if anything pops up.'

'What does she do?'

'She's a sales rep for one of Denmark's largest publishers.'

'Which one?' he said.

Back in his office, he immediately googled the firm. It wasn't hard to tell that a good chunk of its income derived from a single mega star.

Valde Brix.

18

Jensen had wolfed down her cinnamon swirl and was now eyeing up Karo's, which still lay untouched in its bag. They were sitting cross-legged in the shade of a large tree in the King's Gardens, Jensen with Ea babbling on her lap.

Around them, people were basking in the sun, reading, chatting, dozing, but Karo was pensive, biting her lip.

'What's up?' said Jensen.

Karo drained her coffee. 'I didn't sleep a wink last night.'

'Because of what happened on Wednesday?'

'No,' said Karo. 'I've started to bleed. I'm afraid I'm going to lose the baby.' She closed her eyes, wincing the tears away.

'My God, did he hit you again?'

Karo shook her head, unconvincingly. 'I got up early, too anxious to sleep,' she said. 'I'd been walking around for ages when I saw the bakery and realised I hadn't eaten.' She looked forlornly at the uneaten pastry. 'What am I going to do?'

Tears blackened by mascara began to run under her sunglasses and down her cheeks.

'Go and see your GP immediately. They can send you for a scan. I can come if you like?'

'No, I'll be all right. I'll probably have to wait for hours.'

'Then call me afterwards, let me know what they say.'

'Or I could come around to yours?' said Karo. She was biting her lip again. 'It's probably best if we stay off our phones from now on. No texts or calls.'

'Why?'

'It's my boyfriend. I think he's monitoring me. "Who's Jensen?" he asked me last night. He thinks you're a man, and that I'm having an affair or something.'

'Karo, that's not right. He can't do that. It's an invasion of privacy.'

'Don't worry, I didn't give you away. I said you were someone I work with. Not that it helped much.'

'It's not me you should be thinking about,' said Jensen.

Karo looked at her. 'But I do. You're my friend and I don't want you to get caught up in all of this. I've deleted you from my phone. You should do the same with me.'

A young woman laughed uproariously next to them, surrounded by friends in high spirits. Karo looked at them wistfully, wiping snot from her nose with the back of her hand.

She was young, just twenty-seven. She should be carefree, not fearing for her safety, and worrying if her unborn child was going to survive.

Jensen took out her phone and did as she'd been asked. If it came to it, she still had Karo's handwritten note with her mobile number.

For now, it was important that Karo trusted her, and that she got seen by a doctor. They would spot the bruises, question how she'd got them.

Later, Jensen thought, she would make another attempt at persuading her to involve the police.

19

Two things struck Henrik as odd when he visited Valde Brix that afternoon.

Firstly, all the curtains in his swanky Potato Rows home were closed. Henrik assumed no one was in, but to his surprise the author himself opened the door, unshaven and distracted in a creased denim shirt.

And secondly, he seemed highly agitated, looking left and right down the street. No sooner had Henrik held up his warrant card than he found himself being pulled inside.

'Is everything all right?' he asked as they stood facing each other awkwardly in the dark entrance hall.

To Henrik's annoyance, despite his dishevelled appearance, Brix was rather handsome, tall with chiselled features and an intense gaze behind his dark-rimmed glasses. His obvious star power made Henrik feel nervous.

Get a grip, he thought.

'Why wouldn't it be all right?' said Brix, seemingly unsurprised to find a police detective in his home.

'Is there somewhere we can sit down?'

Reluctantly, Brix led them through to a kitchen at the

back. Henrik was relieved to see daylight coming through the windows. There was a highchair in one corner, and he noticed some toys, but saw no other sign of the author's young family.

He wasn't offered a seat; nevertheless he sat, leaning back in his most disarming pose.

Brix remained standing, with his arms folded across his chest. 'Go on, what is it I'm supposed to have done?' he said. 'I take it you're here because someone has reported me.'

'Why do you think that?'

Brix was beginning to look less certain of himself. 'Isn't that normally why you people turn up unannounced?'

Henrik ignored the question, frowning. 'What would someone have reported you for?'

'I asked first,' said Brix.

Henrik stared at him silently for a while. This usually prompted people to volunteer information. However, on Brix it seemed to have the opposite effect.

'At this stage, I was merely hoping that you'd be able to help me,' said Henrik after an uncomfortable pause.

Brix frowned. 'With what?'

'Does the name Mia Steen mean anything to you?'

'Is she the one who has reported me? Because I categorically deny having done anything wrong. In fact, I would like to call my lawyer right now.'

'No one has reported you,' said Henrik. 'Mia Steen is the name of the woman whose body has just been found behind a wall in an apartment in Bredgade. She was twenty when she went missing in the late eighties. Someone murdered her. Don't you watch the news?'

'No, of course, I did see that,' Brix said. 'But why are you asking me?'

'Did you know Mia?'

'Not that I recall.'

Henrik watched Brix closely, but he appeared to be genuinely blank.

'The apartment belongs to your agent, Andreas Lund.'

'Andreas? I don't understand.'

'Lund was very helpful. He told us that you lived in the apartment with your girlfriend for a spell in 1987.'

'That's right, but I don't see . . . what was the name of that woman again?'

'Mia Steen. Wait, let me show you.' Henrik took out his phone and brought up the photo of Mia smiling at her high-school graduation, oblivious to the horror that would befall her only two years later.

'My God,' said Brix. 'I do know her, I think. Did. And you say she was murdered?'

'Stabbed. Beaten. Raped, maybe.' Henrik looked intensely at Brix.

'It wasn't me,' said Brix, handing the phone back as though it had caught fire. 'I didn't do anything.'

He looked utterly terrified.

He was hiding something. But what?

'When did you meet Mia?'

'She must have come along to one of the parties in the apartment.'

'Who invited her?'

Brix shrugged. 'Could have been anyone.'

'Were you and Mia lovers?'

'No,' said Brix, red-faced now. 'I had a girlfriend, Marion.'

'You must have been in your early twenties then, and Mia was a beautiful young woman. Surely, you could have been tempted to stray?'

'I said no.'

'When did you last see Mia?

'You can't seriously expect me to remember that. It was almost forty years ago.'

'You seem very reluctant to talk to me. I can tell that you're nervous. Why is that?'

Brix threw his head back, ran a hand with silver rings through his salt-and-pepper hair. 'I've answered your questions. What more do you want?'

All right, Henrik thought. *I want to know what you're up to with Jensen.*

Of course, he didn't say it. If word got back to Liv that he'd asked Brix to account for his relationship with a *Dagbladet* journalist unrelated to the investigation, he could be in serious trouble. Worst case, if she learned the whole truth, Liv might consider his association with Jensen a conflict of interest and take him off the case. Eventually, word would get back to his wife, and his life wouldn't be worth living.

Instead, he turned to Brix and said as calmly as he could: 'You'll need to come to the station for a formal interview. Your lawyer is welcome to join us. In the meantime, I'd like you to remain in Copenhagen. Got any travel plans?'

'No,' said Brix. He was looking scared again.

'Good, keep it that way.'

Brix followed him back through the hallway. 'I trust this won't get out. I don't want my name dragged through the mud. Whatever you may think, I'm totally innocent.'

'One step at a time,' said Henrik. He said his goodbyes and let himself out, wondering what Jensen's mother would have to say about it all when they managed to get hold of her.

*

He was late for dinner. Not that work had kept him. The team was still collecting information, trying to form a picture of what had happened.

Mia's mother wouldn't be arriving till tomorrow, and Marion Jensen still hadn't been tracked down. A neighbour in North Jutland claimed to have seen her cycling in the direction of the local town, but from there the trace had gone cold.

He and Mark had interviewed Andreas Lund again. Appearing genuinely shocked, the agent had told them that Mia Steen had worked as his cleaner.

'Did she clean for you while Valde Brix and his girlfriend were staying with you?'

'Yes, I think so. Though she later left,' Lund had said. He hadn't been able to recall when this had happened but said it had been her own decision. Later, he'd heard that she'd gone travelling in Asia. 'And to think that all the time she was in that wall. Poor, poor Mia.'

'Brix seemed to recall that she'd come along to a party in the apartment. Did she?'

Lund had looked blank. 'I suppose it's possible.'

Henrik could tell how this was going to go. Without evidence, it all came down to who remembered what. Who was lying, and who was telling the truth.

He paused outside the door to the kitchen, manning up for what was in store. Dinner with his in-laws was usually a trial in patience.

'You could have called,' hissed his wife as he pecked her on the cheek.

'Ah, at last, the hero returns,' bellowed his father-in-law, Knud, large glass of red in hand. 'Been out getting criminals off our streets?'

The old fool still thought he spent his days chasing hooligans and cat burglars with a truncheon.

He'd given up explaining that he was a detective these days, wearing civil clothes and leading a team. If he were a brain surgeon, it wouldn't be good enough for Knud's precious daughter.

Henrik helped himself to a large scoop of meatballs in curry sauce (love of traditional Danish fare was pretty much the only thing he and Knud had in common). His mind was swirling with thoughts of Valde Brix and the crazy coincidence that he, of all people, should once have hung out in the apartment in Bredgade.

Or maybe it wasn't a coincidence. Maybe it was linked to Jensen's interest in the smug prick. He had to speak to her at the earliest opportunity, find out exactly what was going on. As he got busy scooping rice and curry sauce into his mouth, he became aware of someone calling his name.

Looking up, he found his mother-in-law, Jytte, smiling at him from across the table. 'Louise has just been telling us about your exciting plans for tomorrow,' she said. 'Knud and I are looking forward to spending some time with our grandchildren. We're taking them to Tivoli.'

A self-satisfied look passed across his father-in-law's face. Five tickets to the traditional funfair in the middle of the city – not to mention tour passes, ice creams and hot dogs – didn't come cheap, but then Knud loved playing the big man with the chequebook.

'About that,' said Henrik turning to his wife. 'I'm afraid we're going to have to postpone.'

'I knew it,' said Louise, emptying her glass of red. Her slurred voice suggested it wasn't her first. 'What did I just tell you? Henrik's going to let me down again. Looks like I'll be joining you in Tivoli.'

She wasn't taking it as badly as Henrik had feared, though perhaps this in itself was worrying. One way or another, he sensed there would be a price to pay. 'I'll make it up to you, I promise,' he said. 'Only we've just taken on these two new cases, so it's all hands on deck.'

'Ah yes,' said Jytte. 'We saw it on the news. The woman in the wall. How macabre. And then that horrible rape in Frederiksberg Gardens.'

Henrik liked Jytte. To his mind, the woman deserved a medal for making it this far without strangling her husband in his sleep.

'What I want to know,' said Knud, 'is what possesses a woman to walk through a park alone at night.'

Henrik glared at him. 'I can't discuss the details of the case, but women and men are entitled to walk alone where they please in this city without fear of attack.'

'In an ideal world,' said Knud. 'But there is such a thing as taking precautions. You should be careful, Louise. Remember this happened just down the road from here. It could be you next.'

'Way ahead of you, Dad. I never leave home without my trusted pepper spray.'

'Your illegal pepper spray, you mean,' Henrik said. They'd argued about the damn spray ad nauseam, but Louise blankly refused to throw it away.

'I don't care,' she said. 'We have the right to defend ourselves. Especially after this.'

'Quite right,' Knud said, refilling her glass and then his own. Jytte wasn't offered any.

'Henrik thinks he is oh so important,' Louise continued. 'No one else can do what he does.'

'A woman has been killed, another almost died from her injuries,' Henrik said. 'You can't expect me to—'

'Oh don't worry,' Louise interrupted. 'From you, I expect nothing.'

This triggered a belly laugh from Knud, and Henrik imagined leaning over the table and pushing the man's face into the curry sauce.

He finished his meatballs in silence, his mind drifting as the conversation turned to a popular TV programme. He only watched the football and couldn't tell one celebrity from another. Except Brix, whose face was pretty much printed on his eyelids by now.

Suddenly, he yearned very badly to see Jensen. The three people around the table didn't understand him, never had. Not even Jytte, although she at least tried to.

'I'm sorry,' he said, getting up from his chair and taking his plate to the sink. 'I'm afraid I have to get back to the office.'

'You're leaving *now*?' said his wife. 'We've not even had dessert yet.'

'Yeah. Something I have to do. Urgently.'

20

Jensen crawled into bed exhausted. She'd spent the evening researching Brix's stalker and getting progressively more downhearted.

Stalking had been criminalised in Denmark a few years before, and the police had been given more powers to investigate, but this was next to no help, seeing that Brix refused to involve them.

She'd no clue where to start. As promised, Brix had emailed her the list of women he'd known, but this was so long and contained so many blanks that just glancing at it had made her weary. Was Brix some kind of sex addict? Was he being stalked by one of the women he'd bedded and rejected, or was there something else going on?

Brøgger had to know more. To her surprise, the usually elusive lawyer had agreed to meet her in the morning. Afterwards she would be seeing Fie, the hacker from Roskilde who was now working for the police.

And Karo's baby was all right, thank God. She'd called around to the flat earlier in the evening.

'I'm so relieved,' Karo had said.

'What did they say to your black eye?'

Karo had smiled. 'They suggested I be more careful around the house and avoid colliding with my cupboard doors in future.'

'So, you didn't tell them what happened.'

'To be honest I'd rather forget about it. Do you think we could talk about something else?'

Jensen had gone to the kitchen to make tea. On her return, there had been a message from Brix on her phone.

Call me ASAP. PS, wonderful to see you yesterday. Kiss.

She wondered if Karo had read it, but then she would have had no idea who it was from.

Karo had noticed Brix's tome propping open the living room door, though. 'Best use for it,' she'd commented with a laugh. 'I can't stand that man's books.'

Trust Brix to push for answers already. He would just have to wait.

Jensen was drifting off to sleep when her phone pinged with a text message. She couldn't help squinting at the screen. The name and thumbnail photo made her sit up.

Am outside. Let me in?

'What the hell are you doing here?' she said, opening the door.

Henrik was dressed like a caricature of himself in his black jeans, white shirt, leather jacket and beaten-up boots. For a moment it seemed as though he was about to hug her, then he put his hands in his pockets and tried to look nonchalant. 'I'd have rung the bell, but I didn't want to wake the baby,' he said.

She was glad to see him. Despite everything, she'd missed their connection, the strange spark that had ignited when they met all those years ago. 'But waking me up was OK?' she said, trying to smooth down her wild hair as she let him in.

'Jensen, it's half past nine in the evening. There are bars that don't open this early.'

'Says the man who never looked after a baby.'

'You used to be a night owl,' he said.

'Well, I've changed.'

'Not from where I'm standing.'

To her immense irritation, she blushed under his gaze, but then he moved on, walking around her living room and looking at her sparse furnishings and baby detritus. 'I love what you've done with the place.'

'Work in progress,' she said. 'Anyway, why are you here? Ea will be awake again soon, and I really need to get some sleep.'

'It's a bit delicate. That's why I didn't just call. You might find what I'm about to ask a bit odd.'

'What, odder than you showing up in my flat out of the blue?' she said. 'OK then, ask, but be quick about it.'

Henrik hesitated as if searching for the right words. 'I understand that you've been taking an interest in the author Valde Brix.'

A claxon went off in her brain. How did he know about that? Had Brix told him? Had he finally done the sensible thing and reported his stalker to the police?

'Taking an interest?' she said.

'You were seen outside his house.'

Jensen thought of the blonde woman who had stared at her from the doorway across the street. How had she known who she was? How had Henrik found out?

'Seen?' she said.

'If you're just going to repeat every word I say, we'll be here for hours.'

'Who saw me?'

'So you were there?'

'I didn't say that. Who alleges that they saw me?'

'I'm afraid I can't reveal my source, but the person is one hundred per cent reliable. Isn't that what you hacks always say?'

She'd forgotten how utterly annoying he could be. 'OK,' she snapped. 'Say I walked past his house. What about it? Can't I go where I want?'

It was Henrik's turn to look embarrassed. 'Of course. Only Brix's name has come up in connection with a case I'm working on.'

'You mean the body in Bredgade? Not the rape in Frederiksberg Gardens, surely?'

Jensen couldn't believe what she was hearing. Was this what the threats against Brix were all about? Was he involved in those stories somehow? Surely, he would have told her?

Or would he?

The woman in the wall had been identified as Mia Steen, a twenty-year-old reported missing in 1988. Her picture was all over the papers. Would she find the name on Brix's list of conquests?

'I . . . can't go into detail,' Henrik said. 'It's just, I wonder what you know about him?'

'That's my business.'

Henrik's face was now bright red. 'Look, I'm sorry,' he said. 'I can see I've made a mistake . . . only I thought, if you were going to write something about Brix, or whatever, it would be helpful to know, in case it's relevant.'

Was it relevant? Possibly, but she wasn't about to discuss

it with Henrik. She didn't want to tell him about Brix claiming to be her father, not till she had the results of the paternity test and perhaps not even then.

Henrik had decided to stay with his wife. She understood his decision and had made peace with it. But that meant he no longer got to ask her personal questions.

She walked him to the front door and opened it. 'If you won't tell me why you're really here, or how Brix comes into it, then I can't help you.'

She said it knowing full well that the issue wasn't Henrik, but Brix himself and whether she could trust her alleged father at all.

Jensen raised herself on her elbows, heart racing as she listened in the dark. The flat was quiet, but something had woken her up. It wasn't Ea, who was sleeping peacefully beside her, nor Wolfgang, the cat, whom she hadn't seen for a few days now.

Her mobile said it was 01.17.

There was another text message and three missed calls from Brix.

Now someone was hammering with their fists on her front door. In her confused state, she thought it might be him. Was he in trouble in some way? Brøgger had probably told him where she lived.

What if it was Karo's boyfriend?

She moved into the hallway, heart in her throat as the hammering resumed.

'Jensen, it's me. Let me in, please.'

A voice she recognised.

When she opened the door, Karo almost stumbled over the threshold. 'Thank God,' she cried. 'I didn't know where else to go.'

There was blood on her nose. Her forearms were covered in red scratches; her nails were broken. 'He just went mad,' she said.

Jensen helped her into the living room and onto the sofa. 'Now I really am calling the police,' she said.

'No, don't, please don't, you'll only make it worse,' Karo pleaded.

'How could it be any worse?'

'He says he doesn't want me to go out unless he's with me. But I can't just stay in the flat all the time, can I?'

'Could he have followed you here?'

'No. I waited till he'd fallen asleep. Then I ran. Please, I wouldn't have come if I thought you'd call the police. Can I sleep here? Just for tonight, until I get myself sorted?'

'Of course, Karo, you can stay here as long as you like, but—'

'Thank you, I knew you wouldn't let me down. I mean, I feel like I know you, even though we've only met a few times. I think I can trust you.'

Jensen cleaned the blood from her face with cotton wool dipped in lukewarm water, applying antiseptic cream to her scratches. By the time she was done, Karo was calmer. 'Don't worry,' she said. 'He doesn't know I'm here, or who you are.'

'It's not him I'm worried about,' said Jensen. 'You're in danger, Karo. There are places you can go, people you can talk to about this sort of thing.'

They helped each other make up a bed on the sofa, and Jensen found Karo a toothbrush, a couple of painkillers and an old T-shirt to sleep in.

'Thank you,' Karo said when she was tucked up in bed. 'I just want to sleep and sleep. I'm utterly exhausted.'

'Of course. We'll talk about it in the morning.'

They did need to talk, Jensen thought when she was back in her own bed, wide awake and staring at the ceiling. She was glad Karo felt safe with her, but her boyfriend had to be stopped.

Tomorrow, she would call Henrik, ask his advice on how best to help given Karo's reluctance to go to the police. This would also give her the opportunity to make amends for their awkward conversation, and to find out how Brix was involved in the police investigation.

This would have been why Brix had been trying to get hold of her so many times. She picked up her phone and composed a message.

Mad day. Call you first thing.

21

Valde Brix is a rapist. Ask him where he was on Wednesday night.

Henrik stared at his screen. The email was from anonymous56789@hotmail.com. It had arrived just as he'd been about to call it a night.

People sent all sorts of random crap during major investigations. Normally, he ignored the messages or forwarded them to someone more junior to sift through, but this one had stopped him in his tracks.

As far as he was aware, Brix hadn't been mentioned by the press in connection with the Frederiksberg rape case, though Jane Dahl-Thomsen was employed by his publisher.

He had a tentative link to the Bredgade case, but no one aside from Henrik and his closest colleagues knew about that, and there was no way of knowing whether Mia Steen had been raped.

Why accuse Brix? It could be someone carrying a grudge against the man, hitching a ride on the latest major news story, but why now?

Henrik was a big believer in coincidences, but this one stretched even him. The fact that Brix's name had now come up twice had produced a tingle in his palms, the familiar signal from his subconscious that he was onto something.

Upwards of forty years apart, was there a link between the two cases?

What Jensen was doing with Brix remained another conundrum. Of all the stupid things Henrik had done in his life, going to see her unannounced had been right up there.

Her instincts were those of a bloodhound. Now that she knew that Brix was of interest to them, she would keep pushing till she found out why.

Standing in her messy flat, he'd wanted to put his arms around her, but he knew that he'd lost the right to do so.

Afterwards he'd driven straight to the office. Anything to avoid his wife's cold shoulder in the double bed or being forced to look at Knud's smug face over breakfast.

He'd slept at work before, an occasional necessity when they were busy on a case. And last year he'd been forced to do so when his wife threw him out, suspecting (correctly) that he was seeing Jensen again.

This time, he hadn't brought any toiletries or spare clothes.

Thinking the office would be empty, he'd been surprised to see Funder and Mark. 'What the hell are you two doing?'

'Going through the CCTV from Frederiksberg,' Funder had said without looking up from her screen.

'But there's just nothing,' Mark had added.

'The bastard knew there wouldn't be,' said Funder. 'He planned the whole thing that way. Oh, and want to hear something that'll make you cry?'

'Not really,' Henrik said.

'The technical report has come back. No DNA.'

'Shit.'

'He's just playing with us,' said Funder.

'Here you go again,' Mark yawned.

Funder gave him the finger.

'I spoke to Liv,' Henrik said. 'She thinks your Operation Polaris may have merit. I've sent her the report.'

'What?' said Mark, looking put out.

'Really? Are you joking with me?' Funder rose from her chair. 'Because if you are—'

'Really,' Henrik said. 'Now go home, both of you.'

He suspected neither of them had wanted to be first to leave, anxious that this might signal weakness to the competition.

Funder lived alone, but Mark had two young kids, and a wife who expected him to take his share of the broken nights.

Henrik needed them both fresh in the morning.

When finally they'd left, he'd gone to his office to run through his inbox, and that's when the anonymous email had arrived.

Nothing he could do about it now.

He removed his boots and lay down on the sofa, thinking of Jensen.

He'd no clue what was going on, but something told him that she held the answer.

Day Four

22

Of all places in Copenhagen, Brøgger had suggested meeting in Tivoli Gardens, to which he held an annual pass. 'I like their classical concerts,' he said.

Jensen found that unlikely. To passers-by, the elderly gentleman in his neatly pressed blue slacks, crisp white shirt and yellow cashmere jumper tied over his shoulders might look like a pensioner on an outing with his daughter and grandchild. But appearances could be deceptive. Brøgger was very much still active, a lawyer whose tentacles reached far and wide into Danish society. While his clients were no angels (he wouldn't be doing much business if high morals were a criterion), he'd managed to stay on the right side of the law.

Just.

Unlike his estranged brother, Leif Kofoed, a master criminal who had evaded justice in Denmark for decades and was now thought to be residing in South America.

If Brøgger suspected that Brix had broken the law, he would have refused to act for him, wouldn't he?

Brøgger liked a quiet life. She'd never managed to find

out where his office was, or where he lived. She didn't know if he was married and had children. It had never come up, and she hadn't wanted to push, sensing that personal questions would be unwelcome.

Brøgger had insisted on buying them both old-fashioned ice-cream cones and was tucking into his own with gusto: three scoops topped with whipped cream, jam and a chocolate-covered marshmallow.

Jensen had been in two minds whether to come at all, but Karo had insisted that she would be fine by herself. They'd eaten breakfast together, and Karo had said she would spend the morning relaxing.

'Whatever you do, don't go home,' Jensen had said before she left.

She'd called Henrik while going to the shops for milk and bread. He'd apologised for coming round last night. 'It was a mistake. I don't know what I was thinking.'

'I admit I wasn't exactly welcoming,' Jensen had said. 'It was actually nice to see you. If you tell me how Brix is involved in your case, I might be able to help you.'

'It's confidential, Jensen.'

'Never stopped you before.'

There'd been a pause before Henrik had spoken again. 'I can tell you that Brix has a connection to the apartment where Mia Steen was found.'

'What sort of connection?'

'That's all you get. Now your turn.'

'Brix and I, it's a personal matter, nothing to do with your investigation, so you can forget about it.'

The rest of their conversation had been brisk and matter-of-fact. She'd asked him about Karo, and he'd recommended a nearby crisis centre for victims of domestic abuse. 'You need to encourage her to seek professional help.

Be very careful. You know nothing about this woman's circumstances. Don't get yourself in too deep,' he'd said.

Too late, she thought.

Afterwards, she'd finally called Brix, who had sounded agitated but refused to discuss anything over the phone. 'You never know who's listening,' he'd said. 'Come to my place as soon as you can.'

Last night, she'd eventually got around to looking at his list of conquests. There were a total of 122 entries, which Brix described as his 'best guess'.

He'd lost his virginity to a cousin on a camping trip aged fourteen. By the time he turned nineteen and left high school, he'd bedded a further fifteen women.

Aged twenty-four, Marion had been his first serious relationship, defined by Brix as someone he'd slept with exclusively for a period of over a month.

Most of the women in the ensuing months and years had come with the briefest explanation: 'Met in a bar' or 'Met at a party'. Later followed more serious relationships, including his sixteen-year marriage to Lis Vendel and his marriage to Astrid Holst, which had so far lasted three years. However, none of his relationships had stayed exclusive for very long.

During his marriage to Astrid, he'd already been unfaithful five times, including three timeswith women whose names he couldn't recall, though he thought two of them had a name beginning with 'A'.

His flings had lasted from a few hours to several weeks, and all had ended, in his own words, undramatically, aside from his divorce from Lis, which had been acrimonious, though according to Brix they were now on speaking terms.

Brix remembered the names of a total of forty-two women, a little over one-third of those he'd slept with.

Jensen had noted several questions for him, including his definition of 'undramatic'.

His list had left a bad taste in her mouth. She'd tried to count her sexual encounters since the age of fifteen, but couldn't get past eight, and she remembered every single one of the names.

Even accounting for the fact that Brix was sixty-one, she was shocked in equal measure by his promiscuity and his amnesia. Little wonder that he'd been scared of the list falling into the wrong hands.

Tivoli was busy and the air full of noise as she and Brøgger walked among the bumper cars and roller coasters in a cacophony of screaming, beeping, whirring and shouting. There were people everywhere. Jensen could see why he'd suggested meeting here. No one would hear their conversation; they could barely hear each other.

'So when did Brix tell you about me?' she said, as they stopped to look at the pleasure boats gliding around on the small pond beside the pagoda.

'Not long after he did the maths and decided that you had to be his daughter,' said Brøgger, licking his ice cream.

'So you knew when we first met over a year ago. Why didn't you tell me then?'

'We didn't know each other as well then as we do now. Besides, as a lawyer I have a duty of confidentiality.'

'When it suits you.'

'It wasn't my secret to tell. In my profession you learn to keep schtum.'

Brøgger got a pristinely clean handkerchief out of his pocket and wiped a speck of ice cream off the corner of his mouth. Annoyingly, she found it impossible to stay angry with him, though he'd betrayed her. 'I got him to do a test,' she said. 'I should be getting the result back in a matter of days.'

'Probably wise.'

Jensen was surprised to hear him say this. 'Then you don't believe he's my father?'

'Whether or not I do has no impact on the facts,' said Brøgger with his infuriating refusal to answer a straight question.

'It was you who suggested he ask me for help to find his stalker,' said Jensen, exasperated.

'Because I thought it was right up your street. I knew you'd be intrigued enough to at least give him a hearing.'

'Well, I still haven't decided whether to trust him.'

'I don't blame you,' said Brøgger. 'Brix has been a bad boy for many years, and I say that in the nicest possible way.'

Jensen thought of what Henrik had told her earlier. 'You don't think he's done anything sinister then?' she said. 'I heard on the grapevine that he has a connection to the apartment in Bredgade where the woman in the wall was found.'

Brøgger didn't skip a beat. 'I thought you probably would have by now, but no, in answer to your question, I don't think Brix has a criminal bone in his body. Not unless you count caddishness and self-absorption, which some might be inclined to do. And a smidgen of plagiarism.'

'Plagiarism? You mean he steals the ideas for his books?'

'Jensen, Jensen, there are no new ideas. And those who have insisted over the years that the ideas belonged to them have been well compensated.'

'Paid off you mean?'

'You might say that; I couldn't possibly comment.'

'Could that be where the threats are coming from? Someone who thinks their work has been stolen?'

'That's for you to find out,' he said.

'It would be helpful to know what might be motivating whoever is doing it.'

'I'd keep an open mind if I were you. It could be anything from professional jealousy to unrequited love.'

'That doesn't seem like a very wide range, or enough of a reason to threaten to destroy someone's life.'

'You'd be surprised,' said Brøgger, chucking the rest of his ice-cream cone in a bin.

He smiled at Ea, who smiled back. Her daughter was turning into a more sociable creature than herself. When she was old enough, Jensen would need to teach her about stranger danger.

'Let's enjoy ourselves now,' said Brøgger. 'The pantomime is about to start. If we hurry, we might still be able to get some seats up front.'

It was a little while later, when Jensen had made her excuses and left Brøgger to the comedic ballet, that she ran into Henrik's wife.

They'd never met, but she'd googled Louise Jungersen plenty of times: head teacher at a high school in Frederiksberg, pretty, successful, mother of three children, two boys and a girl, who were now crowding around her excitedly with tour passes around their wrists.

The name of the youngest boy was Oliver. He looked like a mini-Henrik with hair.

The couple following a few steps behind were obviously the grandparents; the old man had a strong likeness to his daughter.

Louise looked stressed and unhappy; Henrik was nowhere to be seen. Perhaps the plan had been for him to come along, and he'd let her down?

He was good at that.

For a moment, her eyes met Louise's, and Jensen thought she caught a flicker of recognition in the other woman.

‘I’m the bastard, not you,’ Henrik had always told her, but it didn’t feel like that now, even though they’d both moved on and she had Ea.

Mortified, she lowered her gaze and rushed for the exit.

23

'All right, let's sum up,' said Henrik, standing by the whiteboard in the meeting room.

There were takeaway coffees and half-eaten pastries on the table. It was a Saturday, and the building was quiet, with the exception of a handful of investigators working on the Jane Dahl-Thomsen case.

He'd asked a core team to join him in his office: Funder, Mark and Detective Sergeant Martin Bagger, who was one of his favourite people on the force. Bagger spent most of his time investigating paedophiles but hadn't allowed this to diminish his humanity and warmth. Last Christmas, they'd worked together on a major case, and Bagger had been the only colleague to stand by him when he'd been sent home for disobeying orders.

He wanted Bagger here because of the email he'd received in the early hours calling Brix a rapist. 'We have an unusual situation,' he said. 'And the profile of one of the people involved means that nothing leaves this room. Is that understood?'

Everyone nodded.

'This week, we opened two new investigations,' he continued. 'Two crimes, both extremely violent, against female victims, upwards of forty years apart. In the case of Bredgade we have been told by the owner of the flat that Valde Brix, at the time a fledgling author, was one of three people with undisturbed access to the property in 1987. The apartment was owned by Andreas Lund, who later became Brix's agent.'

Funder put her hand up. 'I read the post-mortem report. Mia Steen's injuries were similar to those of the Polaris victims, suggesting a perp with the same kind of uncontrolled anger.'

'We don't know if Mia was raped,' said Henrik. 'And she went missing a full six years before the Polaris perpetrator became operative, according to your own report.'

Funder shrugged. 'Perhaps she was the first.'

Henrik was about to continue after her interruption when Funder put her hand up once more. 'If we believe Mia was killed in 1987, why wasn't she reported missing until the year after?'

'That's a good question,' said Henrik. 'Mark, you said it was Mia's mother who made the report. Do we know why she waited so long?'

Mark sent Funder an irritated glance. 'We can ask her in the interview.'

Henrik continued his summary. 'Then on Thursday morning, fifty-four-year-old Jane Dahl-Thomsen was found in Frederiksberg Gardens, beaten and raped. We know that she'd been on a date at a nearby restaurant and that she went to the toilet just after nine in the evening. She never returned. It's possible that the perpetrator intercepted her in the basement where the toilets are located and injected her with some substance.'

Funder put up her hand again, earning a tut and a loud

sigh from Mark. 'Just been confirmed. Puncture wound from a needle on her thigh and Rohypnol in her blood.'

'Right,' said Henrik. 'However, no DNA from the perpetrator was found on her, and we've no CCTV of her leaving the restaurant. We've had a mobile police station placed at the main entrance to the park since yesterday, but so far, no witnesses have come forward. The victim has been interviewed but is unable to describe the man, nor recall any detail of the assault. With me so far?'

He looked around the table and everyone nodded again.

'Then last night at close to two a.m., I received an email from an anonymous sender saying that Valde Brix is a rapist and suggesting we look at what he was doing on Wednesday night.'

'Some prankster having a go,' said Mark.

'Why Brix, though? He's not been linked to Frederiksberg and his connection to Bredgade is not in the public domain.'

But you told Jensen, he suddenly thought.

Could the email have come from her? Was this at the root of her interest in the man? She'd asked him about a friend with an abusive partner. Was that somehow also linked to Brix?

He would need to speak to her again as soon as possible.

'Jane Dahl-Thomsen is a sales rep for Brix's publisher. We should find out if the two of them know each other. Our anonymous informant might harbour genuine suspicions about Brix or want to hurt him in some way,' said Henrik. 'Brix seemed shifty when I spoke to him yesterday. I got the impression that he was expecting me.'

His mind kept snagging on this. Brix had seemed genuinely surprised at the news that the remains in Bredgade were Mia Steen's. Yet he'd behaved like a man expecting to be accused.

'Someone as famous as Brix wouldn't need to go and actually rape someone, would he?' said Mark. 'He's well known for being a lothario.'

'What the fuck is that supposed to mean, Søndergreen?' said Funder. 'You think men rape because they don't get enough sex? It's about power and control and utter contempt for women, not sex, you absolute moron.'

'Of course I don't,' said Mark, bridling. 'That wasn't what I said.'

'Idiot,' said Funder.

'Shut up, both of you,' said Henrik.

He was beginning to regret asking the two of them to work together.

'It's more likely to be a random accusation,' suggested Bagger, ever the diplomat. 'Someone as successful as Brix is likely to inspire a lot of jealousy. We always get people writing in to throw celebrities under the bus.'

True, Henrik thought. But the sender had used a VPN connection to conceal their identity, so they weren't the average troll.

Could Brix be a rapist? Funder was right. Rape was rarely just about sex. But someone of Brix's fame? It seemed impossible that he would be able to get away with it.

On the other hand, no one would ever suspect him. An esteemed author, a married man with a beautiful young wife.

'We'll check his alibi, though it seems somewhat far-fetched. In the meantime, let's keep an open mind,' he said looking pointedly at Funder.

He turned to Mark, who was leaning so far back he was almost horizontal, arms folded across his chest. A sulk straight out of the body-language manual. 'Any news on Marion Jensen?'

Mark shook his head without meeting his eyes.

'OK,' said Henrik. 'By this evening, let's start to put together an overview of what happened during those months in 1987. When did Brix and Marion move in, and when did they leave? What was their relationship with each other, and with Andreas Lund? And can we pinpoint the last confirmed sighting of Mia?'

He turned to Funder. 'As for Jane Dahl-Thomsen, we need witnesses. A woman leaves a restaurant, drugged and confused, on a Wednesday evening. Someone must have seen her with a man, looking like she'd had one too many. It wouldn't have been completely dark at that time.'

'Meanwhile, we'll continue to go through her phone records, emails and socials,' said Bagger.

'Good,' said Henrik. 'Get that wonder woman from Roskilde on it, that hacker you got NC3 to hire, what was her name again?'

'Fie Pedersen,' said Bagger. 'I've asked her to come in. If she can't find something to go on, then nobody can.'

'OK,' said Henrik, clapping his hands. 'Let's get back to work.'

24

The vast, red-tiled concourse at the central station was like a giant aquarium, dappled with sunlight and full of milling commuters.

Jensen's arms felt too light. She kept panicking that she'd left something behind or come out half naked.

It had been Karo's idea to leave Ea asleep at home with her. 'You won't be long, will you? With a bit of luck, she will stay down till you get back. If not, I need the practice,' she'd said, placing a hand on her invisible bump.

Jensen suspected Karo felt like she had something to make up for. They had that in common, both loath to be indebted to others.

Karo had already been hard at work while she'd been out meeting Brøgger. The flat had been a bombsite when she left but spotless upon her return. 'I'd rather keep active,' Karo had said, busy hanging Ea's bibs and babygros on the laundry rack.

Jensen had grabbed the moment to suggest speaking to someone at the crisis centre Henrik had recommended.

It hadn't gone down well.

'You want me to leave,' Karo had said, sounding hurt.

'That's not it at all. What your boyfriend did to you last night is not OK. You can't go back to him. There are people at the crisis centre who can help you figure it all out.'

'I know he's not good for me or my baby,' Karo had said. 'But I feel safe here, with you. And it's all happened so fast. I need to think about what I want to do before I take the next step. I promise I'll take my share of the load. How about I start by cooking for us both tonight?'

The exchange had made Jensen feel guilty for pushing. Taking Ea with her would have broken Karo's fragile trust in her still further.

She hadn't left her daughter before, except with Gustav for a short while, but it had to happen sometime, and Ea seemed to like Karo.

Don't fuss, everything will be fine, she told herself as she approached Joe & the Juice.

She'd enjoyed the short bike ride from her flat. It had been a relief not needing to bundle Ea into the sling. She and Fie would be able to talk without stopping for feeds and nappy changes.

The hacker from Roskilde stood by the entrance to the café, dressed in her usual flowing garments, white socks and plastic sliders, a rucksack slung over one shoulder.

Despite her large size, her presence was discreet and apologetic, as if she was determined to leave the smallest possible footprint on her surroundings.

A long-standing agoraphobic, she'd only recently transitioned from assisted living to her own flat in a secure development. Being out by herself, commuting between Roskilde and NC3 in Glostrup several times a week, was new.

Jensen was conscious of the effort it would have taken for

her to be here. A fearless warrior behind a screen, Fie found real life unbearably painful.

'Good to see you.' They hugged awkwardly, and Jensen caught herself wishing that Gustav had been there to make their conversation flow more easily. She envied his ability to tease Fie out of her shell.

'I can't stay long,' said Fie, smiling with her eyes. 'I've been called into work.'

'The rape case in Frederiksberg? So bloody awful.'

Fie looked coy. 'I'm not allowed to say.'

They went inside the café, both relieved to turn the conversation onto Gustav, their common denominator.

'He's hoping that his aunt will make his position at *Dagbladet* permanent,' said Fie.

'Not going to happen,' Jensen said. 'Too many unemployed journalists going around, and he's her nephew.'

'He told me that what he really wants to do is open a detective bureau with you.'

'I know. He even had a sign made for my front door – Skov & Jensen Private Investigators. I told him that, if anything, it should be the other way around.'

'He tried to recruit me too,' said Fie, laughing.

Jensen bought the two of them strawberry and banana smoothies and they found a table in a corner of the dingy room where loud music played to weary travellers. Everyone was staring at their phones. 'So, what's it like working for the police?' she said.

'Better than being caught by them, and nice to be paid for doing my thing,' said Fie, her eyes disappearing into her face as she sucked on her straw.

As a child, she'd got into trouble for breaking into the system to change her mother's criminal record. Since then, she'd learned to be more careful.

'The thing is,' said Jensen, 'I need to identify a stalker from a number of fake social-media accounts. Can you do that?'

Fie's face grew serious. 'Is someone stalking you?'

Jensen decided that she had to trust Fie if she was going to get anywhere. 'The person being stalked is someone called Valde Brix and I've agreed to help him.'

'Valde Brix, the author?'

'Yes.'

'I've read all his books. He's amazing.'

Jensen should have guessed this. She belonged to a small minority of people who hadn't read Brix's books. Now that she'd had a glimpse of who he really was, she doubted that she ever would.

'Why did he ask you?' said Fie.

It was the right question, but Jensen didn't want to answer it. Not yet. 'Someone I know put him in touch with me, suggesting that I might be able to help.'

Fie nodded, seemingly satisfied with the explanation.

'The thing is . . . the stalker is threatening to ruin Brix's career.'

'How?'

'By reporting him for rape.'

'For no reason?'

'If Brix is to be believed,' said Jensen.

'What do you think?'

'I haven't made up my mind yet, but let's just say I'm intrigued.'

'I understand. You want to find out if it's true.'

'You can't tell anyone that you're looking into it. Not your colleagues either. Brix doesn't want the police involved, so you're going to have to do it in your own time.'

'I will.'

'Thank you. I'm not sure where else to turn.' She placed

a memory stick with the stalker's messages in Fie's hand. 'You'll find the information you need here. I've also added a list of people who might be carrying a grudge against Brix.' She looked around the café to make sure no one was listening. 'They're women he's had affairs with. Just the ones whose names he can remember.'

Fie's face fell.

Jensen hated to break her illusions – if she still had any, seeing as she spent her days battling cybercriminals, including those peddling child sexual abuse material.

At the same time, she suspected Fie was as fascinated by the darker side of humanity as she and Gustav were. The three of them were the same: loners, watchers, skirters on the outside of life.

They made a good team.

On the way back to her bike, Jensen saw a missed call from Gustav. She rang him back.

'Where are you?' he said.

'Coming back from meeting Fie. Why?'

'I dropped by your flat on my way to the newspaper, but you weren't there, so I just wondered.'

'Didn't Karo say where I was?'

'Who?'

'The friend I told you about. She's looking after Ea.'

'Wait, you left your daughter with a complete stranger?'

'Karo's not a stranger. She stayed with me last night, hiding from her violent boyfriend.'

'Well, she wasn't there when I called round earlier. I let myself in and your flat was empty.'

Shit.

Jensen could hear Gustav shouting something as she ended the call and began to run.

25

Andreas Lund waited patiently as Mark removed the police tape and wrestled with the new front-door lock to the apartment.

Henrik had decided to kill two birds with one stone: Lund needed to collect a few belongings, and he wanted to watch Lund's face when confronted with Mia Steen's makeshift tomb.

The door finally yielded, and the three of them stepped inside. The air had a dank, chalky smell to it. Soon mildew would be forming on the carpets.

Lund picked up a pair of expensive-looking leather shoes and poured water out of them. He looked surprised at the extent of the damage.

'This way,' said Henrik.

Lund gasped when he saw the broken wall. Mark placed a chair under him just as he looked as though he was about to keel over.

'We're unable to determine whether she died before or after she was bricked up,' said Henrik.

Lund had begun to cry. 'I can't bear it. Who'd want to do something like that to an innocent young woman?'

'I was hoping you'd tell me,' Henrik said. 'I'm having trouble picturing it. While you're away, someone moves the back wall of your larder forward by a foot, carefully bricking it up, sealing it with plaster, painting it over, remounting the shelves, all that, and you don't notice a thing?'

'I know,' Lund said. 'It's so grotesque, I can't comprehend it. It must have happened while I was away on one of my longer trips up the Swedish coast. I was a more adventurous sailor in my younger days.'

'Only Valde Brix and Marion Jensen had keys to this place. You're saying one of them did it?'

'Yes. I mean no. God, I don't know. I've known Valde for most of my life. Without him, his stupendous talent, I'd be nothing. We trust each other implicitly, he'd never . . .' He trailed off.

'His girlfriend then?'

'But why?' said Andreas. 'What had Mia done to deserve this from anyone?'

Henrik sighed and looked out of the window. The dome of the Marble Church sparkled green and gold in the sunlight. There were people up there, in the tower at the top. The thought of a slow climb up a claustrophobic staircase several hundred feet above ground turned his stomach.

'I did think of something, though,' said Lund after a while. 'Last time you said that Brix remembered Mia coming along to a party. Actually, I believe he's right. If you'll let me have a look in my office, I think I may even be able to find a photo from that time, if you're interested?'

They went through. It was one of the only rooms in the apartment that hadn't been affected by the flooding.

Pia Øster's team had been over every inch of it and found nothing that incriminated the man in any way.

Henrik hadn't noticed before that most of the bookshelves were dedicated to works by Brix, hundreds of them, in all languages imaginable.

Lund reached for a white ring binder on a top shelf. It contained printed photographs, each in their own plastic pocket. 'I kept this. Photos from my childhood, snaps I took myself. There aren't many, but there should be some from that summer. It was good fun.'

'In what way?'

'We had lots of parties. The apartment was always full of people. Brix charmed everyone. Have you spoken to him yet? If so, I'm sure you've seen for yourself.'

Have I heck, thought Henrik.

'Ah, here's one,' said Lund, holding up a photo of a group of people laughing at the camera, eyes red in the flashlight. The photo was grainy.

'That's Brix there,' said Lund. 'And, oh God, he was right, there's Mia.' He pointed to a girl with long blonde hair to the side of the group, smiling, if a little less broadly than the others.

'Who's that?' said Henrik, pointing to a stunning, tall woman next to Brix.

'That's Marion. They broke up not long after this picture was taken.'

'Why?'

'You'd have to ask her that. I haven't seen her since.'

'You said Mia was your cleaner for a while?'

'For over a year. She was wonderful, if rather shy. God-fearing, I seem to recall.'

'How did you find her?'

'I must have put an ad in the paper. Or maybe someone recommended her to me. I don't remember.'

'Did you invite her to the party?'

Lund shrugged. 'Might have done. Or maybe Brix did.'

'I'll take that photo album,' said Henrik. 'Now, I believe you wanted to collect a few things?'

A few minutes later, the three of them descended in the lift, Lund carrying a small leather travel bag.

As they watched him disappear down Bredgade in the direction of his hotel, Henrik saw a call coming in from Liv.

Her voice was strange, as though she couldn't quite believe the words coming out of her own mouth. 'A woman has been found dead in an Airbnb in Kronprinsessegade. I need you to go there immediately.'

26

Jensen bounded up the stairs, taking the steps two at a time. Pedalling home at top speed, she'd kept calling Karo's number, almost crashing her bike several times as she jumped red lights and swerved in and out of the traffic.

Gustav had been right. How could she have been so stupid?

She didn't even know Karo's surname, or where she lived.

Her mind was racing through the possible scenarios. It felt like she was going to pass out.

What if Karo's boyfriend had followed her there last night after all? What if he'd returned for what he considered his? Maybe Karo had managed to flee with Ea?

She dared not think the thoughts that appeared in her head.

Her future life passed like a film in front of her eyes. Tearful interviews with the police. The years of not knowing, wondering what Ea would look like as a grown-up. Talking to the press on every anniversary – twenty years, thirty, forty – while clutching a faded baby photo to her chest: Ea, the tiny human she'd sworn would never come to any harm as long as she lived.

She let herself into the flat and ran through the rooms. Ea's cot was empty, but all her things were there: sling, pram, nappy bag, clothes, toys and dummies.

There were also several of Karo's belongings in the room where she'd slept last night.

Jensen was dialling 112, when something made her look out of the window of the room, which faced the courtyard at the back of the building.

What she saw was so wonderful that she almost laughed out loud when a woman's voice answered the emergency call.

'I'm sorry, I made a mistake,' she said, hanging up.

Because all the way down there, at the wooden picnic table, sat Karo in her enormous sunglasses, with Ea on her lap, looking at the pictures of animals in her cloth book.

Jensen's phone pinged.

Gustav.

Please tell me you found her?

She quickly texted back, relief rippling through her body.

False alarm. They'd just gone outside.
Ea's safe.

'I'm so sorry, I wasn't thinking,' said Karo, when Jensen had run down the stairs and given Ea the biggest hug of her life. 'I left my phone on silent earlier when she was asleep. You must have been going out of your mind.'

'No harm done,' said Jensen, inhaling her daughter's milky-sweet scent.

'No, it was thoughtless of me,' said Karo. 'Only the weather was so good I couldn't resist it. I thought we'd be safe down here.'

'Of course you are,' said Jensen.

'I'd never harm Ea,' Karo said, sounding close to tears. 'I'd never harm anyone.'

'It's OK,' said Jensen, but she could tell that Karo was feeling hurt. She tried to explain. 'I thought that maybe your boyfriend had found out where you were and come after you.'

'I told you, he's not going to. I was extremely careful when I left home last night.'

'He must have contacted you, though?'

'Loads of times. He says he's really sorry, and wants me to come back, but I'm not falling for it any more.'

'Good,' said Jensen.

'He's never going to change, is he? I've got to leave him. For my baby's sake. Honestly, I don't know what I would have done if I hadn't met you. You're so brave, bringing up your daughter on your own.'

Jensen had never considered herself brave. She'd been ambivalent about her pregnancy. Unable to decide whether or not to keep her baby, she'd simply let time pass until it was too late. Some would call it cowardice.

She felt guilty that she'd suspected Karo of putting Ea in danger. Karo was a victim of domestic abuse and deserved sympathy, not mistrust. 'Look, I'm sorry I overreacted. Can we just forget this ever happened and start again?'

'I'd like that,' said Karo. 'And you're right, I do need to see the people at the crisis centre. As soon as I've got my head together. Tomorrow maybe?'

'Works for me,' said Jensen. 'Now, I'm famished. Did you say you were going to cook for us this evening?'

'Absolutely,' Karo smiled. 'But first I want to go home and collect a few things, and then I need to shop for food.'

This sounded like the world's worst idea to Jensen. 'Are you sure that's wise? I mean, what if he's there?'

'I checked. He's at work, on a job out of town.'

'Then let me at least come with you?' Jensen pleaded.

'I'll be fine by myself. It's bright daylight, plenty of people around. You need to go and cuddle your daughter. Nothing's going to happen to me,' said Karo.

Famous last words, thought Jensen.

She had a plan, though, and Karo didn't need to know about it.

27

What the hell is happening? Henrik thought, as he pulled into Kronprinsessegade, a row of tall red-and-white apartment blocks facing the King's Gardens. For the third time in a week, he was about to enter a major crime scene.

The hordes of people sunning themselves on the lawns of the park had no idea of the horror that had occurred only metres away from them.

For a moment he envied their innocence. The city they lived in was safe, beautiful and full of light. His was a dark place where bad people hurt each other out of greed, jealousy and rage.

As a cop, he was condemned to moving between the two. He couldn't unsee the horrors he'd experienced.

He and Mark parked behind Funder. In the stairwell, as they climbed to the top floor, they could hear a woman crying. It turned out to be the cleaner who had found the body. She was sitting on the stairs, trembling as a uniformed officer tried to calm her down with offers of tissues and bottled water.

The flat was much smaller than the luxury apartment

in Bredgade. It had a sloping ceiling and bland, modern furnishings.

Funder greeted them in the hallway, where the smell of putrefying flesh was unmistakable. As they stepped into their protective gear, Henrik was grateful for his facemask.

'The woman had rented the place for just one night,' said Funder. 'The cleaner discovered the body when she arrived to turn the place around for new guests arriving this afternoon. The bedroom is to the left, but I need to warn you, she's . . .'

'Yes, yes,' said Henrik irritably, as he began to sweat inside his space suit. For some reason, it was a hundred degrees inside the flat, which explained the stench of decay.

Though he'd been warned, he still froze on the threshold to the bedroom, the tableau in front of him clashing horribly with the idyllic spring day outside.

The woman was spreadeagled on top of the mattress, hands and feet tied with a harness disappearing under the bed. She was naked, except for a T-shirt that had bunched up across her chest.

Her face and blonde hair were a bloodied mess. A pair of tights had been knotted around her neck.

Funder came up behind him. 'Raped and strangled, I'd say. Looks like she tried to defend herself,' she said, pointing to red marks on the woman's hands and forearms.

'So she wasn't out of it.'

'At least not at first,' said Funder. 'We can't be sure that she was drugged until we have the toxicology report.'

Henrik knew she was thinking of Polaris, but the defensive injuries, and the fact that the woman had been killed, made this feel different.

He felt an overwhelming urge to throw up, but he couldn't, not in front of Funder, who was looking at the body with the detached interest of someone studying a new species of butterfly.

Instead he moved to a set of French doors, which some considerate soul had opened to let in the air.

Removing his face mask, he took a couple of deep breaths, while he concentrated hard on the verdant view of the gardens and Rosenborg Castle from the world's smallest balcony. 'Why is it so bloody hot in here?' he said, as vomit-heralding saliva began to run in his mouth. He swallowed it back.

'The heating was left on full blast,' said Funder. 'That's what's caused the body to be so—'

'Yes, thank you,' said Henrik. It could have been a naïve attempt to destroy evidence or confuse the timeline of the killing by speeding up putrefaction. All the same, it struck him as rather amateurish. 'Do we know who she is?'

'Vivian Sejer, according to her driving licence,' said Funder, who had found a wallet in the woman's handbag. 'She was forty-six. From Aarhus.'

Henrik forced himself to turn from the view, his eyes avoiding the body. He picked up a mobile phone from the bedside table.

There were a couple of WhatsApp messages from this morning, possibly from friends or family members wondering if the woman was OK.

A laptop bag had been left against a chair by the window. On the chair was a pile of clothes. A pink dress, trainers, a denim jacket. A small suitcase on wheels was open on a low table. It contained the usual spare clothes, a hairdryer and a pair of smart shoes.

In the pocket of the laptop, Henrik found a piece of paper that seemed to have been torn from a book. He didn't recognise the words, but across the page, someone had written a name and phone number followed by a heart. He could scarcely believe his eyes.

Valde Brix.

For the author's name to turn up twice in connection with a crime investigation could be written off as a coincidence. Three times, and it was a pattern impossible to ignore.

He showed the piece of paper to Funder and Mark.

'Him?' said Mark, surprised.

'And here he is again,' said Funder holding up a slim diary. 'Yesterday's entry: "VB". I told you. Rapists can hide in plain sight. They can be anyone.'

'Let's not get carried away. We don't know that Brix was here, or that he even knows this woman. Get her phone and laptop back to Bagger and ask him to get her chat history checked out. We need to know why she was in Copenhagen, who she'd been in touch with, why she rented this place. And get forensics to fast-track any traces – prints, DNA, fibres, the lot.'

'If this is a Polaris case, the perp won't have left any, and there'll be no CCTV,' said Funder. 'There's a half-empty bottle of water in the fridge, but it's odds on to be hers.'

'Just do as I say. Mark, get Brix to come in for an interview in the morning. I'll attend the post-mortem as soon as it can be arranged. Preferably tomorrow.'

'You're the boss. Goldschmidt's already on his way,' said Funder.

'Tell him to contact me as soon as. I'm heading back to the office, you two stay here.'

He got his phone out to call Liv. The press coverage was already mental. With this new case, the third in a week, it would explode.

28

Following Karo with Ea in the sling was harder than Jensen had imagined. By the time she took up pursuit, Karo was already far down the gravel path.

Jensen had to break into a run to catch up with her before the bridge. Though she took care to stay in the dappled shadow of the trees, she had to duck fast a couple of times when Karo glanced over her shoulder.

You'd make the world's worst private detective, she told herself.

On the bridge, Karo turned left and continued in the direction of Nørrebro, her bobbing red hair almost disappearing a couple of times, before she turned up again among the throng of pedestrians.

She was wearing wide-legged jeans and trainers with a cropped green top she'd borrowed from Jensen because her own T-shirt had blood on it. It stretched taut over her chest, and she kept pulling it down.

Suddenly, she made a right turn, then another, and for a minute Jensen lost her completely, until she spotted her again some distance away, unlocking the door to a block of flats. Karo looked up and down the street before disappearing quickly inside.

Jensen waited for a few minutes before creeping up to the door.

Karoline & Jonathan read a hand-written sign next to the doorbell for the flat on the third floor to the right.

So the arsehole's name was Jonathan.

Jensen walked further down the street and took shelter in a doorway. She decided to give Karo half an hour before ringing the doorbell in case Jonathan had surprised her inside the flat.

It turned out not to be necessary. In under twenty minutes, Karo re-emerged with a large holdall. Jensen followed her as far as the Co-op, before heading back to her own flat. Karo would be safe in the supermarket with lots of people around.

Tonight over dinner Jensen would ask her some more questions about herself, find out what her plans were.

Taking the lift back up to her flat, she was surprised to see someone sitting on the top step, leaning against the wall, asleep: a woman with long grey hair, a floor-length skirt, a woollen jumper, scuffed walking boots and blackened silver bangles on her suntanned, bony wrist. By her feet was a well-worn travelling bag. The scent in the air was at once foreign and familiar: salt, woodsmoke and patchouli.

'Marion? What are you doing here?'

'Darling,' said Marion, smiling as she stretched and blinked herself awake. 'I've been waiting for you.'

As far as Jensen was aware, her mother hadn't been to Copenhagen since the two of them moved to North Jutland all those years ago.

She was tired of the city, Marion had said then, and

yearned for space and sky, but the real reason must have been Brix's attempt to make contact.

Jensen recalled Brix's words: *You don't know what your mother is capable of.*

Did she know Marion at all, when it came to it?

Marion had been an only child. Her father had died when she was young, and her mother had passed away when Jensen was small.

The family albums had got lost in the move to Jutland, and the only mementoes Jensen had of her childhood were a couple of dozen photos, mostly taken by Marion's friends: a picture of herself bathing as a toddler in a red plastic tub on someone's lawn, skipping in the courtyard in Copenhagen, standing with her bike in front of the Jutland cottage.

There was never anyone else in the photos. No friends, no other people she was close to.

Only one photo existed of herself and Marion together. It was taken on a beach somewhere north of Copenhagen. Jensen was eight and wearing a yellow bathing suit. Her mother was squinting into the camera, holding a hand over her eyes.

The two of them were leaning away from each other; Jensen had always thought this symbolic of their relationship. Over the years, their distance had continued to grow.

Marion made smiley faces at Ea who was smiling back. 'Look, she likes me.'

She likes everybody, thought Jensen.

'I'm glad you're here,' she said. 'This whole business with Brix has been so weird. I know you don't like me seeing him, but can't we just talk about it?'

'Maybe another time,' Marion said. She stroked Ea's fine, golden hair. 'I just didn't want to come all the way without at least seeing you two.'

‘What? You’re not staying?’

‘I’m tired. Hitchhiking all the way here took me ages. Lisette and Bo are putting me up, but you and Ea can walk me to the Metro, if you like?’ She looked awkward all of a sudden, and Jensen wasn’t sure she wanted to hear what came next. ‘This isn’t a social visit,’ her mother said. ‘I’ve come to speak to the police about Valde.’

29

Mia Steen's mother had been waiting in the family room for hours by the time Henrik finally found the time to see her. It was the last thing he wanted to do at seven thirty in the evening with no end to the working day in sight, but the eighty-two-year-old woman was refusing to leave before they had spoken.

She'd driven herself to Copenhagen, a four-hour journey from her home in Randers.

'I am sorry you've had to wait so long. I'm afraid we've been dealing with an emergency this afternoon,' said Henrik.

Grethe Steen was a trim, upright sort of woman with coarse grey hair cut in a short bob. She was wearing a black anorak, sensible shoes and glasses with metal frames, and she looked exhausted.

He knew that she had a daughter and a son besides Mia and wondered why she hadn't asked them to accompany her on the journey.

'I would like to see my daughter as soon as possible,' she said.

'Are you sure? You should know that your daughter's remains are … it's been nearly forty years, so they won't be very—'

'Detective Inspector Jungersen, I was a farmer's daughter and a farmer's wife, you don't need to pussyfoot around me. I know we're talking about little more than bones, but I need to see for myself that she really is dead. My heart just won't take it in otherwise.'

'Mia has been identified by her teeth, and also the fracture to her leg that she sustained in childhood. We're confident that it's her, but I can arrange for you to view the remains, if that's what you want?'

'It is. How did she die?'

The old woman was blunt, unusually so for a grieving relative, but then she'd had many years to get used to the idea. Part of her might even be relieved. There were instances when knowing the truth was preferable, no matter how abhorrent.

'Your daughter was strangled. That's all we know for now. We're still trying to understand what happened to her.'

Grethe closed her eyes.

He thought she was going to cry after all, but when she looked up her eyes were dry.

'When did you last see your daughter?'

'Late July 1987. She came home for a few weeks, before returning to Copenhagen to continue the second year of her German and English business studies.'

'But you spoke to her after that?'

'Yes. She used to call from the payphone in her student halls every Friday, until … Well, we argued and then she stopped calling. The last time I spoke to her was towards the end of September.'

Henrik frowned. 'Hang on, you didn't report her missing

until August 1988. Do you mean that by that time you hadn't spoken to her for almost a year?'

'Yes.'

'Must have been a bad argument. What was it about?'

Grethe looked at him for a long time as if she couldn't decide where to begin a long and difficult story. 'We're Jehovah's Witnesses in my family. Mia had stopped going to her weekly meetings. That was exactly what I feared would happen when she first moved over here. I begged her not to leave, but she wouldn't listen.'

The Devil's Island.

Henrik recalled that this was how some people in Jutland referred to the island of Zealand, home to the capital. Supposedly as a joke.

'Why fear it?'

'I knew she would be far away from home, surrounded by temptation. She could have studied in Aarhus, which was much closer. But she argued that the business school in Copenhagen was better. She said that she wanted to give back to the faith, and that the languages would be useful for missionary work. In hindsight, I think she may have been telling us what we wanted to hear. I believe her real intention was to get as far away from us as possible.'

Henrik felt irritated. If Grethe had reported her daughter missing much sooner, the case could have been solved before any trace of what had happened went ice cold.

'So when Mia stopped calling you, you just accepted it. Is that it?'

'What do you think?' said Grethe, looking at him sternly. 'Mia was my daughter. I wasn't going to give up on her. I left messages, I wrote, I even drove to Copenhagen myself to see her.'

'When was that?'

'January the following year. But I was too late.'

'How so?'

'Mia had gone by then, and there was another student living in her room. We found out that Mia had left her course and given notice at the student halls. The other students thought she must have moved out over Christmas when everyone would have been home for the holidays. They said they'd heard that she'd travelled to Asia.'

So someone had gone and emptied Mia's student room and made it look as though she'd gone travelling, when in fact she was slowly rotting behind a wall.

'What did you do?'

'I spoke to the elders about it. They said that she'd chosen to leave the community. My husband and I, and her siblings, were to stop contacting her. It had to be as though we didn't know her.'

She closed her eyes again.

What a terrible waste of life, Henrik thought. He was starting to feel angry. 'But in August that year you decided to report her missing after all. Why?'

'I couldn't stop thinking that something must have happened to her, something terrible. She wouldn't just have taken off without telling me. None of her old friends from home had heard from her either.'

'Were they Jehovah's Witnesses too?'

'Some, but not all. Mia was well liked at school.'

'So what did you do?'

'I appealed to the elders, but no one would listen to me. My husband, Mia's father, didn't want to know. We had to do as we'd been told, and Mia was old enough to make her own decisions. But in the end, I reported her missing anyway, and began to look for her myself. Eventually, I stopped attending meetings and left the faith voluntarily in 1990.'

'What took you so long?

Grethe looked sad. 'I don't think you understand what I'm saying. I had to leave everything I'd ever known. My husband, my two other children, my relatives and my friends. Not one of them has talked to me since I left. I sometimes go and see my children, without them knowing, just to make sure they are healthy and happy.' She paused for breath and took a sip of water, her gaze distant. 'Of course, by the time the police began to look into it, Mia had been gone for so long that there was almost nothing they could do. Because her student room had been cleared, and notice given, they assumed she really had gone backpacking and decided to start a new life.'

'Did anyone check if it was actually her who gave the notice?'

'I did. I got them to give me a copy.' Grethe opened her handbag and handed him an A4 sheet of paper in a thin plastic pocket.

It was a typewritten letter dated Friday 27 November 1987, carrying Mia's name and an address in Randers.

'That was where we used to live,' said Grethe. 'It gave me hope when I first saw it, like she still regarded it as her home. Maybe it meant that she was planning on returning one day. But of course, she never did.'

There was no signature on the letter, and the message was matter-of-fact and brief. Anyone could have sent it, thought Henrik.

'Mia didn't own a typewriter, to my knowledge. I said as much to the police, but no one cared. They told me to move on and live my life, but I never stopped looking, and when I saw the news . . . they said she was found in someone's apartment? Whose was it?'

'It belongs to someone called Andreas Lund, who has owned it since 1985. He was twenty-three when Mia disappeared two years later. He had two friends staying with him at the time. Mia had been cleaning for him for a while by then. Did she ever tell you that?'

'Not who he was, she wouldn't say. But I knew it was a man, and we argued about that when she was home for the holidays. She told me that sometimes, after she'd finished cleaning, the two of them would talk over a coffee. I think he must have put ideas into her head. That summer, it was as if she began to question everything – her faith, her future, us, her family.'

'You think they were in a relationship?'

Grethe shook her head. 'No. Perfectly innocent, according to Mia, but that kind of close friendship between two unmarried young people is discouraged by the faith. I tried to find him after she went missing, but without a surname, it was impossible.'

Henrik felt angry. He wanted to go back and see who had dealt with the misper case, though he knew the exercise would be pointless.

'I don't think it could have been this Andreas who hurt her, though,' said Grethe.

'Why not?'

'I could tell from what she said that he was very fond of her. He treated her with kindness and paid her well. Maybe she got involved with one of his friends?'

'We're trying to find out what happened,' said Henrik. 'But we're certain Mia came to at least one party in the flat.'

He put the picture of Mia with Brix and Marion on the table. Grethe picked it up, mouth agape. 'Oh,' she said.

'There is something else you should know,' Henrik said. 'And this will be difficult, so brace yourself. Your daughter was between ten and twelve weeks pregnant when she died.'

Grethe stared at him as her hands flew up to her mouth. Now the tears came. It was as if she'd had a puncture, slowly sinking into herself, trapped in her own misery.

No one could help her now.

But he wanted to, desperately, so he said what no policeman should ever say. 'I promise you that we will find your daughter's killer.'

30

After seeing her mother to Nørreport Station, Jensen went straight to Brix's house in the Potato Rows, fuelled by red-hot anger.

'I'm going out of my mind here. Why couldn't you have come sooner?' he said, as he opened the door.

She pushed past him. 'I've just had a really interesting conversation with Marion,' she said. 'Told me all about you and Mia Steen. How you slept with her, while you and Marion were living with your agent in his apartment in Bredgade. And sure enough, she is on your list.' She got out her phone, opened his email and read aloud. 'Let's see now. "Girl with long blonde hair. Don't remember the name. Timid. Sweet. Met at Andreas's." You're actually beginning to disgust me. I really hope we're not related. Who'd want a father like you?'

'Can I speak now? Are you done?' said Brix. He looked as though his head was about to explode. 'Yes, I knew Mia Steen. Yes, I slept with her. But I didn't strangle her and put her in that wall. Why would I have done that?'

'Maybe she became trouble. Fell in love with you or something equally inconvenient and refused go away.'

'No, no, no!' shouted Brix. 'We slept together and then we moved on, and I didn't see her again, end of story. And if you would stop to draw breath for a second, you would know that it was precisely because of Mia that I wanted to speak to you. The police came here to question me.'

'Let me guess. Detective Inspector Henrik Jungersen?'

'Yes, how do you know?'

'What did you say? What did he ask?'

'He showed me a picture of Mia and asked if I knew her.'

'Did you admit it?'

'Of course. Though I was so flustered because of that business with the stalker that I made a mistake and denied that we'd been lovers.'

'You and Marion were living together.'

'Yes.'

'But then this other pretty girl turned up, and you dropped Marion like a hot potato?'

'It wasn't like that.'

They stared at each other for a while, until Brix looked away.

'Maybe the whole stalker thing is about Mia,' Jensen said.

Brix dropped onto a chair, head in his hands. 'I didn't rape her. It was consensual. I've always fallen in and out of love quickly. That first rush, it's like a drug. I know the feeling won't last but still I go back for more,' he said. 'Maybe Marion is my stalker. She was very angry. Wouldn't talk to me after it happened. Left the next day, took all her things.'

Jensen had never considered her mother digitally literate (her only known method of communication was an old Nokia phone) but maybe Brix was right that she was capable of far more than anyone gave her credit for.

Marion had seemed so determined earlier as they'd said

goodbye on the steps to the Metro. 'I'll see you soon and then we'll talk. Once I've told the police everything I know. I love you.'

'What's going to happen now?' Jensen asked Brix.

'I expect they'll arrest me. Marion will say it was me who did it,' he said. 'Have you made any progress on your investigation yet?'

Jensen shook her head.

Brix's list was next to useless. Her only hope was that Fie would be able to work a miracle. 'No progress,' she said with a sigh. She would have to feed Ea and change her nappy before she could leave. 'Like I said before, I really don't know why you think I'm able to find whoever is after you. Your best bet is to call Henrik Jungersen at once and tell him everything.'

By the time she finally returned home, Karo had set the table in the kitchen with paper napkins, candles and a bunch of tulips in a vase.

The crockery and glasses were familiar to Jensen; she hadn't seen them in almost two years.

'I hope you don't mind that I unpacked your stuff,' Karo said, pointing to the cardboard boxes that she'd flattened and left neatly stacked in one corner. 'You have so many gorgeous things, I thought it was a shame to keep them all packed away, so I put them in the cupboards for you.'

'I don't mind at all,' said Jensen, yawning. Ea was in bed, and she was ready to follow as soon as she had finished eating. 'To be honest, I don't think I would ever have got around to it myself.'

In the end, she'd stayed for ages at Brix's house, going over everything again.

And still he'd refused to involve the police.

'How far did you get?' she asked Karo.

'Oh, just the kitchen stuff and some of the boxes in your office. You have so many books.'

'You were meant to be resting,' said Jensen. 'I hope you didn't carry anything heavy?'

'Don't worry,' Karo said, offering Jensen garlic bread from a woven basket that she'd once bought at Camden Market. 'I didn't know if you were a vegetarian, so I kept dinner meat free. It's just mushroom pasta, so nothing special, but at least it's hot. Oh and I bought us alcohol-free beers.'

'It smells amazing,' said Jensen.

Karo smiled broadly. 'I wanted to show you my gratitude.'

Her left eye had gone from black to bluish-green and the scratches and cuts on her face and arms were healing nicely. 'Cheers,' she said, as they clinked bottles.

The pasta was delicious, and Jensen had a second helping. 'There's chocolate for dessert,' said Karo.

Jensen leaned back in her chair and unbuttoned her jeans. 'I can't eat another thing,' she said. 'But give me an hour and I'm all yours.'

Karo laughed and Jensen was glad to see that she hadn't lost her sense of humour. 'So picking up your things went OK?'

'Yes, I did it all quickly and got out,' Karo said, sipping her beer. 'The flat was a mess. My boyfriend is useless without me.'

Jensen attempted her most disarming smile. 'You've never even told me his name.'

'Jonathan,' said Karo, biting her lip.

'Jonathan . . .?'

'I think it's better if you don't know his full name. That way you can't be put in any awkward position for not reporting him.'

'Because that's what should have happened,' said Jensen. 'You do know that, don't you?'

'Yes,' said Karo and now her eyes were filling with tears. 'I know, and you're right, of course you are. I will speak to the people at the crisis centre about how best to deal with it. I'll go on Monday.'

Jensen was relieved. She shouldn't have doubted Karo's resolve.

Karo got up and began to carry the dirty plates and cutlery to the sink. 'By the way, did you hear anything yet about Ea's paternity test?'

'What?'

'The DNA test you posted the other day?'

'Oh that, no,' said Jensen.

'It must be unbearable to wait for the result. I mean, it could change everything.'

Yeah, Jensen thought. *It could mean that I have a rapist for a father.*

31

Henrik closed the front door as quietly as he could and sat down on the steps to remove his scruffy Timberland boots.

It was almost midnight, and he didn't want to wake Louise and the kids. In fact, he thought he might sleep in the spare room. The day had been brutal, and all he wanted was to collapse into bed and sleep like the dead.

Vivian Sejer's sister had told them that she'd left for Copenhagen on the train on Friday morning, excited about some mystery man she was going to meet.

They would know more when Bagger's team had been through her phone and laptop, but it was odds on to be Brix.

On the way into the kitchen for a glass of water and a couple of painkillers, Henrik stopped in the shadowy hallway. There were suitcases there, and bags and shoes that belonged to his in-laws. Had they stayed an extra night after the Tivoli trip?

His heart sank. He'd been hoping they'd have gone home.

Now he thought he heard something – another person breathing? 'Anyone there?' he said into the dark, feeling ridiculous.

A creak on the floor in the living room, a weight shifting. Bunching his fists, he went through to investigate, trying to orientate himself in the dark.

The streetlight was reflected in the TV and in the armchair a figure moved, a skein of long dark hair falling across a face.

'Louise?'

'Don't turn on the light,' she said.

'OK.' He held up his hands. 'Has something happened? Is it your parents? Are the kids all right?'

'I saw her,' she said.

'Who?' But he knew the answer. His scalp prickled coldly; he wanted to turn and run.

'Jensen.'

The name sounded wrong in Louise's mouth, grotesque almost. She'd never said it before.

In their past conversations about his indiscretions (Jensen was the only one who had amounted to anything serious) it had always just been *she* or *her.*

The same had been the case whenever he and Jensen had discussed his marriage. Thus, he'd been keeping the two women in his life apart, and now their worlds had clashed together horribly.

'Where?' he said, though he wasn't sure he wanted to know. Had Jensen turned up here, at his home? Had Louise gone to see her in the flat by Peblinge Lake? The thought of either made his flesh crawl.

'At Tivoli. By chance. Or maybe divine intervention. I'll let you decide. I'd just arrived with Mum and Dad and the kids, and she was on her way out.'

Louise's voice was robotic. He wondered if she'd taken a tranquiliser or been drinking. She didn't sound like herself at all and was beginning to frighten him.

How did she even know what Jensen looked like? The implications of this filled him with dread.

'She's shorter than I thought, but pretty in her own way. She had her baby with her. In a sling. A daughter, I think, or at least she was wearing a pink sunhat.'

'Why are you—?'

'Is she yours, the baby?'

'Categorically no,' he said, his voice firmed by righteousness at last. 'The father is an entrepreneur who is awaiting trial for killing his parents and ordering the death of numerous other people. They were an item before she realised what he was up to.'

This wasn't public knowledge, and he shouldn't be telling her, but how else could he prove her wrong?

'Are you sure about that?' she said.

'One hundred per cent.'

His certainty didn't stem from innocence but from the timing of when he and Jensen had last been together. There simply was no way that he could be Ea's father.

He still found it hard to believe that Jensen, normally so strong and self-sufficient, had fallen pregnant with a man she'd only known for a short while. He'd tried telling her, to no avail.

She never listened.

'There is nothing going on between me and her, I swear,' he said. 'I mean there was that horrible business before Christmas . . . when she got caught up in—'

'But there was something between you once,' said Louise in her sleepwalker voice. 'And you saw her recently. Perhaps as recently as last night when you left in the middle of dinner.'

Again, he felt a spike of fear. She'd never challenged him so directly before, so dispassionately.

'Wow,' he said, trying to make light of it. 'Amazing that you could tell all that from a fleeting meeting.'

'You still love her.'

'I don't know what makes you—'

'Please don't insult me by denying it,' Louise said. 'She knows it too. I could see it in her eyes. I've always known about it, of course, since you went to London all those years ago, but I didn't want to admit it to myself, because I knew it would ruin everything, everything we've worked for and built up, the trust between us.' She shook her head. 'How stupid we are when we deceive ourselves.'

He wanted to drop to his knees, beg her to stop what he knew was coming, but his instinct told him it would never work. Nor would kissing her passionately, his usual method of distracting her from suspicion.

He knew she still fancied him; their sexual attraction had always been the glue that had held them together. Now even that appeared to be failing. 'Louise, I love you,' he said, truthfully.

'I know,' she said, surprising him.

'You do?'

'Of course. Only you don't just love me. You have feelings for her too.'

'Listen,' he said. 'It's late, you're upset, though you've no need to be. We clearly need to talk about this, but I've just worked a fourteen-hour shift, I'm knee-deep in three major cases and to be honest I could do with some sleep.'

Work, tiredness, major new cases. The usual excuses washed off her.

'It's not your fault,' she continued. 'You can't help who you love.'

'Maybe not,' he said quietly, knowing that denying his feelings for Jensen would be pointless. 'But I chose you, and I still do. This house. Our kids. Us. I've no plans to go anywhere.'

'The thing is,' she said. 'I'm not sure that's enough for me any more. You're not the only one with a choice.'

He grabbed her hands. They lay in his like dead birds. 'Remember last spring when you threw me out and I went to live with my dad for a while?'

'Yes.'

It had been a horrific time, never to be repeated. All he had been able to think of while lying in the single bed in his boyhood bedroom in Brøndby was how to get home.

'And then you took me back because you said the children needed a father,' he said.

'Yes. They do need you.'

'Well, nothing's been going on with Jensen since then. While I may not always have succeeded in your eyes, I've tried to be a good husband. So why throw me out again? Why now?'

She looked up in surprise. 'Oh but I'm not throwing you out.'

Now he didn't understand anything at all. He put his hands on top of his head. It was as if his brain was on fire. 'You're not? So what is this all about?'

'I'm the one who's going away. My deputy head has agreed to cover for me for the remainder of term. Officially I'm going on medical leave for minor surgery. It's only a few weeks of exams and then it's the summer holidays.'

'But you love the end of term, the graduation ceremony, watching your students pass their exams and enjoy themselves. You always said it's your favourite time of year.'

Louise carried on as if she couldn't or wouldn't hear him. 'My parents have moved in. They'll look after everything and stay here as long as necessary. It's your choice whether you remain or go somewhere else. I know you don't like my dad.'

There was no sense denying it, and Knud had never hidden the fact that the feeling was mutual. Staying in the house with him and Jytte quietly reproaching him for their daughter's departure would be sheer hell.

'When are you coming back?' he said, though he was conscious how pathetic he sounded, like a boy whose mother was leaving on a trip.

'I don't know yet, but I'll be absolutely fine, and so will you and the kids. I've told them that I'm going on a course in the US.'

Henrik's mouth was dry. All the saliva seemed to have drained out of it. 'Is that where you're going, to the US?' he said.

Before they'd had kids, she'd spent six months working at a school in San Francisco and always raved about it. Perhaps she was going back there. It would be difficult, but he thought he could cope with that.

Perhaps he could even overcome his fear of flying to visit her during the holidays. They could find their way back to each other, spend some time together, just the two of them.

'I'll FaceTime the kids regularly, so you've no need to worry on that score.'

'But what about me?'

'You'll live.'

She got out of her chair and crossed the floor of the dark living room like a sleepwalker. He reached out and seized her arm, but she twisted free without effort.

'I made your bed in the spare room. Don't come upstairs, and don't try to persuade me to stay because it won't work.'

She paused briefly in the doorway. 'Goodbye, Henrik, take care of yourself.'

Day Five

32

Sunday morning, and Ea had gone back to sleep. Jensen could hear Karo moving about in the kitchen, filling the kettle and taking two mugs from the cupboard for tea. These gentle sounds of domesticity filled her with a deep sense of happiness. No one had ever looked after her before. Not like this.

Her mother had brought her up to be independent and, from when she was old enough, she'd shopped and cooked for both of them, looking after their laundry and trying to keep their place tidy, an uphill battle against her mother's disinterest and an endless stream of visitors.

Maybe when Karo had finally left Jonathan and retrieved the rest of her things from their joint flat, she could move in as her lodger.

There was plenty of space for the two of them, and she would be able to help Karo with her baby when it arrived in November.

Last night's conversation over dinner had felt good, as if Karo was finally listening to her and starting to think about her future.

Her phone began to vibrate on the bedside table.

Fie.

Jensen felt a burst of excitement. Perhaps she had already made progress.

'Have you found something?' she said.

'It was a long night,' said Fie. 'I'm still in the office. There's been a murder. Perhaps you've seen it on the news?'

Jensen hadn't. She quickly looked up *Dagbladet*'s front page.

WOMAN, 46, FOUND MURDERED IN AIRBNB.

'What the hell?' she said, sitting up and casting the duvet aside.

Three new major investigations in one week. And she was on maternity leave and wouldn't be covering any of them.

'Yeah, it's pretty bad,' said Fie. 'Anyway, I managed to look at the stuff you sent, and it's not easy to see who it's coming from. If you want my opinion, I think the stalker is a pro.'

'What do you mean?'

'Someone who knows how to cover their tracks, use a VPN connection, a burner phone, working across all platforms.'

'A hacker?'

'Could be. I'm following up through my connections, but it's going to take time, and work is pretty busy.'

'What about the names I shared?'

'Could be any or none of them, if they have the right skills. I'd have to look at them more closely.'

When the call had ended, there was a knock on the door, and Karo entered with a tray: a mug of tea, a glass of orange juice and a bread roll with cheese.

'Breakfast,' she said, putting the tray on the duvet next to Jensen.

'So kind of you.' Jensen smiled as she reached for the bread roll. 'You shouldn't have, but I'm glad you did.'

'What were you doing?' said Karo. 'It sounded like you were on the phone just then.'

Jensen wondered if she'd overheard the conversation, but decided that even if she had, it wouldn't have made sense to her. 'Oh, just something I'm working on.'

'I thought you were on maternity leave.'

'I am. This is something private,' she said, sipping her orange juice. 'By the way, did you see the news about that woman who's been murdered in an Airbnb?'

'No,' said Karo her eyes widening. 'That's terrible.'

'She's the third female victim this week, and those are just the ones we get to read about in the press. On Wednesday, they found the remains of a woman behind a wall in a flat, Friday there was a violent rape in Frederiksberg Gardens, and now this. It a dangerous time to be a woman, but then it always has been.'

Karo looked uncomfortable. 'Jonathan would never actually have killed me,' she said.

He might have done if you hadn't run away, thought Jensen. And he still could if Karo didn't report him.

The news was full of stories of men killing their partners or exes. Jensen would do anything to ensure that didn't happen to Karo. 'Promise me that you really will go to that crisis centre tomorrow?'

33

'Brix is in the interview room, Boss,' said Mark, as Henrik arrived at the office.

He hadn't slept at all. It felt like the floor under his feet was liquid. The latte he'd chucked down in the car on the way here sat in his belly like a stagnant pond.

The conversation with Louise had been playing on a loop in his head for hours. Why hadn't he fought harder to change her mind? Why hadn't he just denied everything?

He knew why, of course.

By speaking the truth, she'd finally made them both face it, and she was right: they couldn't go on living like this.

He'd watched helplessly from the window in the spare room as just before six a.m. she'd left in a taxi with two suitcases. She hadn't looked back or hesitated as she'd stepped into the black Mercedes.

His first instinct had been to go after her, drive to the airport and create some tearful Hollywood-movie scene in the departure hall. But he knew there would be no point.

It was no longer up to him; it was up to Louise, and there was nothing he could do to influence her decision.

In this respect, his wife and Jensen were the same: once they'd set their heart on something, it happened.

So instead, he'd showered and got dressed, packed a bag with a few clothes and toiletries and sneaked out of the house before the kids and his in-laws woke up.

He'd left a note addressed to Jytte on the dining table.

I'll be very busy at work the next few days, so you won't be seeing me. Call me if you need anything, and thank you for helping us out. We're very grateful.

He'd used the plural deliberately to suggest that he and Louise were intent on working through their problems together, but he wasn't sure if there even was a 'we' any more.

There was no way he could stay overnight at home with Knud and Jytte there, not without committing an act of violence against his father-in-law.

All he could do was throw his energy into work.

He sensed that the arrival of the celebrity author had created a buzz in the office. Even Liv had come in, despite it being a Sunday. He caught a glimpse of the back of her cream silk shirt as she disappeared into her office.

There was no reason at this stage to believe that Brix was implicated in the murder of Vivian Sejer. The author was merely helping them with their enquiries.

Not even the bleak décor of the interview room was enough to diminish his star power, though Brix looked anxious.

'Ernst Brøgger,' said his lawyer. 'Finally we meet in person.'

Henrik momentarily lost his cool. Brøgger had played a small but significant part in the harrowing investigation last Christmas that had seen Henrik suspended from his job.

The solicitor to the rich and powerful looked as though he was about to board a cruise to the Norwegian fjords, with his slacks and V-neck jumper. The scent of his lemony aftershave filled the room.

His brother Leif, who went under the surname Kofoed, was a top-class crook who had evaded Danish justice for years by hiding out in South America.

Brøgger claimed to be as clean as his brother was dirty. Henrik wasn't so sure. Lawlessness was a sliding scale.

'If you don't mind, I'd like to get this over with quickly,' said Brix.

Henrik took his time sitting down and making himself comfortable. He opened his laptop, pretended to look through some notes and drank from a bottle of water, until he saw Brix's legs begin to bounce.

'OK,' he said. 'Does the name Vivian Sejer mean anything to you?'

Brix looked like this wasn't what he'd expected. He frowned. 'Why do you want to know that?'

'Just answer the question please.'

'Yes,' he mumbled.

'How do you know her?'

Brix glanced at Brøgger, who nodded slightly.

'I had an affair with her.'

'When?'

'Last year. I don't remember exactly.'

'And when you say an affair . . .?'

Brix snapped. 'We slept together. She's a fan. I met her at a signing event.'

Henrik pushed the photo of Vivian Sejer across the table. 'This woman?' he said, and Brix nodded miserably.

'And where did you sleep together?'

'At my hotel, but what—'

Brøgger cut him off, smiling magnanimously as he held up his hand. 'Detective Inspector Jungersen, my client has answered your question. Now, unless you want to know what colour undergarments he was wearing, why don't you tell us what we can help you with?'

Henrik looked at Brix, who kept biting his lip. The eyes behind the stark, black-rimmed glasses were shifty, glancing this way and that.

'OK,' Henrik said, keeping his gaze fixed on the author. 'You may have seen the news about a woman found murdered in an Airbnb. It was Vivian Sejer. She was discovered by a cleaner in a top-floor flat in Kronprinsessegade yesterday. We believe she was subjected to a sexual assault before she was killed.'

Brix looked shocked. Whatever he'd expected the interview to be about, it wasn't this.

'Killed?'

'And you are telling my client this, because . . .?'

Henrik ignored Brøgger's overbearing interruption and continued to focus on Brix. 'We found your initials in the woman's diary. Under yesterday's date.'

The author looked confused as he exchanged a glance with Brøgger.

'And this,' said Henrik, pulling out his pièce de résistance, the page with Brix's name and number, now wrapped in an evidence bag. 'Recognise it?'

'That's from my latest book,' said Brix after studying it for a few seconds.

'Any idea how your personal phone number came to be in Vivian Sejer's possession?'

'Must have been when we . . . during the affair.'

Brøgger put his hand on Brix's arm. 'Let me,' he said, turning to Henrik. 'A murder is always tragic, and our hearts go out to Ms Sejer and her family, but you still haven't answered my question. What makes you think my client can help?'

'I just told you. Vivian Sejer was due to meet your client yesterday.'

'No, that's not what you said. You said that my client's initials were in her diary. VB could be anyone.' He turned to Brix, whose eyes looked as though they were about to fall out of their sockets. 'Did you meet Vivian Sejer yesterday?'

Brix shook his head. 'I haven't set eyes on her since last year.'

'Where were you last night?' said Henrik.

'Home alone.'

'Can anyone verify that?'

'I was alone, so no.'

Henrik reminded himself to check whether Brix's mobile had been anywhere near Kronprinsessegade.

'There you go,' said Brøgger. 'My client was at home minding his own business. Now, will that be all?'

Henrik looked at Brix. 'You seem anxious. Is something on your mind?'

Again Brøgger spoke for him. 'With the greatest respect, if there's something on my client's mind, it's of no concern to you or the matter at hand.' He began to get up, gesturing at Brix to do the same.

Henrik knew that asking about Jensen would be highly unprofessional under the circumstances, but he'd taken an intense dislike to Brix, which had only grown in the past few minutes.

He simply had to know what Jensen was doing with him. As soon as he had an answer, he would put the matter to one side and forget about it.

'Just one more question,' he said as casually as he could. 'Do you know *Dagbladet*'s chief crime reporter? Her name is Jensen.'

Brøgger smiled knowingly, but Brix looked rather

disinterested in the question. *So it's true*, Henrik thought. *She really is romantically involved with the sleek bastard.*

'I'm sure you'll have a good reason for asking?' said Brøgger.

Henrik felt himself blush. He tried to sound confident. 'As you can probably guess, we in the police sometimes cross paths with members of the press who write about crime. I can't disclose any further details.'

'Of course. Though, if I'm not wrong, I believe the young lady is on maternity leave at present,' said Brøgger, clearly enjoying himself.

Henrik squirmed.

Might as well go the whole hog.

'That's correct, but I happen to know that she's been showing a close interest in your client recently. I'm purely wondering if she's working on a story that could be relevant to our current investigations.'

'How considerate of you,' said Brøgger. He turned to Brix, his smile broadening. 'Why don't you tell the Detective Inspector how you know Jensen?'

'I don't see why not,' Brix said. 'If it doesn't leave this room.'

Henrik nodded, holding his breath.

'The thing between Jensen and myself is personal.'

Here we go.

Jensen had said the same.

He wasn't prepared for what Brix said next.

'She's my daughter.'

34

Jensen had brought Ea to see Gustav at *Dagbladet*. In a desperate bid to keep the business afloat, the Swedish owners had rented out the top floor of the building, and the editorial staff were now squeezed into a single open-plan office downstairs.

As she stepped out of the lift, Jensen found herself face-to-face with the bronze bust of the newspaper's founder, relegated from the lobby to reflect the building's new shared occupancy.

How the mighty have fallen.

She found Gustav in a corner, frowning at his laptop. The rest of the room was empty, except for a couple of subs engrossed in a heated conversation.

'I thought I might find you here,' she said, hauling a bag with cold drinks and a couple of large chicken sandwiches with curry mayonnaise onto the desk. 'I brought sustenance.'

Gustav tutted as he peeked into Ea's pram. 'Couldn't you have made sure she was awake this time?'

'What are you working on?' she said, taking a seat and biting into her sandwich.

Gustav took off his bucket hat, scratched his shaved head and reached for the food. 'This new Airbnb murder,' he said. 'I think I know where it happened. Look at this picture someone shared on X.'

There was an ambulance and several police vehicles. A person dressed in a white coverall and facemask could be seen entering a block of flats.

'When and where was it taken?' she said.

'Yesterday, in Kronprinsessegade. The police won't comment and, before you ask, I did ring your boyfriend. He's not even picking up. Like the last time I rang him, and the ten times before that. Perhaps you could . . .?'

'Absolutely not,' she said, taking a sip of her lemon-flavoured sparkling water.

'Not fair,' said Gustav. 'I went down there, shot a video of the street and the building, but no one would let me in, or tell me anything, so it's completely useless.'

'What about the Mia Steen case? And the rape in Frederiksberg Gardens the other day?'

'Nada. I'm told there won't be an update until tomorrow at the earliest.'

'Any relatives you could interview to find out more about the victims?'

'I've tried, but they don't want to talk yet. The only upside is that our competitors are no further. We're all just running around in circles, regurgitating the same information, which wasn't much to start with.'

'Sounds like just another day at the office. Welcome to your life as a reporter,' Jensen said. 'Perhaps you should take the day off.'

Gustav shook his head. 'I can sleep when I'm old.'

'Jensen, is that you?' A booming voice from the other end of the room announced the presence of Margrethe Skov.

She was wearing her usual business attire, a navy dress and court shoes, as if expecting to be called in to interview the prime minister or the king at any moment. Her only concession to the weekend was an old scarf wound twice around her neck.

'When are you coming back to work?' she said, like she'd done every time they'd met since Ea was born.

'And what do you suggest I do with my daughter?' Jensen said, pointing to the pram.

'Put her in a nursery. It's good for children to be exposed to others from an early age.'

'Nursery spaces in Copenhagen are like gold dust. You should know. You've written several leader columns on the subject.'

'Then bring her to work,' Margrethe said. 'I need you back here pronto. I commissioned a feature yesterday from one of your colleagues, who shall remain nameless, on violence against women in all its forms. Rape, domestic abuse, partner murders.'

'And?'

'It's abysmal. Written with all the enthusiasm of a third-division nil-nil match report, and totally missing the point. I simply can't run it,' said Margrethe. 'And my leader column tomorrow is all about that. How many more years must we endure the same horrifying statistics in an enlightened society like ours? When will it ever stop?'

Jensen looked at her boss in awe. *Dagbladet* had weathered crisis after crisis in recent years. The newspaper was being run by a skeleton staff, and subscriber numbers were at record lows, but Margrethe was still on the barricades, undeterred in her mission to speak truth to power.

This time, she was going all out on behalf of Karo and

the thousands of women like her who weren't safe at home, forced to flee, scared of their own shadow.

'If you can lend me a laptop, I could have a look at the article, if you like?' Jensen said, throwing the remainder of her sandwich in the bin. 'I mean as long as Ea stays asleep.'

She looked up in time to see a smile slowly spreading across Magrethe's face. 'That's my girl.'

35

'I'm sorry to see you again so soon,' said Goldschmidt as he led them into the post-mortem room for the second time in a week.

'Not half as sorry as I am,' said Henrik, nodding at Goldschmidt's assistant Layla and the photographer from forensics as he averted his eyes from the shape under the sheet.

'Are you sure you're OK to do this? You look a little pale,' said the pathologist.

'I'm fine. Let's just get it over with,' said Henrik. Any more concerned probing by Goldschmidt and he would collapse in a heap.

No more bombshells please.

Three women brutally attacked, two of them dead.

A possible serial rapist.

His wife gone.

Brix and Jensen, father and daughter.

He was struggling to get his head around it all. And to think that barely five days ago he'd yearned for a new case to absorb him.

It had always seemed unlikely to him that Jensen's father

was a complete unknown. Why hadn't she just told him the truth on Friday night?

To make a bad day worse, Jensen's mother, Marion, had turned up at the office just as he was setting off for the post-mortem, demanding to speak to him.

He'd told her to come back tomorrow. There was only so much he could take in one day, and right now Marion Jensen was the least of his problems.

No sooner had he seen Brix and his lawyer out of the building than Liv had asked for a word.

'What was that question about *Dagbladet*'s crime reporter about?' she'd said, a deep frown on her face.

She'd been watching the interview next door.

Of course.

And so had Funder and Mark, judging by the embarrassed glances they'd sent him on his way to Liv's office.

'She was seen loitering outside Brix's house. I wanted to know why,' he said to Liv, trying to brazen it out.

'Seen?'

'It was an unofficial report that I . . . er . . . received,' he said. 'I thought it could be important to the case. I had no idea that he's her father.'

Liv looked at him sceptically, leaning against her desk in her cream-coloured shirt and slacks. 'Is this Jensen someone you know well?' she said.

Yes, and she's a pain in the arse, Henrik thought.

'I know *of* her,' he said. 'I know most of the crime reporters in this city, as you'd expect.'

'I don't encourage ad hoc conversations with journalists. Every communication to the press must be controlled, agreed, vetted and channelled centrally. It's not like the bad old days.'

Henrik was well aware of that. When he'd first started

out as a detective, it had been common for higher-ranking murder investigators to take calls from individual journalists. He sometimes still did but only when absolutely necessary.

'Understood,' he said.

'Unless . . . are you and Jensen in a relationship? Because that would be a clear conflict of interest.'

'There is nothing for you to worry about.' he said.

Thankfully, Liv had dropped the subject. 'OK, I trust you. You look done in. Can't someone else attend the post-mortem, so you can go home and rest?'

'No. I want to be there. I'd rather be working.'

It was a case of bearing witness, of paying his respects.

Besides, he didn't have a home to go to. Not one that he was capable of running like his wife did. He loved his kids enough to know that they deserved better.

As soon as he was done at the Forensic Institute, he was going to find a cheap hotel and try to sleep.

He grimaced as Goldschmidt pulled away the sheet, revealing Vivian Sejer's body; it was in a terrible state.

'She fought back,' said Goldschmidt. He pointed to scratches and cuts on Sejer's hands and forearms. 'Those are defensive wounds. If we're lucky, there'll be DNA and fibres under her fingernails.'

Henrik looked at the ligature marks around her wrists and ankles, and the horizontal line across her neck where the pair of tights had been.

'Could it have been a sex game gone wrong?'

'I'm sceptical,' said Goldschmidt, beckoning Henrik closer. 'See these marks and tiny red pinpricks across her face? I believe she was asphyxiated by hand. Her veins would have been squeezed so hard that blood was unable to flow back to her heart, causing all these superficial blood vessels in her skin to burst. The CT scan showed fractures to her tongue bone and thyroid cartilage, classic signs of strangulation.'

'So?'

'The perpetrator would have had to apply constant, immense pressure to her throat for three to four minutes before death occurred. It's not something that happens by accident.'

'And the tights?'

'Could have been added later to make it look like an accident during sex.'

'Was she raped?'

'Her injuries suggest rape, yes. The samples will show us more.'

As Goldschmidt and Layla got on with their slow, methodical work, Henrik let his mind drift. Trying to ignore the noises and smells around him, he focused his gaze on the light coming through the row of narrow windows on top of the wall.

His thoughts were chaotic, darting and clashing.

Brix had turned up again and again, like a joker in a card game. Was he behind Polaris? Was Funder right that Mia Steen had been the first? Had Brix developed some sort of sick hatred for the women he'd had affairs with, going back to hurt them afterwards?

It seemed to him as if everything that had happened was connected. There was a bigger picture; he just couldn't see it yet.

'Henrik?'

Goldschmidt was trying to get his attention. 'You seemed far away there,' he said. 'Penny for them?'

'I wouldn't waste your money,' Henrik said. 'What were you saying?'

'That her multiple injuries suggest the use of significant

force. Punches and kicks. This was an extremely savage attack.'

Henrik nodded to himself. It was almost as if Vivian Sejer had been punished for something. 'Could she have been drugged?' he said.

'Funny you should ask.' Goldschmidt pointed to a red spot on the woman's thigh. 'See that?'

'What is it?'

'Something was injected into her bloodstream. But my guess is that it didn't happen immediately. Like I said, she fought back.'

Henrik thought about the implications of this.

In the Polaris cases, the victims had no defensive wounds. They'd been beaten and raped, but the perpetrator hadn't given them a chance to fight back. Nor had he killed them.

Had Vivian Sejer surprised him before he'd had a chance to inject her with a drug to render her defenceless? Had she seen his face, and that's why she had to die?

They would have to go through her entire personal history. Hopefully, they would find more clues in her laptop and phone. Her sister was travelling to Copenhagen to formally identify the body and might tell them more.

Still, the task ahead of them was overwhelming.

As Henrik watched Goldschmidt and Layla examine Vivian's Sejer's broken body, he felt at a complete loss.

Day Six

36

'Fuck, fuck, fuck, fuck.' Jensen was swearing all the way to the Potato Rows.

Copenhagen was heaving in the morning rush hour, as though every single citizen was on the move, choking the streets with bikes, cars and yellow buses.

Ea was at home with Karo, showing off her new trick on a blanket on the floor – rolling from her tummy onto her back. Soon, Jensen would need to start thinking about weaning her.

But right now she'd something more pressing to deal with. Half an hour ago, police had released the name of the woman who'd been found murdered in an Airbnb on Saturday: Vivian Sejer.

Reading the news, Jensen had almost choked on her tea. Quickly she'd opened Brix's list and sure enough, the name had been near the top among his newest conquests:

> Vivi something. A fan I met at a reading event in Aarhus. We went back to my hotel. Returned again a few weeks later and stayed with her in the same hotel for two nights.

She wanted to see me again, but I declined, and we split amicably, with no further messages exchanged.

First Mia Steen, and now this woman. What were the chances?

She'd called Brix immediately, but he'd refused to speak over the phone (again), so she'd thrown on some clothes and jumped on her bike.

She was going to give him an ultimatum: either he told the police about the stalker, or she would.

If he was innocent, it couldn't hurt him, but what if there was more to it? What if the stalker's allegations were true, and that was why he'd refused to involve the police?

Either way, she'd had enough.

Yesterday, she'd ended up spending four hours in the office, while Gustav looked after Ea. The article Margrethe had passed to her needed to be rewritten from scratch.

It had felt amazing to be working again, and she was pleased that her piece had made it onto the front page.

Sadly, it had only become more topical overnight, she thought as she locked up her bike next to Brix's picture-postcard house and knocked on the door.

Brix had a haunted look about him. 'Did anyone follow you?' he said, double-locking the door after her.

'I didn't look,' she said. 'This crap has got to stop.'

'Where's Ea?'

'At home with a babysitter. I assume you saw the news about the Airbnb murder?'

'Yes,' he said, rubbing a hand over his chin.

'You slept with that woman. She's on your list.'

'I know. I was interviewed by the police yesterday.'

'What did you tell them?'

'That I didn't do it. I'm being set up, Jensen. Don't you

see? The stalker threatened to report me for rape. This is it. It's happening.'

'So you finally told the police about the threats?'

'No. They'll think I'm guilty. Brøgger believes it'll be OK, if I just hang in there. Never volunteer information, he says.'

'If only you had, you wouldn't be in this mess, don't you see?' she said. 'You couldn't look more guilty if you tried.'

'This whole business could finish me.'

'It will if you keep sticking your head in the sand, and it's about to get a whole lot worse. Marion is in town, and she's talking to the police.'

He looked at her in astonishment. 'Say that again?'

'You can't be surprised. That's what she said she'd do if you ever got in touch with me. Does she know something about the rape allegation?'

'No.'

'Well I'm sure the police will love to hear what she knows about Mia Steen. Her side of the story won't look good for you.'

Brix shook his head. 'Marion doesn't have anything incriminating on me. Just stuff I wouldn't want in the papers.'

'Your careless behaviour with women, for example? Use and throw away. Next. What else? Drugs?'

'As long as she doesn't talk to the press, we'll be fine.'

'I wouldn't put it past her. I've never seen her more determined. She's a different person.'

Brix looked genuinely terrified. 'I know what you think of me, but I swear to God I haven't done anything. I love women, I respect them.'

'Really? Let's do a poll, shall we? Bet you anything those 122 women on your list don't agree, including your wife,' she said, her voice rising. 'And do you know what? I'm actually on their side. I think you're a giant self-absorbed prick. I can't believe you got me involved in your shit.'

She paused for breath, collapsing into a chair. Brix sat down next to her, shoulders slumped. When he spoke, his voice was thin and weak. 'I deserved that,' he said. 'But I repeat, I'm not a rapist. I didn't do anything those women didn't consent to. What the hell am I going to do, Jensen?'

37

Henrik was sitting in his office staring blankly at the sun-drenched street where somehow life was carrying on as though nothing had happened.

The bread roll someone had brought him from the canteen sat untouched on his desk. There was so much coffee and adrenaline in his system that he couldn't imagine ever sleeping again.

He'd checked in with his mother-in-law by text (he didn't trust himself to talk to her without crying). The kids were at school and there was nothing to worry about, she'd replied.

Nothing to worry about.

As if.

A triple knock and Mark stuck his head around the door. 'We thought you'd want an update on everything before you brief Liv,' he said.

Funder pushed past him, nabbing the visitor's chair before Mark could react. The atmosphere between the two of them had got worse, and so far Funder was coming out on top.

'Did you see this article in *Dagbladet*?' she said, throwing the paper in front of him.

His eyes widened in surprise when he saw Jensen's byline.

'I like her,' said Funder. 'Finally someone who gets it. Wasn't she the one you were asking Brix about? We should talk to her, find out what she's working on.'

Already way ahead of you, Henrik thought.

Mark sent him a funny look. Jensen had cropped up in other investigations. It was unusual but not unheard of that reporters obtained knowledge of interest to the police, but had Mark sussed that there was more to it?

Henrik didn't have time to dwell on it. There was going to be another press conference in an hour. Thank God, this time his presence was not required (his dismal recent performance had made sure of that), but he'd promised Liv to brief her beforehand.

'Talk,' he said.

'Grethe Steen saw her daughter's remains,' Mark began.

'How did it go?'

'It was dreadful. I tried to deter her, but she wouldn't hear of it. She took a lock of her daughter's hair as a keepsake.'

'Where is she now?'

'On her way back to Randers. We got the names of Mia's friends, and also some of her family members, and will be speaking to them in the coming days.'

'I spoke to the forensic geneticists, and they've managed to get the DNA of Mia's foetus after all. Might help us determine who the father was,' said Funder.

Mark continued, clearly annoyed at her interruption. 'We have to assume that Mia was murdered sometime between arriving back in Copenhagen after her summer holidays in late July 1987, and her student room being cleared by the first of January the following year,' said Mark.

'The letter giving notice on her student room was sent on the twenty-seventh of November. I reckon she'd been dead for weeks by then,' said Henrik.

'We can't rule out that she sent the letter herself,' said Mark.

'She'd been in the habit of calling her mother once a week and suddenly in late September she just stopped.'

'Because they'd had an argument.'

'No, because she was dead.'

'You think Brix, Andreas Lund or Marion Jensen killed her?' said Funder.

'Yes,' said Henrik.

'Marion Jensen has come back. She's waiting downstairs,' Mark said. 'I could talk to her, see if she can shed some more light?'

'No,' Henrik said. 'I want to do it, but it'll have to be later.' He closed his eyes. When he opened them again the room swivelled and listed for a while before falling into place. 'Please tell me that we're further ahead on Jane Dahl-Thomsen.'

'Well, I found out that she and Valde Brix definitely met in person. There was a big event last year at the publishers where both she and Brix were in attendance. I was shown a photo of him talking to her.'

'Nothing more than that?'

'I'm still digging,' said Funder. 'However, in other news we had a call from a member of the public who remembered seeing a drunk couple heading into the park sometime after nine p.m.,' said Funder.

'Good. That's a start.'

'But they were unable to describe the man, except that he wore dark clothing and some sort of headwear, maybe a baseball cap.'

'Excellent,' said Henrik. 'It's a proper shit show.'

'But hear this,' said Funder. 'One of the staff at the restaurant said they saw a man in hi-vis hanging around earlier in the day. They assumed it was an electrician, as they'd had a few problems with a fuse box, but we checked with the proprietor who denied having called anyone.'

'A stake-out, getting to know the lie of the land, where the cameras were, which exit to use?' said Henrik, more awake now.

'That's what I think,' said Funder. 'You remember the broken camera in the courtyard? It's possible the guy disabled it when he called round earlier.'

Henrik felt like the floor was rushing up to meet him.

'Oh, and by the way, I checked, and Brix doesn't have an alibi for Wednesday night. Claims he was at home by himself, but is unable to verify it,' said Funder.

Same story as with Vivian Sejer, Henrik thought.

'That doesn't mean he did it,' said Mark.

'I'm not saying it does,' snapped Funder. 'I'm just relaying the facts.'

'Relaying the bullshit more like,' said Mark under his breath, his face turning bright red.

They both looked at Henrik as if expecting him to settle the matter.

He opened his mouth to tell them both to get lost.

He needed to think. Perhaps lie down on his couch with his eyes closed for a few minutes. But before he could speak, another visitor arrived.

It was Bagger, with his calm voice and perpetually smiling eyes.

'I've found something you need to see,' he said.

He opened his laptop and clicked on an email. 'Vivian Sejer received this two days ago. Three guesses who it's from.'

Valde Brix.

The man who was everywhere.

Dearest Lisa

I can't stop thinking about you and what we did last Christmas. I know what I said, but I'm going to be on my own on Friday night. Would you like to come over and play? I miss you.

VB

Vivian Sejer had sent two emails by way of reply. The first was a gushing acceptance, the second the booking confirmation for the Airbnb in Kronprinsessegade.

'What the hell?' Henrik said. 'The bastard lied to us.'

He marched to Liv's office, closely followed by Bagger. All his tiredness had gone. At last, a breakthrough.

Liv was at her desk.

'Valde Brix had arranged to meet Vivian Sejer on Friday night.'

'What?'

Henrik reckoned that the look of shock on her face was a mere taster of what the reaction in the general public would be. The story would go around the world.

FANTASY AUTHOR ARRESTED FOR RAPE AND MURDER

'All hell will break loose now,' he said.

'Yep,' said Liv. 'But we can't be seen to be giving celebrities preferential treatment. Not on my watch. We'll postpone the press conference. Go and bring in Brix.'

38

Jensen was about to leave Brix's house when she sensed that something was happening outside. Through a gap in the living-room curtain she saw that a car had pulled up.

Brix was trembling and looking close to collapse. 'Expecting anyone?' she said.

He shook his head.

'Could it be your wife coming back?'

Another shake of the head. 'I spoke to her this morning. She's still at her sister's house in Roskilde. I told her to stay put.'

Jensen felt her pulse rise when she saw Henrik get out of the passenger seat and head for the front door, followed by a younger male detective she'd seen before.

Another car pulled up, and a squat woman with short hair got out, a grim expression on her face.

'It's the police,' Jensen said. 'And I don't think it's good news.'

Henrik rang the doorbell twice, then hammered on the door with his fist.

'Oh God, oh God, oh God,' said Brix.

'Try and stay calm,' she said. 'Open the door.'

Henrik was holding up his warrant card. 'Valde Brix, I'm arresting you in connection with the murder of Vivian Sejer.'

So they had something on him now, something linking him to the crime.

Behind Henrik and his colleagues, she recognised the neighbour who'd been watching her when she first visited Brix. The woman was holding up her phone, filming.

It wouldn't be long before the whole world knew. Exactly what Brix had been so afraid of.

Henrik had finally spotted Jensen. 'Step aside please,' he said gruffly, as though the two of them were complete strangers.

More officers slipped into the house, black warrant cards dangling from their necks. She assumed they would be searching the place and confiscating Brix's laptop and phone.

In a way, it was a relief. Now they would discover what had been going on.

Brix was taking it badly. 'I haven't done anything. I'm being framed. Jensen, tell them!'

Thankfully, Henrik interrupted before she could say anything. 'Let's calm right down,' he said. 'You'll have ample opportunity to explain everything with your lawyer present. I'll remind you that you've not been formally charged with anything yet.'

The word 'yet' hung in the air in the narrow hallway. 'Jensen, help me! Call Brøgger,' Brix shouted as Henrik led him out.

She watched as they put him into the car. Henrik took a seat next to Brix, and his colleague drove them off.

More neighbours had emerged from their houses. They

were talking to each other, pointing to Brix's property. Soon there would be reporters all over the street.

Jensen quickly composed a message for Brøgger, telling him what had happened. His remark that Brix didn't have it in him to commit a crime rang in her head. Brøgger was seldom wrong, and what he'd said had chimed with her own gut feeling.

A thought occurred to her. It felt like a betrayal of Brix, but he would be all over the news anyway; she might as well give Gustav a head start on the story.

'Margrethe loves your article,' he said when he answered her call. 'Hasn't stopped talking about it all morning.'

'Shut up for a minute,' she said. 'I have a scoop for you. Valde Brix has just been arrested.'

'What, your dad?'

'The man who may or may not be my father, yes. Get yourself down to the Potato Rows. I'm texting you the address now. I'll tell you as much as I can.'

39

Brix had pushed himself so far down that he was half lying in the footwell with the seat belt around his neck. 'I don't want anyone to see me,' he kept saying, covering his face with his hands.

His desperate attempts at hiding were futile. As they drove away, his neighbours were already gathering around his house like flies on a corpse.

The news would be out soon. Henrik knew Jensen would make sure to put it on the front page of *Dagbladet*.

It had been weird seeing her at Brix's house, and even weirder pretending they didn't know each other.

'Be quiet,' he said to Brix.

The author ignored him. 'I have a stalker,' he shouted. 'I've been harassed for months by this person threatening to report me for rape. They must have set me up, you've got to believe me. Ask Jensen, she knows.'

I did, thought Henrik. *If only she'd said something.*

'Why didn't you tell us before?'

'Because then the stalker would have won. No smoke without fire. I'd be branded for life, and my career would be over!' He almost screamed the words, his voice hitting an undignified falsetto.

'Oh yeah? How's that working for you so far?' Henrik mumbled under his breath.

Chaos reigned back at the office. The staff of the violent crimes unit took pride in being an unflappable bunch, but not today. People were rushing between desks, shouting. Someone had turned on the TV news on the big screen.

Henrik recognised a politician from one of the opposition parties calling for new legislative powers to tackle violent crime against women.

The interview was interspersed with pictures of Mia Steen, Jane Dahl-Thomsen and Vivian Sejer, as well as footage from the three crime scenes.

'Everyone's jumping on the bandwagon now,' said a voice behind him.

Liv.

'And see this.' She held up her phone, showing him a garish tabloid news site with a picture of Brix being led out of his house. 'Famous author arrested,' said the headline under the 'Breaking' banner.

'We've got to manage the media,' said Liv. 'I'll speak to the leadership and put a few words together for a press release.'

In the incident room, separate whiteboards had been arranged to capture evidence from the three investigations.

As Henrik stepped in, he saw Funder coming towards him. She looked sheepish. 'Appears our man might have made a mistake after all. The technicians managed to get DNA from the water bottle in the fridge at the Airbnb, and it's not Vivian Sejer's. If it's Brix, we've got him.'

They were yet to interview the author after his arrest. His lawyer, the erudite Ernst Brøgger, hadn't arrived yet.

Now Mark approached, looking pained. 'Marion Jensen's still here. What shall I say to her?'

'Not now, for God's sake, Mark,' said Henrik. 'Tell her I'll call when I'm ready. I must speak to Brix first. If you want to be useful, get me a coffee.'

40

'Did you get what you needed?' said Jensen when Gustav returned from interviewing Brix's nosy neighbour.

They'd crawled inside the red wooden playhouse in the middle of the street to hide from the gaggle of reporters who had assembled outside Brix's house.

Gustav looked like a giant as he ducked under the ceiling with his long limbs folded awkwardly.

'More than,' he said. 'She gave me her video recording of Brix being led away. I don't think she likes him. Apparently, he's not very sociable. There was a party here recently. Chairs and tables all the way down the street, live band and everything, and Brix and his wife didn't even show. Also, she asked him for a selfie once, and he just walked off. He used to be much nicer when he wasn't so well-known, according to her.'

'He'll be wary of strangers because of the stalker.'

'I wish we knew why he'd been arrested.'

'They must have something concrete on him. Still, you can break the news that he knew Mia Steen and Vivian Sejer personally, which is a story in itself.'

'Not the whole story, though.'

'It's more than the rest of the media have.'

'Why can't I say that he had affairs with them?'

'Because his wife has a right to know before everyone else does.'

Gustav tutted and began to scroll through his footage.

The police still hadn't left Brix's house. A couple of neighbours, one of them with a small dog in tow, stood about chatting as if expecting more excitement.

'You'd better get that video edited and posted,' Jensen said, watching a TV broadcast van turn into the street.

'Yeah,' said Gustav. 'And you'd better get back to Ea. I can't believe you left her with that woman, not after last time.'

'Her name is Karo, and nothing happened, remember? It was just you getting worked up over nothing.'

'You barely know her,' said Gustav, glued to his screen. 'So do you think Brix has been lying?'

'I don't know,' she said. 'I mean, I think he's an arsehole, but I can't believe that he's an actual rapist or murderer. I'm not sure the police agree though.'

'They'll let him go as soon as he tells them that this is all down to the stalker, won't they?'

'He'll have to hope so,' said Jensen. 'Unless they believe the stalker has something on him, which they might.'

Gustav put away his phone and climbed out of the playhouse, slowly unfolding his limbs. She followed, checking her watch; she'd been gone for more than two hours.

'So what are you going to do now?' said Gustav.

'Get back home. Let's keep each other posted, shall we? I'll show you mine, and you show me yours?'

'You got it,' he said, smiling broadly. 'Say hi to Ea from me.' He stepped on his e-scooter and sped off as if the tarmac was on fire.

She was about to press Fie's number when she saw an incoming call.

Brøgger.

'I'm on my way to the police station,' he said. 'But I've just received a strange text message from an unknown number.'

'Strange how?'

'It says, "Tell Brix I have his kid. Time to confess or else." I don't like the sound of that.'

'Shit,' said Jensen. 'It's the stalker.'

'Any idea where his wife and son are?'

'They're in Roskilde, with his wife's sister.'

'Ah yes, that's right. I'll call the police now and tell them to go there immediately. Little August could be in grave danger,' said Brøgger. 'And tell Andreas Lund that Brix has been arrested, would you? This is going to get very ugly, he needs to handle the press, and I haven't been able to get hold of the man.'

How had the stalker managed to find the boy and his mother? Brix had thought he was keeping them safe when he sent them away, and now his toddler, just two years old, was being held to ransom.

It seemed grossly unfair.

The son shall not bear the sins of the father.

Suddenly, Jensen was anxious to get home to Ea, but first she had to call Andreas Lund.

Brix had forwarded his details; she was reminded that she needed to talk to him at some point, find out if he had an idea who the stalker could be.

Her call rang for ages. She was about to end it when Lund finally picked up. He sounded breathless, as though he'd been running.

There was no time for small talk. 'Brix has been arrested,' she said. 'Brøgger told me to let you know.'

'But what for?' said Lund.

'The murder of Vivian Sejer. That's all I know.'

She ended the call. A cameraman and a reporter were busy setting up in front of Brix's house. She ran past them and jumped on her bike. If she got a move on, she could be back at the flat in under ten minutes.

41

Henrik was on his way to the interview room when he saw Funder and Mark come running towards him. Mark was pressing a phone to his ear.

'Something's happened,' shouted Funder. 'Apparently, the stalker has taken Brix's two-year-old. His lawyer received a message on his way here and called the police. Brix is beside himself.'

'What? Where?'

'Brix says he sent the boy and his mother to her sister's in Roskilde to keep them safe, but now it seems the stalker's found them.'

'What exactly did the message say?'

'"Tell Brix I have his kid. Time to confess or else,"' said Funder. 'Perhaps they mean time to confess to the rape they're threatening to report him for?'

'Brix says he's being framed. Perhaps the stalker staged Vivian Sejer's murder to look like he did it, and that's what they want him to confess to?' said Mark.

'Why would they kill a completely innocent woman just to get at Brix? It makes no sense.'

Henrik held up his hand. 'Stop, both of you. Let's find the boy first.'

'I'm on hold with the control room now,' said Mark. 'Local officers are on their way to the sister's house as we speak.'

They retreated to the incident room to wait for news.

Henrik noticed that a fourth whiteboard on wheels had been added to the other three. 'What's this?' he said to Funder.

Photos of eleven women had been arranged side-by-side with magnets. Below each there were images of horrific injuries that Henrik tried not to look at.

'Polaris,' said Funder. 'These were the victims mentioned in my report. I thought it worth reminding ourselves. Do you know if Liv has read it yet?'

'Funder, we're in the middle of a media shit storm. She will have other priorities.'

'But this could be important,' she said, pointing to the board. 'Everything could be linked to Polaris.'

'Or it isn't,' said Henrik. 'And it's a massive distraction.' Soon, he'd have to find a hotel room and get some sleep, or he wouldn't be able to function, let alone think.

'I've been through it again,' Funder said. 'I still believe these crimes were all committed by one man.'

'What sort of man?'

'An entitled one. He has anger issues, gets into these uncontrollable rages. Hates women. Perhaps a sadist. To the outside world, he comes across like a normal, well-adjusted individual, but he's living a secret life, and he's getting off on fooling us and avoiding justice.'

Henrik didn't believe in psychological profiling, had seen perpetrators prove the theorisers wrong too many times. Funder carried on regardless.

'He's well-educated, with the brains and resources to cover his tracks successfully. He could easily be married with kids.'

'Shut up, we've got something,' shouted Mark. He put his phone on speaker. A uniformed police officer was live on a video call. 'We're at the address. You wanted to know if August Brix is OK?'

'Is he?' said Henrik.

The officer didn't reply but changed the orientation on the camera and panned it to his left. They could now see a toddler playing on the floor with a wooden trainset. An attractive woman next to him was glancing anxiously at the camera. Brix's young wife, Henrik assumed.

'As you can see, he's perfectly safe. No one has noticed anyone hanging around outside the property. Looks like it was a false alarm.'

'Thank God.'

'I wonder what that was all about,' said Funder.

'Putting the frighteners on Brix,' said Henrik. 'And it clearly worked.'

He was relieved. They had enough madness to deal with without adding a child abduction.

He quickly composed a message to let Jensen know that August Brix was safe. Then he headed for the door.

'Let's go and give Brix the good news. Then we'll hear what he has to say for himself.'

42

Jensen let out a sigh of relief on seeing Henrik's message. August Brix was safe, and the police would be staying at his aunt's property in Roskilde until further notice.

She parked her bicycle in the courtyard behind her block and climbed the kitchen stairs, looking forward to seeing Ea's face again after the turmoil of the past two hours.

Gustav had been wrong; it was good for her daughter to get used to other people.

Parenthood was a slow loss of control, she reminded herself. She didn't own Ea; she was merely helping her daughter grow safely into adulthood.

She let herself into the kitchen. It was clean and swept and the tulips from Saturday night had opened fully and were hanging low on the table.

'It's me, I'm home.'

There was no reply. Karo and Ea were probably sleeping. In a minute they would wake up, she would have a cuddle with Ea, then devote the rest of the afternoon to catching up on the news and making a more determined effort to find Brix's stalker.

Maybe Karo could help, if sworn to secrecy. She would probably be glad to be of use in some way.

'Karo? Ea? Are you there?' she shouted as she walked through the flat. The door to the bedroom was closed. She opened it gently, a smile already spreading across her face, but the bed and cot were empty.

She broke into a run. Ea's pram was in the entrance hall, but her changing bag had gone, and so had her sling, pink sunhat and yellow blanket.

She already knew that Karo and Ea weren't in the courtyard, but she looked out of the window anyway, in case they'd just missed each other.

There was a strange sound now; it was coming from herself, a strangled yelp on every in-breath.

She'd not had any messages or missed calls from Karo, but then she'd been worried about them using their phones in case her boyfriend was intercepting their messages.

Maybe he'd finally found her. But if she'd been in a mad rush to escape from him, then she wouldn't have had time to take Ea's things.

Tell Brix I have his kid.

Jensen felt an icy prickle on her scalp as the past few days ran like a film in front of her eyes. Her gratitude for Karo's company – for having made a new friend – had dulled her senses.

Karo's interest in the paternity test and who Ea's father was should have made her suspicious. She'd let Karo unpack her boxes and go through her private things, her laptop and mobile phone left unguarded.

It seemed so obvious now that Jensen felt ashamed to have missed it.

The violent boyfriend, the injuries, the pregnancy. They'd all been lies to put her off the scent.

She screamed.

Karo was Brix's stalker.

And she had Ea.

43

Out of the corner of his eye, Henrik noticed an incoming call from Jensen and turned his phone face down.

As nothing had happened to Brix's kid, he saw no immediate urgency to speak to her.

Brix had finally calmed down enough to be interviewed, but it wasn't going well, and Henrik was getting fed up with Brøgger's patronising tone.

'Perhaps now you believe that my client has a dangerous stalker?'

'If he'd said so a lot sooner, we might have avoided the last half-hour of panic,' said Henrik.

Now he understood why Brix had behaved so weirdly when he'd first been to see him at his house – the closed curtains, the expectation that he was going to be arrested for something.

On the other hand, why would an innocent man be so terrified?

'My client is not at fault,' said Brøgger.

'Oh yeah? What was it that the stalker wanted him to confess to then?'

'Who's to say what's in the mind of this clearly deranged individual. Why don't you ask them?' Brøgger smiled. 'Now, would you kindly tell us what you've got, as today has already been upsetting enough for my client and he'd like to rest now.'

'All right then,' said Henrik. 'We were here yesterday, discussing Vivian Sejer. We're now in possession of an email from your client to Sejer, inviting her to Copenhagen. An invitation she gladly accepted, whereupon she booked the Airbnb in which she was found murdered on Saturday morning.'

Henrik pushed a printout towards Brøgger. He looked it over for what seemed like ages, then said, 'This was not sent by my client.'

'It comes from his email address,' said Henrik pointing to the top line on the print-out.

'Then the stalker must have hacked into my client's account and pretended to be him. I'd say they probably assaulted and murdered the poor woman to make it look like my client did it.' Brøgger stared at him obstinately, not a flicker of doubt in his eyes.

It was as if Brix had woken up from a daydream. He got out his phone and began to scroll through his emails. 'My God,' he said. 'It's true, here's the email exchange.' He passed the phone to Brøgger. 'I never saw it before now.'

'We found DNA on a water bottle in the Airbnb. I believe you've now kindly given us a sample. Will we discover that you drank from that bottle?'

'No!' shouted Brix. 'It wasn't me. I was never there.'

'Let's see, shall we?' said Henrik. 'The results should be in soon.'

He looked at Brix and smiled. 'Now, I'd like to turn to another matter. On Wednesday night, a fifty-four-year-old woman named Jane Dahl-Thomsen was brutally raped and assaulted in Frederiksberg Gardens. I understand the two of you know each other. Is that correct?'

Brix looked like someone had punched him.

'It's a simple yes or no,' Henrik said.

Brix nodded. 'We work for the same company.'

'You're sure that's all?'

'What's this about?' said Brøgger. 'Are you accusing my client of something else? I must say it's hard to keep up.'

Henrik kept his eyes on Brix. 'I'm just asking how well you know Jane Dahl-Thomsen.'

'Well, I think he's answered you,' said Brøgger.

'As I understand, you don't have an alibi for last Wednesday night,' said Henrik to Brix.

'I assume you're asking because you have something concrete that connects him to the crime scene?' said Brøgger. Henrik was enjoying the fact that he was no longer smiling.

'Just asking questions,' Henrik said.

'I was at home on Wednesday night,' said Brix. 'I haven't done anything.'

'Well, if there's nothing else,' said Brøgger. 'I take it my client is free to go?'

'For the time being,' said Henrik, getting to his feet.

Looking at his phone on the way out of the interview room, he saw seven missed calls from Jensen.

He knew deep inside his being that this couldn't be anything good.

44

After a moment of blind panic, Jensen surprised herself by switching into action mode. Karo wasn't completely unknown to her; she knew where she lived, and she had her phone number.

She called 112, heard herself say: 'My baby has been taken.' It took a while to answer all their questions and get them to take her seriously. No, she didn't have Karoline's full name. Yes, she had looked everywhere. No, she knew of no other place they could be.

She gave them the address of Karo's flat – the only firm ground she had to stand on – and told them to meet her there. Karo wouldn't be stupid enough to return home, but maybe they could search the place.

Jumping on her bike, she cycled to Nørrebro as fast as she could. All the way, she kept looking for Ea's pink sun hat, trying not to become consumed with the horror of it all.

She got there before the police and rushed to the door where she'd seen the name tag. But perhaps she'd misremembered the street number because there was no

Karoline & Jonathan now. She ran from door to door checking the entire street but drew a blank.

So Karoline and Jonathan were a lie, like everything else. Karo, or whatever her name was, had known that she was being followed, and like a total amateur Jensen had fallen into the trap.

Which of the women on Brix's list was Karo? Most likely one of the many he couldn't even remember the name of.

But he'd made a mistake. This one wasn't willing to go away quietly.

Why? Because he'd hurt her feelings? Or was there a more sinister reason?

The police arrived. 'Jensen?' said a muscular officer with frameless glasses, as he got out of the patrol car and walked slowly towards her.

Why was he not running? What did he not understand? And why wasn't Henrik here?

She'd called and called.

'She took my baby,' she shouted at him. 'And I don't even know what she's called. She just said her name was Karo, short for Karoline.'

'Whoa, take a deep breath,' said the officer who was towering above her. 'This Karoline has your baby?'

'Yes,' she said. 'I already explained all that. Except her name isn't Karoline, and she doesn't live here. She lied.'

He looked at her like she was mad. People were walking past staring at them.

It was a nightmare.

'You live by Peblinge Lake, is that right?' said the other officer, who had a spotty face and looked not much older than Gustav.

'Yes. I told them that over the phone. Listen, just listen for one second.' She was trying to control her voice. 'I'm a journalist. I work at *Dagbladet*. I'm on maternity leave. The other day, I met this woman who had an obvious injury to her face. She told me that she was pregnant and that her boyfriend had struck her. I tried to make her call the police, but she wouldn't, and I didn't want to scare her off. Then on Friday night she turned up at my flat in a complete state, saying he'd beaten her up, so I let her stay at mine for a few days. This morning I had to go out, so she offered to babysit for my daughter Ea, but when I got back there was no sign of them. Ea's just five months old, but small for her age. She was premature, you see?'

'What made you think that the woman who called herself Karo lived in this building?' said the officer.

'Because I followed her here on Saturday. She'd told me that she was going home to collect a few things, and I was afraid that her boyfriend might hit her again. But she must have known I'd be there, because she'd put a sticker with 'Karoline & Jonathan' on it right next to that bell. No idea where she'd got the key from, but I saw her let herself in. Maybe she picked the lock.'

Jensen pointed to the panel with the names of the people who lived in the flats. The name tag for the third floor to the right now said *Ole Madsen*.

One of the officers rang the bell. Ole Madsen said he'd lived in his flat for eighteen years and had never heard of anyone called Karoline or Jonathan.

The officer with the glasses turned to Jensen. 'Can you give us a description of this woman?'

'She has long red hair and blue eyes, and she's taller than me, slim built. She has a bruised eye and scratches on her hands and arms, and a tattoo here, right across her collarbone, saying "Not all those who wander are lost." It's from the Lord of the Rings.'

She watched as if from behind glass, as the officer passed on the details through the radio. He and his colleague both moved slowly and deliberately, as though acting out instructions from a textbook on how to calm people down.

It wasn't working. She felt like she was going to throw up. 'What about the phone number I gave you?' she said.

'Not in use.'

She let out a frustrated cry.

'You're upset and that's completely understandable,' said the spotty-faced officer. 'There'll be units all over Copenhagen looking for your daughter now. Let's get you back to your flat in case your friend returns. There might still be a natural explanation for all of this.'

'My friend? Have you been listening to a word I've said?' Jensen was about to scream again when she heard a car coming to a screeching halt.

Henrik.

He ran towards her.

'Brix's stalker,' she cried. 'I know who it is, and she has Ea.'

45

Henrik had never seen Jensen in this state before. He could barely get her to look at him; she sat as if in a trance, staring out of the window in the family room, only turning her head when the door went, or a phone rang.

He'd had all manner of trouble persuading her that driving through the streets looking for her baby in random places would be pointless, and that they'd be better off waiting back at the office.

A nationwide search was well underway but hampered by the lack of any useful information about the kidnapper, such as her name and photo.

Jensen's description had been vague, except for the woman's tattoo: 'Not all those who wander are lost'.

It was Funder who had pointed out that this was a quote that featured prominently in Brix's first novel.

Henrik questioned himself. Should he have been more suspicious when Jensen had asked his advice about the domestic-abuse victim she'd made friends with?

His wife had friends – an endless parade of overpoweringly talkative women whose names he always got wrong – but he'd never heard Jensen mention anyone outside of work that she was close to.

If Brix was telling the truth, the stalker had intercepted his email. Perhaps that's how they'd found out about his correspondence with Jensen and got the wrong end of the stick.

Henrik had made the same mistake after all, thinking that she was having an affair with Brix.

What a mess.

Jensen wasn't gullible, but she was famously a sucker for the underdog, and the stalker had built a convincing narrative.

'I thought we could be friends,' Jensen said. 'I wanted to help her.'

'You were being kind,' he said. 'And she used that against you.'

But Jensen wasn't listening to him. 'I wasn't sure if I wanted Ea when I first fell pregnant. And now . . . I feel so guilty.'

She refused the coffee and sandwich he'd brought and hadn't touched the bottle of water someone had placed in her hands.

He'd managed to get hold of Gustav Skov, who had told him that he'd warned Jensen about her new friend. The lad had seemed extremely upset. To make him feel better, he'd asked him to go to Jensen's flat.

A team was already there, searching for clues to the woman's identity, along with DNA and fingerprints.

'Wait there in case she returns,' he'd told Gustav.

'I'll kill her if she does.'

There was a gentle knock on the door and Bagger entered the room followed by Fie Pedersen, the hacker whizz-kid from Roskilde.

On seeing her, Jensen came alive and rose to her feet. 'Have you tracked her down?' she said, and the hope in her voice was unbearable. 'Do you know who she is?'

'Not yet,' said Fie. 'I'm trying as hard as I can.'

They'd spoken to Brix, who remembered meeting a blonde woman with a similar tattoo last November. 'This can't go any further, but we met at Café Nytorv and went to a hotel. I was drunk. Don't remember her name. She was a big fan, she said. A rather intense person. Never heard from her again.'

'I've sent someone for the CCTV, though we should brace ourselves that her picture won't be very clear,' said Bagger.

The door opened again, and Liv entered the room, her face full of concern. Henrik quickly removed his hand from Jensen's shoulder.

'We're getting a slot on the radio news now. We'll find them, sooner or later,' she said to Jensen, and the word 'later' hung in the air with all its horrifying implications.

Jensen hung her head, and Henrik had never felt more powerless.

'Come outside with me for a minute,' said Liv.

They waited for a couple of colleagues to pass.

'I would like an explanation,' she said. 'You asked Brix about that reporter yesterday. He told you that he's her father. Did you know all along that she was trying to help him find his stalker?'

'No,' said Henrik, feeling his cheeks grow hot. 'I swear I didn't.'

'Did you know that she'd been befriended by the woman who called herself Karo?'

He shook his head. He couldn't tell her the truth without revealing that he knew Jensen personally, and that he'd failed to spot that she was in danger.

'So why did you ask him about her?'

'It was Goldschmidt, the pathologist.'

'I know David,' she said. 'What about him?'

'He lives in the same street as Brix. He said he'd seen a reporter behaving suspiciously outside his house.'

'Very neighbourly of him.'

'Well he wondered what was going on, so he told me. He recognised Jensen from . . . from . . . her picture in the newspaper. I thought it might have some bearing on the case, so I asked Brix about it.'

Liv looked at him, eyes narrowing. She might not believe him, but at least he seemed to have earned a stay of execution. 'All right, but you'd better be telling the truth,' she said.

All they could do now was wait.

46

The call came just before half-past nine in the evening. Ea Jensen had been missing for more than twelve hours.

Henrik immediately jumped in his car, speeding to Søndermarken, closely followed by Mark and Funder. The park lay between Frederiksberg Gardens and the Carlsberg city district where pricey new flats had sprung up between restaurants, bars and manicured green spaces on the old brewery site.

Patrol cars were on the scene already, as was an ambulance, their blue blinks illuminating the tall blue-grey trees. It was almost completely dark.

Through the open doors to the ambulance, he saw a paramedic holding a stethoscope to a baby's chest, talking in soothing tones. The paramedic nodded at him. 'She's fine,' he shouted.

Only then did Henrik feel like he was able to fully let out the air in his lungs.

A woman with a restless Labradoodle on a lead was talking to the uniformed officers. He introduced himself.

'I understand it was you who found the baby?' he said to the woman.

She nodded, wide-eyed. 'Yes. Who'd do something like that to a child?' she said.

'Tell me exactly what you saw,' he said.

'I didn't want to come in here at first. Not after what happened to that woman in Frederiksberg Gardens last week. There were no other dog walkers that I could see, and it was so eerily quiet. But Monty needed his walk, so we went,' she said, looking at the dog.

'I heard a sound from the bushes. Then Monty took off and his lead slipped out of my hand. When I saw him up ahead, sniffing the ground, I thought he'd caught the scent of a fox.' She shuddered, patting the dog's fur. 'If he hadn't refused to come back when I called him, she might not have . . .' She closed her eyes, pressed her lips together.

'Show me where you found her,' Henrik said.

They walked across to a clump of low bushes under some trees.

'There.'

He shone his torch at the spot.

'She was wrapped in a yellow blanket. I picked her up, then I rang you.'

'What else?'

'That's everything,' said the woman.

Henrik began to walk away. 'Get the park shut,' he shouted to Mark and Funder who were walking across to him. 'Tape off those bushes and get the team to search the whole area.'

He headed back to the ambulance. If Ea was OK, she should be returned to her mother. He would follow along behind.

'Wait,' shouted the woman with the dog. 'I've remembered something else.'

'Yes,' he said, feeling hopeful.

'When I went across to see what Monty was looking at, I saw someone run through the trees.'

'Man? Woman?'

'I wasn't close enough to see, but I'm pretty sure they were running away. Do you think it was them who put the baby there?'

Yes, Henrik thought. *And they waited until they were sure you'd seen her.*

47

Jensen hugged Ea one more time until she began to wriggle free, arching her back.

The whole day had been a blur. All she remembered was looking out of the window at Henrik's office and seeing the ambulance pull up, then the paramedic with a bundle in his arms, Ea's pink sun hat sticking up from her yellow blanket.

Outside her bedroom door, she could hear Gustav talking quietly with Margrethe, who had just arrived from the newspaper. 'How is she?' she said, and Jensen realised it was her that Margrethe meant.

Ea had been found completely unscathed with a clean nappy and showing no signs of hunger or distress. The police believed that Karo, or whatever her real name was, had stayed until she'd seen the dogwalker pick her up.

Now that her fear had gone, Jensen was feeling angry. The past twelve hours had been the worst of her life. Karo had done that to her, and for what? Just because she hated Brix? Surely, nothing justified taking a child.

Above all, Jensen was angry with herself for letting Karo trick her. Henrik had tried to comfort her by pointing out that Karo had been extremely devious. Hence, not even Fie had been able to find her.

Yet Karo had made one big mistake; she'd left her fingerprints and DNA all over the flat. With a bit of luck, the police would know who she was.

Why had she made such an error when she'd been so careful about everything else?

Either she'd burnt her bridges and didn't care, or she'd been forced to flee and take Ea with her.

Whichever way, it seemed out of character, and Jensen's mind kept returning to it.

Stroking Ea's hair, she vowed never to leave her in danger again.

Margrethe knocked on the door and entered, almost completely obscured by a bouquet of flowers. 'Jensen. What a horror show,' she said. 'When you come back you must write your personal account of it.'

Typical Margrethe.

Everything was a story to her.

It had just been announced on the radio that a baby missing for twelve hours had been returned to its mother safe and sound. Jensen was grateful that her name hadn't been disclosed, nor the link to Brix's stalker.

The latter was now all over the media. She detected Ernst Brøgger's legwork in the headlines, or was it Andreas Lund pulling the strings? In any case, the objective was clearly to garner sympathy for Brix.

VALDE BRIX: STALKER IS MAKING MY LIFE HELL

There was no mention of the rape allegations, nor the stalker's identity. After all, neither Brix nor the police knew who Karo was.

'We'll see,' she told Margrethe. 'For now I just wish they'd find her. I can't rest before that happens.'

Ea began to babble happily. Gustav pushed himself in front of Margrethe. 'Can I hold her?' He threw himself on the bed and held her high above him, making aeroplane noises. Ea laughed, oblivious to the drama she'd just been at the centre of.

'I don't understand,' said Margrethe. 'Who was the woman again? Some stranger you were trying to help, Gustav said. But why take your baby?'

After swearing both her and Gustav to silence, Jensen told them that the woman who called herself Karo was Brix's stalker.

'So Brix gives her the cold shoulder, and then she sees you outside his house and assumes that you're his new love interest, instead of his daughter?' said Gustav.

'Yes, and that Ea is his child.'

'Wait, you're Brix's daughter?' said Margrethe.

'Alleged daughter. I'm still waiting for the result of the paternity test,' said Jensen.

'But who is she really, this woman, and what does she want with Brix?'

'I'm pretty sure it's someone he slept with at some point. Let's just say he's fond of the opposite sex.'

'Ew,' said Gustav.

'So Brix is a womaniser,' said Margrethe. 'Doesn't surprise me. I met him a few times and thought he was rather in love with himself. Still, why stalk him?'

'I don't know,' said Jensen, running her hand over Ea's golden hair. 'Maybe he ghosted her, and she got angry. For whatever reason, she decided to give him a real scare, and it worked.'

'How do you mean?'

'She threatened to report him for rape. We don't know if there's something to it.'

'Except now he is the victim,' said Margrethe. 'Hounded by a crazy fan. Can only be good for book sales.'

'Unless everyone catches wind of his infidelities,' said Gustav.

'Would make a great story,' said Margrethe.

Jensen's phone pinged.

Unknown number.

It was a text message.

> *Am outside by the lake. Come down alone.*
> *Important. Liron*

'It's Liron,' she said. 'He says he's downstairs. But where did he get my number from? How does he know where I live?'

'Ah,' said Gustav. 'That would be me.'

'You?'

'Yeah, I told him earlier that Ea had been kidnapped. I thought he might be able to help find her.'

'Help how?'

Gustav shrugged. 'Dunno, but he's helped us before, and I was desperate. He told me he saw you and that woman only the other day. Maybe he's found out who she is?'

Liron refused to come up, so Jensen left Ea with Gustav and Margrethe and took the lift downstairs.

48

Henrik sensed the meeting room slowly filling up around him. Seeing Ea reunited with Jensen had sapped what remained of his energy. He could no longer remember what day it was, nor what he was supposed to be doing.

Mark and Funder entered the room. As usual, they were arguing about something and only stopped when Liv entered the room and formally started the meeting.

'As everyone will know, earlier this evening Ea Jensen was returned to her mother.'

At the mention of Jensen, Liv glanced at him meaningfully, and Henrik tried to force his face into neutral folds.

Liv had seen how emotional he'd been when Ea had been handed into her mother's arms. He would have to watch himself from now on.

Across the table, Fie Pedersen from NC3, sitting next to Bagger, looked at him with sympathy. Did she already know what Jensen was to him, or had she worked it out for herself? The girl was smart.

'We know that the kidnapper used a false name when befriending Ea's mother, who happens to be *Dagbladet*'s chief crime reporter. We're looking for a white woman between twenty-five and thirty, medium height. Beyond this, we're in the dark. We have reason to believe that she may be in disguise.'

Bagger raised a hand. 'Actually, we now have a photo of her.' He handed a grainy black-and-white print-out to Liv. 'The quality is poor, it's a CCTV image from Café Nytorv, but the facial features are clear enough.'

'Get it distributed,' she said.

'Already done. By the way, the bartender remembered Brix speaking to the woman. He said that he recognised Brix, and that he'd been to the bar before.'

Liv summed up what they had: a collection of loose ends.

Though they had no witness statements, CCTV or mobile-phone traffic to connect Brix to the crime scene in Kronprinsessegade, he was still technically a suspect.

Though everyone now believed it was the stalker who'd invited Vivian Sejer to Copenhagen, pretending to be Brix, he could still have gone to the flat and killed Vivian.

'Brix remains a suspect in Vivian Sejer's murder, and it's clear that he knew both Mia Steen and Jane Dahl-Thomsen. He denies any involvement.'

'Yeah, he would do,' said Funder.

Mark rolled his eyes. 'It's a coincidence. Brix is clearly a womaniser. He gets around.'

'Some coincidence,' Funder shot back.

'And we can't ignore that Brix's stalker threatened to report him for rape,' said Liv. 'Could there be something to it?'

'Well, yes.' Funder's tone was impatient.

'It's possible that she simply sought to harass him by making a false accusation. The point was to show him that she was in control,' said Bagger.

'By kidnapping what she thought was his daughter,' said Mark.

Liv held up her hands: 'Then why leave the baby in the park?'

Mark shrugged. 'Perhaps she realised that she was mistaken and that the baby wasn't Brix's after all.'

'Or she got frightened by the amount of press attention and police. She hadn't intended to harm the baby; she just wanted Brix to notice her, to pay attention,' said Bagger.

Henrik glanced at him appreciatively. He too thought it was significant that Jensen's daughter had been found without a scratch on her.

'Maybe Brix is right that the stalker intended to frame him for the rape and murder of Vivian Sejer. She could have set the whole thing up, even deliberately left evidence on the scene,' said Mark.

Henrik shook his head. 'I don't think that whoever gave Vivian Sejer those horrific injuries before strangling her could be the same woman who left Ea Jensen unscathed to be found by a member of the public. Something doesn't add up there.'

'Well, until we have something more substantial to go on, we'll continue working on the basis of those two suspects for the Vivian Sejer murder,' said Liv. 'On Bredgade, I believe you're yet to interview Marion Jensen. As for the Dahl-Thomsen case, we'll continue to look for evidence. Now, go home everyone and I'll see you back here in the morning.'

She gathered her papers and rose to her feet.

Henrik was on his way out of the room, intent on returning to his hotel and crashing into bed, when Funder intercepted him.

The last thing he had the energy for now was to listen to her going on about Polaris. She wouldn't be happy that this had taken a back seat with everything else going on, but so be it. There was no way Liv was going to approve funding now.

'Look, whatever it is, can we pick it up later?' he said. 'My head is splitting, and you heard what Liv said. You should go home.'

Funder wasn't having it. She seemed excited and, despite himself, he got curious.

'OK,' he said. 'Two minutes.'

'The eleven Polaris rape cases. I've been looking at Brix and his history with women. One of the eleven was Iben LeFevre, who reported a rape in 1996 after a night out at a bar in Østerbro. It happened at her flat. She claimed that she'd been drugged at the bar and followed home.'

Henrik's palms began to tingle. 'What about her?'

'The year before, 1995, Brix went out with her for a few weeks.' Funder pulled a print-out from a folder. 'This is a photo from one of the weeklies of her and Brix arriving at the Royal Theatre hand in hand.'

'Doesn't mean he had anything to do with raping her.'

'But what if he did? Do you not think it would be worth following up on? I mean, including Mia Steen, Dahl-Thomsen and Vivian Sejer, that's four victims he's been connected to.'

'Why would he rape women he'd previously been in a romantic relationship with?'

'Some sort of fetish or trophy collection. Or maybe he hated them for making him want them. The women had to be punished for what they'd done to him.'

'I can't see it,' said Henrik. 'And without evidence, we're nowhere.'

Funder was undeterred. 'I'm going through the rest of the cases now to see if there are any more hits.'

'By all means,' said Henrik as he headed for the exit, already dreaming of throwing himself into crisp white hotel sheets. 'But in your own time, and don't tell Liv.'

49

On Henrik's orders, a uniformed officer had been posted by the entrance to Jensen's block of flats, though she doubted that Karo would try to return.

'I'm meeting a friend,' she said to the officer, pointing to a dark figure stepping out from behind a tree. 'Don't worry, I'll scream if anything happens.'

She walked towards the lake. 'Liron,' she said.

He hugged her, then pulled her towards a bench a little further along the path.

It was freezing cold. Jensen shivered and Liron put his arm around her. A vaguely rotten smell was coming from the water, mixing with his scent of tobacco, coffee and spices.

'Why didn't you bloody come to me for help?'

'It all happened so fast. I couldn't think straight.'

'I feel bad. When you came to see me with that woman, I kept thinking, "Liron, you fucking saw her before", but I couldn't tell for sure because of her sunglasses.'

'You asked her to remove them,' Jensen said.

'But she bloody ignored me, which should have told

me something. She said she was pregnant, but she wanted strong coffee? I didn't believe a word of it. I should have said something. It's all my fault.'

'Don't be daft,' said Jensen. 'You weren't to know. She was very convincing.'

'But luckily, I have remembered now where I saw her before.'

Jensen sat up abruptly. 'You have? Where?'

'She used to work for an office along the street from my van. It's a while now since she stopped by for coffee. Always black, always as strong as possible.'

'Which company?'

'DX Digital. Some sort of marketing firm.'

Jensen stood up, kissed him on the cheek. 'Liron, that's amazing, thank you. I'll tell the police at once.'

'You can do even better than that,' he said, holding up his phone. 'She gave me a weird feeling, so I took this picture, just in case.'

Jensen looked at the screen and saw herself from the back with Ea in the sling. Karo was looking over her shoulder at Liron. It wasn't a great picture, but it would help. She felt her phone buzz in her pocket as he airdropped it to her.

'Liron, you're a star.'

'And tell that bastard cop that if he doesn't find her, then I will.'

Jensen smiled as she walked back to the flat. She was already forwarding the photo to Henrik, having cropped herself out of it.

Day Seven

50

Jensen and her mother looked nothing like each other, Henrik thought as he walked into the interview room. The woman with the long grey hair who was snoozing on the chair against the wall was tall, long-limbed and feminine while Jensen was boyish and short. But then Marion opened her eyes and looked at him, and he saw Jensen's intense dark-blue gaze.

It threw him for a few seconds, but then he pulled himself together. Liv would be watching, and she was already on to him.

After a solid night's sleep, he'd woken up in the hotel to find a message from Jensen with a photo of the as-yet unidentified stalker and kidnapper, along with the name of a company she used to work for.

Of course, she'd refused to say where she'd got the information from, but Funder and Mark were now busy following up. At least it was progress.

'I'm Detective Inspector Henrik Jungersen. Sorry you've had to wait so long,' he said as he sat down. 'I'm sure you're aware what happened yesterday. Everyone's very relieved your granddaughter is safe, as I guess you must be.'

Marion was wearing a long skirt with walking boots and a tatty jumper. There was paint under her nails and a faintly musty smell coming off her clothes.

He gathered she'd more or less checked out of society and was living hand to mouth as an artist. Jensen had given him the impression that she was the adult in the relationship, and not especially close to her mother.

'Yes, my daughter told me. I spoke to her this morning,' said Marion, her accent betraying her inner-city Copenhagen origins.

She was not at all eccentric as he'd imagined, but matter-of-fact, almost cold. Maybe she was uneasy with the authority he represented. Or maybe she knew about him and Jensen. If so, she was unlikely to be happy about it. 'You seem very calm,' he said. 'Your granddaughter was kidnapped. She was missing for twelve hours.'

'She's fine. That's all that matters,' said Marion. 'And waiting a few days is nothing to me. I've waited years to say what I'm about to tell you.'

'About Mia Steen?'

'And other things.'

'Andreas Lund told us that you lived in the Bredgade apartment for a spell back in 1987.'

'That's correct. I shared a room there with Valde for about four weeks.'

'When was that?'

'Would have been sometime in July.'

'What made you leave?'

'Finding out that he slept with other women. Including Mia.'

'Tell me when you first met her.'

'She came along to a party in the apartment. Valde was forever having parties. He was very popular.'

'And Andreas Lund?'

'A useful idiot. Still is. Valde didn't even like him, but he had the apartment, and he had money. Andreas was so in awe of him that he did whatever Valde wanted, like some kind of puppy dog.'

'What do you mean, still is?'

'I hear that he worships the ground Valde walks on. Can't do enough for him. That makes him an idiot in my book.'

'What was he like when you lived there?'

'Amenable to the point of being obsequious. The poor guy had lost his parents and didn't know what to do with himself. Valde took advantage.'

'Did you meet Mia while she cleaned for Andreas?'

'Once or twice. She was very quiet, almost afraid of her own shadow. She and Andreas used to sit and whisper together in the kitchen.'

'Was there anything between them?'

'Not that I saw. But then, with Valde around, he wouldn't have got a look in.'

'What did he and Mia talk about?'

Marion shrugged. 'I got the impression she came from a rather strict home. She wanted to break free and live her own life.'

'And he encouraged that?'

'He was kind to her. But then he was kind to everybody. Too kind. Especially to Valde.'

Henrik turned over the photograph he had brought in with him and pushed it across the desk to her. 'This photo was taken at a party in the apartment in 1987.'

Marion studied the photo. 'I've never seen this before,' she said.

'Mia was Lund's cleaner, but here she's clearly a guest at a party. Do you remember who invited her?'

'That would almost certainly have been Valde. I should have known he'd go for her; she was just his type – young, blonde, innocent.'

'Did he sleep with her at this party?'

'Oh yeah. That's why I left. I walked in on them, on the couch in the spare room. I went to sleep, and when I woke up the next morning, he hadn't returned to our bed. I moved out that day, and later I heard Brix had got Mia pregnant.'

'You believed it?'

'Yes.'

'It must have upset you, given that you were yourself expecting his baby at the time?'

Marion glanced at him sharply. 'What makes you think that?'

'He told me he's your daughter's father.'

'Well he's not.'

'Now I'm confused. Then who is?'

'None of your bloody business. I'm not here to talk about that.' There was real anger in her eyes now. Did she hate Brix so badly that she was refusing to accept that he'd fathered her child?

'OK,' he said, letting it go. 'Tell me about what happened to Mia Steen. When did you last see her?'

'I didn't see her again after that night. I met Brix at a party somewhere else about a month later. He tried to get back with me.'

'And did you?'

'What do you think?' said Marion, her eyes flashing with contempt. He'd seen that hard glance a hundred times before from Jensen.

'You told him to go to hell,' he said.

'Well done, Einstein. I heard from Andreas that Mia had

stopped cleaning for him. I believe she eventually tried to get her job back, but Andreas had hired another cleaner by then, so it didn't work out. Later he said Brix had told him she'd gone travelling.'

Henrik paused. Mia hadn't had many friends at the end of her life, but they'd managed to track down an old classmate from Randers whom she'd spoken to around the same time as her last call with her mother.

The woman had recalled Mia being upset, saying that she'd done something terrible, and that she wouldn't be able to return home.

Henrik guessed she'd discovered that she was pregnant, and that Brix didn't want to know.

Marion's story was consistent with Lund's, but Brix had denied knowing Mia intimately. Why?

'When I saw on the news that Mia had been found behind the wall in the apartment, I just knew that Valde had something to do with it. He's a total bastard who treats women appallingly. So was Mia really pregnant?'

'I ... err ... I can't disclose details of that nature.'

The look in Marion's eyes was one of disgust. 'I take it from that answer that she was. Well, perhaps you can find out who the father of her baby was, and then you'll be closer to finding out who killed her.'

'You think it was Brix?'

'I think he was the father of her baby.'

Marion stared at him and for the first time he saw a flicker of doubt cross her face. It seemed it was only now that she realised the implications of what she'd been saying. She was condemning a man on the basis of ill feeling towards him; she'd no proof that he was a murderer.

He decided to pressure her a little. 'Did Brix ever display violent tendencies towards you?'

'Not that I recall,' she said.

'Did you witness him being violent to others?'

'No, but that doesn't mean he wasn't capable of violence. He could be incredibly cruel, especially to Andreas.'

'How so?'

'Belittling him in front of others, making him do his bidding.'

'What motive would Brix have had for killing Mia?'

'Maybe it was an accident. I always thought that story about Mia going travelling on her own was utter bollocks. She was a timid, innocent little creature. And it was Valde who started the rumour. Doesn't that tell you something?'

'We don't know for sure that he did start it. He claims it was something he'd heard on the grapevine.'

'Oh yeah, sure, and you believe him, of course.'

'I'm not saying that I do. I'm saying that in my line of work, all that counts is evidence, and if you don't have some sort of proof to back up your theories then that's what they'll remain – theories.'

He studied her closely, reminding himself that it was too soon to rule anything out. 'Speaking of theories, who's to say it wasn't you who did it?' he said. 'You'd have had plenty of reason to hate Mia for getting in the way. Lund tells me that both you and Brix had keys to his apartment. You look strong, and as an artist you'd be well used to working with materials. Building a wall would present no problems for you, I'm sure.'

Marion looked at him dispassionately. 'Detective Inspector, why would I have taken it out on Mia? I'm not a violent person, but if I was, it's Valde I would have killed. If he hadn't done what he did, if I hadn't left him, then I wouldn't have been ...' She trailed off. 'No, it doesn't matter.' She picked her bag off the floor and stood up. 'I've said what I came to say. Evidence is your department. I'll be staying with my daughter and grandchild for the time being, so you know where to find me.'

When Henrik emerged from the interview room, he found Mark waiting for him.

'I've been in touch with the company in Sankt Peders Stræde where we think the stalker worked. They're expecting us.'

51

Jensen woke up and immediately panicked. It was after nine o'clock, and Ea's cot was empty.

She jumped out of bed and ran down the corridor to the living room, only to find Gustav sitting on the sofa with Ea in his lap, bathed in sunlight from the open windows.

He was singing a nursery rhyme, and Ea was as content as Jensen had ever seen her.

'Morning,' said Gustav. 'You looked exhausted, so I stole this one to let you sleep.'

'Not the best choice of words after what happened yesterday,' she said as her pulse slowly returned to normal.

'Sorry,' said Gustav. 'Did they catch her yet?'

'I don't know,' said Jensen.

There was no message from Henrik and a quick scroll through the news sites suggested nothing had happened since last night.

Dagbladet led the coverage with Liron's photo of Karo. She'd given Gustav the scoop last night.

ALL-OUT POLICE SEARCH FOR 'DANGEROUS' STALKER

'Well done on getting the front page,' she said. 'Though I'm not sure Karo really is dangerous.'

'She took your baby!' Gustav cried.

'But she didn't harm her,' she said, stroking her daughter's hair. Her anger had subsided in her sleep, and now she couldn't help wondering what Brix had done to Karo. It had to be more than hurt feelings.

'Where do you think she is?'

'I don't know. Hiding from the police, obviously. Working out her next move.'

There was a text message from Marion.

> *Finally spoke to the police. It's done. On my way to yours.*

'My mother's coming over,' she said.

'Good,' said Gustav. 'I need to get to work, but I bought you breakfast. It's in the kitchen. Oh, and the police are still outside.'

'I'm sure that's not necessary. She won't be coming back here.' Surely, now that they had a photo and a former place of work, it would only be a matter of time before they found Karo.

Gustav stood up.

'Oh, before I go. This came for you.'

He pulled something out of his back pocket.

A white envelope.

'Is it what I think it is?' he said.

In the melee of the past few days, Jensen had managed to forget about the paternity test. She was no longer sure that she wanted to know the answer.

Brix had turned out to be self-absorbed and manipulative. If he was her father, she would have the certainty she'd yearned for, but she couldn't imagine building any kind of relationship with him. Not any more.

And did any of it really matter? Her family were the people she cared about. Whether they were blood relations didn't come into it: her mother, Ea, Gustav, Fie, Liron, Margrethe.

She tore open the envelope and pulled out the letter, running her eyes down the page. When she saw the result it was like a punch to the stomach.

52

Henrik pulled up outside the old building in Sankt Peders Stræde, and he and Mark got out.

A little further along the street, by an old-fashioned streetlamp, he saw Liron Vaknin, the coffee seller, sitting on a folding chair in front of his coffee van, waving at him.

So this was who Jensen had the information from. Henrik didn't wave back.

He didn't like the strange Israeli with the bangles and the ponytail who seemed to know everything and had inveigled himself into Jensen's life as one of her closest confidants. Vaknin had skills no one got from making coffee all day: stakeouts, fist fights, handling a gun. This had become apparent during last summer's heat wave when Liron had played a crucial role in an investigation involving the abduction of a Syrian refugee and a member of parliament. Where had he learned those things, and what was he doing in Denmark?

One day I'll find out who you really are, he said to himself, as Mark rang the bell for DX Digital.

The door buzzed open, and they climbed the stairs to a room that looked more like a yoga studio than an office.

Benjamin Trads, the CEO, was in shorts and T-shirt, had pierced ears, and looked as if he had no more than a couple of years on Mikkel, Henrik's eldest boy, who was now officially a teenager.

Trads was guarded, looking nervous as he checked their warrant cards. 'So what was it you wanted to see me about?'

Henrik thrust the photo 'Know this woman?' he said. 'We believe she used to work here, and we need to find her, urgently.'

'I don't know her,' Benjamin said.

'Look at the photo again.'

'I don't have to. We're a small business. I know all our staff personally, including the ones who've left.'

'A client then?'

Benjamin took the photo. 'Not that either.'

'A cleaner? Someone's girlfriend?'

Benjamin shook his head and handed the photo back.

'And it's just your company in this building. No one else?'

'That's right. She's the one who kidnapped that baby, isn't she? I saw it in my feeds this morning,' said Benjamin.

A woman with short purple-coloured hair had appeared behind him. 'Can I see the photo?'

'Who are you?' said Henrik, irritated at the interruption.

'Cecilie is our creative director,' said Benjamin, handing the photo to her.

The woman studied it. 'It could be Petra,' she mumbled to her colleague. 'You remember, she came in for that consultancy job last summer. Can't have been more than a month.'

'Oh yeah,' Benjamin said. 'She didn't have red hair, though.'

'Must be a wig,' said Cecilie.

'Excuse me, Petra who?' said Henrik.

'She called herself Petra, but that isn't necessarily her real name. She's an ethical hacker, a white hat,' explained Benjamin.

'What?' Henrik felt like he'd entered some parallel universe.

'They're hackers, but in a good way. Companies employ them to test their security by seeing if they can break through their cyber defences.'

'That's right,' said Cecilie. 'We had a client who was looking for that, but it's not our area of expertise, so we got Petra in. It's normal for people like her to keep a low profile,' said Cecilie.

'How did you find her then?'

'Through the grapevine. We got an email address and there was a phone number, but those would have just been temporary. And we paid her in cash.'

'So if you wanted her back, what would you do?'

'Put the word out, I guess,' said Benjamin.

Henrik rubbed his temples with thumb and forefinger. Petra, or whatever her name was, was unlikely to be dumb enough to reply.

'Look,' he said. 'What do you know about this Petra? Did she say where she lived? Maybe she made some comment about her commute, or a partner? Plans for the weekend? Anything could be important, anything at all.'

Benjamin and Cecilie looked at each other, two human question marks. It was a wonder they were capable of running a business.

Eventually Benjamin shook his head. 'I don't think we can help you. Petra was professional, incredibly good at what she did, and that's all that really mattered to us under the circumstances.'

Henrik had heard enough and headed for the exit.

Mark lingered. 'Thank you,' he said and handed Benjamin his card. 'It's really important that we find her. Speak to your staff and if anyone remembers anything, no matter how small, call us immediately.'

They were in the car heading back when Bagger called. 'We think we have something,' he said. 'I'm here with Fie Pedersen.'

'They told us at her former workplace that she's some sort of good hacker,' Henrik said. 'But they've no clue where to find her. Complete Mickey Mouse outfit.'

'I reached the same conclusion,' said Fie. 'I mean the way she was able to hide and intercept Brix's emails told me that she had to be a pro. So when I looked into it more closely I saw something . . . let's say a call sign . . . and I realised that I knew who she was, because I'd come across her before, online. She helped me once or twice.'

'What's her name?'

'She uses aliases, like I do. Petra was one of them, but I've put some feelers out in the community, and I should be getting something back soon.'

Henrik felt his hopes rise once more as he stepped on the accelerator.

53

Marion put a mug of tea on Jensen's bedside table and sat down gently on the side of the bed.

A smell of chamomile filled the room and Jensen was reminded of when she was a child, off sick from school, and chamomile tea with honey had been her mother's trusted remedy. Though she'd always thought it tasted like dried grass, it was strangely comforting now, and she sipped from the mug gratefully.

'Are you very upset?' said Marion.

Was she?

Jensen didn't know.

Most of all, she felt a fool for getting excited. The desire to know who her father was hadn't been there before – at least not until she'd had Ea – but lately it had been all she could think about.

'No,' she said, attempting a smile. 'In a way I'm glad it's not Brix. From what I've seen and heard, I don't actually like him very much.'

'That makes two of us,' said Marion.

'What I don't understand is why he was so certain.'

'Arrogance. He simply couldn't imagine that it could have been anyone else than him.'

Jensen took her hand and looked at the long, bony fingers, the nails with half-moons of paint, and her mother's strange silver rings with stones in turquoise, amber, jade and topaz.

'I wish you would tell me the truth,' she said.

'I have. I am sorry that I don't have the answer you want.'

'You and Brix were together.'

'Yes. I loved him. There'd been others before him, of course, but he was the first man I really loved. I thought he was beautiful, not just on the outside, but in his soul. He knew all this poetry by heart, and he really understood my art, or at least he pretended to. My friends tried to open my eyes to what he was really like, but I couldn't hear them. Then one night I finally saw it for myself. Mia was incredibly beautiful, with her long blonde hair, just twenty, and I saw the way he looked at her, like he wanted to possess her. He loved making people fall in love with him, and he was very good at it.'

'What happened?'

'I walked in on them. They hadn't seen me, so I left them to it, but I was shocked. It was like I couldn't breathe. The next morning I packed my things and left.'

'Where did you go?'

'I stayed with friends. I was twenty-seven years old, four years older than Valde. I'd finished art school and begun to paint for money, but I made hardly anything from it, so I worked in a café in the evenings to make ends meet.'

'You must have fallen pregnant with me around that time?'

Marion pressed her lips together and looked away. She

looked vulnerable all of a sudden, old and dog-tired. 'Don't live your life in the past. You'll miss out on Ea's childhood and everything you have to be grateful for: this flat, your daughter, your job at the newspaper.'

Jensen felt the wall between them go back up.

Marion rose from the bed. 'I've decided to stay here for a while, at least until they find the woman who took Ea. You must have been so terribly worried.'

Jensen set down her tea. 'Do you think Brix killed Mia? It's so strange that he knew both her and Vivian Sejer, who was murdered in that Airbnb. He wouldn't have asked me to find his stalker if he'd done something for real, would he?'

'I only know that he has no conscience. He's an accomplished liar who has let down every woman he has known. I'm afraid that, for that reason, I just don't believe anything the man says, and neither should you.'

Marion moved towards the door. 'If you want my advice,' she said, 'leave him to the police. Forget this . . . this quest you seem to be on to find your father and live your life. Not all truths are worth knowing.'

54

In the end it was the DNA she'd left in Jensen's flat that led them to the stalker.

Elise Berg had been arrested five years earlier in connection with a violent demonstration where a police officer had been seriously injured.

She'd ended up walking free from court, but her DNA had remained on the police database along with around 160,000 other individuals who'd been charged with crimes carrying a potential sentence of eighteen months or more.

They were now checking whether the DNA left on the water bottle in the Airbnb fridge was hers.

Elise Berg lived in Emdrup in a one-bedroom flat near the S-train station.

By the time they were ready to force entry into her flat, it was late in the day and kids were beginning to come home from the neighbourhood schools.

Some stopped on the way to watch the excitement and had to be moved on before the operation could begin in earnest.

He didn't know what he'd expected to find in the home

of a stalker. Some sort of evil lair, full of computer screens and dodgy gear?

There was none of that. In fact, the flat was nothing special, moderately messy and looking recently lived in. There was milk in the fridge not yet past its sell-by date.

'She must be working out of an office somewhere,' said Mark, voicing what Henrik was thinking.

Apart from a battered MacBook there were no electronic devices in sight.

With a gloved hand, Henrik opened a drawer in the desk in the living room and found a passport and a thousand kroner in cash.

'Boss, you need to come here,' shouted Mark from the bedroom.

At first Henrik couldn't see it. The curtains were drawn, and it took time for his eyes to get used to the dark. Then he whistled. The walls were covered in posters from the TV series of Valde Brix's books, and on a shelf was what looked like a shrine to the author. Henrik knew that Brix had written twenty-eight books, but Elise Berg had amassed what looked like three times that number.

He took a volume down from the shelf, and saw that Brix had signed it to Elise, adding a kiss after his name. So the two of them had definitely met.

Henrik reminded himself that, without the knowledge of what Elise Berg had done, and what she might have been capable of, there was nothing unusual about a fan developing a crush on an author she idolised.

If anything, the room seemed rather girlish, with jewellery and make-up and dried flowers scattered across the bedside tables.

Where was she?

They would have to take her life apart, speak to her

friends and family. Without money, and with her face plastered all over the media, it would be extremely difficult for her to stay on the run for long.

On the other hand, Elise Berg was obviously extremely resourceful and well used to hiding.

'OK, I think we have something.' Mark's voice could be heard from deep inside the wardrobe.

When he emerged, he was holding a hooded black zip-up top in his gloved hands. There were brown stains down the front; they looked like blood. Mark was smiling. 'If this matches the black fibres we found under Vivian Sejer's fingernails, then we've got her.'

55

'Elise Berg,' said Jensen. 'I wonder where she is.' She was sitting on the front seat in Henrik's black car, her feet on the dashboard as they drove across the dark city.

They'd spent a good part of their relationship here; it was the only place he felt safe from being recognised. The smell of leather and air freshener brought back memories of being so hard in love that she couldn't eat or sleep.

For most of her adult life he'd been there, in her thoughts, at the end of the phone, sending her heart racing with late-night messages. Neither of them had been able to end it.

He'd picked her up from the flat, and they were now heading north towards the coast. She'd left Ea asleep with Marion, and the police standing guard outside.

Henrik looked at her sideways. 'She can't hide for long.'

'I don't know,' said Jensen. 'She managed to hide from Brix for months.'

'We're talking to everyone she knows. She hasn't used her bank card in a while, but she's bound to eventually.'

'You think something could have happened to her?'

'Anything is possible,' said Henrik.

He looked exhausted and drawn. 'I'm glad to see you,' he said, reaching for her hand, then regretting it mid-move and leaving it on the gearstick.

She ran the tips of her fingers briefly over his knuckles. 'I actually feel sorry for her,' she said. 'She threatened to report Brix for rape. Maybe she had good reason to?'

'Why not come straight to us then?'

Jensen thought about it. Elise Berg had been in trouble with the police in the past, and she was part of a community that operated on the edge of the law. 'She probably didn't think she'd get a fair hearing against the mighty Brix. Maybe she knew it would be his word against hers, and that she didn't stand a chance of seeing him convicted. So she used her knowledge and resources to put the fear of God into him. She wanted him to confess of his own volition.'

Henrik swerved to avoid a cyclist. Ahead of them, the road was opening up, the sea on the right, expensive villas on the left. 'Before you get all dewy-eyed, can I just remind you that she kidnapped your baby? There are those who believe that she also killed and assaulted an innocent woman after luring her to Copenhagen under false pretences.'

'But you don't believe that?'

'I don't know.'

Jensen looked at the sea; it was as flat as a mirror. 'Maybe she did write to Vivian Sejer,' she said, 'but I don't believe she killed her. It was Brix she was after, and I don't see why she would have hurt another woman to get at him. Although . . .'

'Yes?'

'When she turned up at my flat in the early hours of Saturday, she had these scratches and marks all over her hands and forearms, like she'd been in a fight.'

Henrik looked at her pointedly but said nothing.

'What is it?' she said. 'Do you have something on her? You do, I can see it on your face.'

'I can't tell you, except that it's not clear cut, by any means.'

The road had begun to undulate. They lost sight of the sea as tall hedges screening even more expensive properties began to emerge alongside them.

'It must be hard,' Henrik said after a while. 'Finding out that Brix is your father, and now all this with his stalker.'

She frowned at him, then remembered that he didn't know yet. 'Well, turns out he's not my father after all. I got him to take a test and it came back negative.'

'Really? Your mother said as much, but I thought she was just angry with him.'

'So did I. Should have listened to her.'

'But why did he think he was your father? He seemed so certain.'

'Arrogance, according to my mother. He simply couldn't imagine that she would have slept with anyone else that summer. She'd been madly in love with him.'

'Who do you think it was?'

'She won't say. Still insists she doesn't know.'

'Could it have been revenge gone wrong? Get drunk, sleep with whomever, only to find out later that she'd got herself pregnant?'

Jensen looked out of the window at the dark hedges looming against the deep-blue sky. Even if Henrik was right, it would bring her no closer to knowing who her father was. Marion had insisted it didn't matter, but it did.

She was a journalist; she couldn't just let things lie. Especially because she had a strong sense that her mother had left something important out of the story.

'It's late,' she said. 'Shouldn't you be getting back home?'

He kept driving. Now they were passing a marina, lights glistening in the dark water. They'd walked there once, him glancing over his shoulder all the time.

'Louise has gone,' he said.

Louise. He'd never used her name before. It had always been *she* and *her.*

'Gone? Where?'

'I don't know. She left on Sunday morning, wouldn't say where.'

'What happened?'

Henrik sent her a look that made her feel cold all over. She pushed her hands under her thighs to stop them from shaking. 'Apparently, she saw you in Tivoli. She said she could tell that you recognised her too.'

'Oh God,' said Jensen. 'I did see her, but it was a few seconds at most, and neither of us said a word. I'd been meeting Brøgger. It was his idea to go there.'

'Well, she says I still love you, and that you know it.'

'But we haven't done anything. Not for a long time.'

Even as she said it, she knew that wasn't the point. It had never just been about sex; it was far worse than that.

'It doesn't matter,' said Henrik. 'She's gone away to think about what she wants. Her parents have moved in to look after the kids. I'm in a hotel for the time being.'

'Why don't you just go home?'

'I can't stand my father-in-law or the thought of him crowing every time he looks at me. He never thought Louise and I would work, and now he's been vindicated, and it's all my fault.'

'You could tell them to leave?'

Henrik looked at her as if the idea had never occurred to him. 'How would I cope on my own with the kids? I don't know how.'

'You'd work it out. Like everyone else.'

Like I have, she thought.

They passed the rest of the journey in silence.

She says I still love you.

Henrik hadn't said whether his wife was right about that, and she hadn't asked.

They both knew the answer.

Day Eight

56

'So we think Elise Berg killed Vivian Sejer,' said Liv. 'Let's go through the evidence.'

The meeting room was full to bursting. It had only been a week since Henrik climbed the stairs to Andreas Lund's apartment in Bredgade to inspect Mia Steen's remains, but he felt like he'd grown older by a decade.

'Forensics have confirmed that the black fibres found under Vivian Sejer's fingernails were identical to the blood-stained jumper found in Elise Berg's flat, and the blood on the jumper was Sejer's. The half-empty bottle of water found in the Airbnb had Elise Berg's DNA on it, and we think it was her who sent the email to Sejer from Brix's address, inviting her to Copenhagen.'

Bagger put up his hand. 'We can't be certain of that,' he said. 'Elise Berg definitely had the skills to hack into Brix's email, but without access to her computer, we're unable to confirm it.'

'What about the laptop we found in Elise Berg's apartment?'

'That was old and had nothing on it of any use. She must

have another computer somewhere, or perhaps she carried it with her when she went on the run.'

'So it could have been someone else who wrote the message?' said Henrik.

'Can't rule it out,' said Bagger.

'Who else would have benefited from Vivian Sejer coming to Copenhagen?' asked Mark.

'Well, Brix, obviously,' said Funder.

'Who didn't write it,' said Mark.

'So he says, but do we actually know that for sure?' She looked at Bagger, who was shaking his head.

'Isn't it more obvious why Elise Berg wanted Vivian Sejer in Copenhagen?' said Mark.

Henrik shrugged. 'To embarrass Brix?'

'To set him up. She wanted to frame him for rape,' said Mark.

'Isn't it a little self-defeating to hurt another woman in order to get at him?' Funder echoed Henrik's thoughts. This was what Jensen had said last night.

'We'll know more about her motives when we speak to her,' said Liv. 'For now I believe we have enough evidence to charge her, whereas we've no evidence connecting Brix to the crime.'

'Aside from the email,' Funder reminded her. 'And the fact that he'd slept with her before.'

'Which was precisely why Elise Berg wanted her in Copenhagen. The whole point was that it was someone he knew,' said Mark.

'Thank you,' said Liv. 'Let's move on.'

'Were there any foreign skin cells under Vivian Sejer's nails?' asked Henrik.

'No,' said Mark.

Liv looked at him. 'Why do you ask?'

'I recall Jensen telling us that Elise Berg had scratches on her forearms and hands when she turned up at her flat in the early hours of Saturday.'

'Could she have got the scratches through her clothing?' said Liv.

Funder made a note. 'I'll check with forensics.'

'It's obvious she made the scratches herself,' said Mark. 'To make her story of domestic abuse appear more credible. Like she gave herself a black eye.'

The conversation moved on to the search for Elise Berg. So far there'd been no sightings, and she still hadn't used her phone or bank card. They'd taken her flat in Emdrup apart.

'I think we have to be prepared for the fact that it could take a long time to find her,' said Fie Pedersen. 'She's very good at what she does.'

'In the digital world at least,' said Mark.

'In any world,' said Fie. 'She has a lot of friends and they'll be people with bad experiences of police and any kind of authority.'

'What do we know about her?' said Liv.

Mark cleared his throat. 'Twenty-seven years old. Born in Kalundborg. Parents both drank. Home was chaotic, she ended up responsible for her younger brother. She and the brother went to live with their aunt when the dad died and the mother was unable to cope. Elise was smart, though. Passed her high-school exams and moved to Copenhagen aged eighteen. Her mother died shortly afterwards. From there things grow more obscure.'

'Where do we know this from?' said Liv.

'The aunt. Claims she hasn't seen Elise since.'

'Did they fall out?'

'According to the aunt, Elise went crazy when her mother died and rejected her family's way of life. She preferred her new friends and adopted their ideals. It was all a fantasy that she escaped into, the aunt said.'

Explains her fascination with Valde Brix, thought Henrik. *How disillusioned she must have been when he turned out to be just another jerk.* 'What about the brother?' he said.

'They're still close, according to the aunt. We haven't got hold of him yet. Lives in Albertslund.'

It would be too obvious for Elise Berg to go there, surely?

'We need to speak to everyone she knows,' said Henrik. 'Let's get it started.'

'Any development in the Mia Steen case?' said Liv.

'Marion Jensen pointed the finger at Brix. No love lost there. Of course, she's a suspect herself, so she may just be trying to deflect blame. If she's this angry forty years later, she must have been in an absolute rage back then. She could have killed Mia, and so could Brix.'

'Why?' said Liv.

'According to Marion he tired of Mia and tried to get back with her. Mia could have become troublesome. A religious girl with a crush, and she may have been carrying his baby. Not what he wanted, an aspiring author hoping for a big breakthrough. She wouldn't have wanted an abortion,' said Henrik. 'Did we find out whether he was the father of Mia's baby?'

Funder shook her head. 'I'll check.'

'And of course we can't rule out Andreas Lund,' Henrik said. 'It's his apartment after all, and would he really not have noticed a new wall going up in his own larder? His motive is a bit more obscure though. Mia was his cleaner, and by all accounts they were friends. Why kill her?'

No one said anything. They were all exhausted.

'OK,' said Liv. 'I take it no news on Jane Dahl-Thomsen?'

'No,' said Funder. 'But she's out of danger; her condition

is now stable. I hope we'll be able to interview her properly before too long.'

'Good,' said Liv.

Funder began to speak again. 'Can I just—'

'Unless it's urgent, can it wait, Funder? I really must go and update the Commissioner.'

The meeting broke up and Liv hurried away. Henrik headed for his own office, but Funder caught up with him. 'So everyone just thinks it's Elise Berg now, and Brix is off the hook,' she said. 'What about Operation Polaris?'

'What about it?'

'You said Liv was keen and now it's like she just doesn't want to know.'

'She's not long in the job and she's dealing with a lot. Give it time.'

'We don't have time,' said Funder. 'And if Brix is still behind all of it? It'll make her look stupid.'

Henrik massaged his temples. Funder might be right, but for now they had no choice but to carry on as Liv had asked.

'Go and check those things with forensics,' he said. 'Something will turn up.'

57

Jensen sat at her desk in the flat and looked out at Peblinge Lake. It was only eight o'clock in the evening, but she already had the lights on.

Spring had faltered, the sky over Copenhagen was leaden, the leaves of the chestnut trees turned inside out. Rain spattered the windows at regular intervals and the cyclists on the other side of the lake were leaning into the wind.

Elise had now been missing for two days. No one had a clue where she was, and you couldn't open a newspaper or a TV news channel without seeing her mugshot. It had been taken four years ago when she'd been arrested in connection with a demonstration. Her hair was green and short, and she'd not yet had the Tolkien tattoo.

A few papers, including *Dagbladet*, had interviewed her aunt about her difficult upbringing. Hidden deep in the articles was the fact that the aunt hadn't seen Elise for more than nine years. She was hardly a well-informed witness.

Dagbladet's closest competitor carried a double-page interview with Brix. He'd been photographed with his wife

Astrid inside their Potato Rows house, which according to the newspaper was now under round-the-clock police protection.

He and Astrid were holding hands; Jensen guessed that he hadn't told her very much.

I FEEL SORRY FOR MY STALKER

The headline made Jensen gag, knowing how he'd treated the women in his life.

He still didn't know the result of the paternity test. Now that the stalker story was out in the open and he was able to milk it for every drop of publicity, he'd stopped contacting her.

It still horrified her that she'd been taken in by Elise to the extent that she'd left Ea alone with her.

Margrethe had tried to comfort her when she'd come around the previous night. 'You showed that you still have a heart. Most people, including yours truly, lose theirs by the time they're thirty. The world turns them into cynics, but not you,' she'd said.

'I'm a journalist. Am I not supposed to be cynical?'

'No,' Margrethe had said, shaking her head vigorously. 'That's a common misunderstanding. You're supposed to be curious. The problem with cynical people is that we lose our curiosity.'

Jensen was definitely still curious to understand why Elise had acted like she had, and what part Brix had played. She was glad that Margrethe had refused to give him any more column inches.

Elise still seemed to be the chief suspect in the murder of Vivian Sejer. Jensen found it impossible to get her head around that.

There was a gentle knock on the office door and her mother came in. 'There you are. What are you reading?' She looked over her shoulder at the laptop screen and made a face when she saw the picture of Brix. 'Odious man. I bet he's stopped calling you now that he no longer wants something.'

'I'm sorry I didn't believe you,' Jensen said. 'Is Ea asleep?'

'Just gone down. She reminds me of you that age. Always refused to settle,' said Marion.

'You know,' said Jensen, 'sometimes I look at her and I wonder what's in there. You know, from her father. Did you ever do that with me?'

'No,' said Marion. 'I always regarded you as an original. You're you, and Ea will be just the same.'

'Don't shut me out, please,' said Jensen. 'Not this time. There must be something in me, things I've done or said over the years that have made you wonder?'

Marion looked away, her mouth a thin horizontal line. She closed her eyes.

Suddenly, it seemed so simple, and Jensen had to ask. She might not get another chance. If anything was to happen to her mother, then she would never know the truth.

'If you don't know who my father is then I can think of only two reasons. Brix hurt you. You went out and got drunk and had sex with the first man you met. You never asked his name. Or . . .'

'Jensen, please don't. When you go there, you can never go back.'

'. . . or you were raped.'

The word was out, and Jensen realised that she'd always suspected this. It hadn't just been her mother not wanting to tell her; she hadn't wanted to hear it.

She reached for her mother's hand. It was bony and cold,

her silver rings hard against her palm. 'You were raped, weren't you?' she said very quietly.

Her mother nodded without opening her eyes.

'How did it happen?'

'My periods stopped, but I didn't think anything of it. I didn't think I could be pregnant. I must have been about ten weeks along when I finally went to the doctor. It was only when I thought back that I remembered when it could have been . . .'

'Yes?'

'After I left Brix, I sofa-surfed for a while until I got my own place. One night, while I was staying at a girlfriend's place, we went to this dive bar in Vesterbro. We got really drunk and she went home with some bloke. The last thing I remember was drinking shots at the counter, but I must have made it home somehow, because I woke up back at my girlfriend's place the next morning with the worst hangover of my life. I was naked, and I had all these bruises on me. I'd broken a tooth and had a split lip and had bled all over my pillow. It's the only time it could have happened.'

'What did you do?'

'I had a long shower and patched myself up. I thought I'd fallen over somehow when making it home, but it was so strange that I just couldn't recall any of it.'

'Why didn't you go to the police?'

'I was embarrassed. It just never occurred to me that I could have been raped. Not until I found out that you were on your way weeks later.'

'You could still have had an abortion. It wasn't too late.'

'No. I thought the best thing I could do under the circumstances was to have the baby. To change my narrative and turn bad into good. I gave you the name of the goddess of luck for a reason.'

'Maybe I shouldn't have stopped using it.'

'I know you don't like it.'

'It's odd.'

'Luck can be both good and bad.'

'Tell me about it.'

'But with the force of your will, you can change it.'

Jensen looked at her mother's hands. They were long and delicate, like a pianist's. Her own were small but strong. 'So you were right. You really don't know who my father is.'

'I went back to the bar, tried to find out who was there that night ... but of course no one could remember anything so long afterwards. The security recording had been taped over. So I decided to get on with my life, and that's what I've done.'

'How did you manage not to hate me?'

Marion opened her eyes. 'I always loved you. Just like you love Ea. I think that now you understand what that means.'

Yes, thought Jensen. *Now I understand.*

'Why didn't you tell me?'

'Because I was afraid that you'd feel ... unwanted. And, to be honest, you never seemed to be curious about it. Not until you had Ea and that bastard got in touch.'

She got up and hugged her mother and their limbs slotted into place perfectly. Nothing had ever made more sense.

Day Nine

58

Mark had asked for a meeting. Henrik's instinct had been to put him off, but Mark had insisted. In the past few days, he'd become more and more irritable and reluctant to take orders. This wasn't like him at all.

Now they were seated across from each other in Henrik's office, with the rain tapping on the window and obscuring the desolate view of the car park.

Somehow it had become Thursday. His wife had been gone for four days without as much as a word. According to his mother-in-law, she seemed happy.

Happy without him.

What if she never came back? The thought of losing Louise and the life they'd created together left him breathless. She'd always been there, as much a part of his life as their four walls in Frederiksberg: solid, reassuring, not going anywhere. But wasn't that exactly the problem? He'd taken her for granted.

What if she was with another man? Perhaps Bo Petersen, the teacher from her school that he'd always suspected her of liking?

He knew the thought was undignified – after all, he'd cheated way before she had – but still it sent a chill down his spine.

He focused on Mark. In spite of the scowl on his face, he looked as fit and cocky as a premier-league footballer. Dark jeans, a white polo shirt stretched taut across his chest and biceps. To think that this was the same bundle of nervous energy who'd joined his team years ago, so eager to please.

Like Louise and his home, he'd always thought of Mark as solid and dependable.

'So, what do you want to talk about?' he said, without really wanting to know the answer.

'I think I've stepped up recently, tried to lead,' Mark said.

'You've worked hard, it's true.'

'You just can't say it, can you?'

'What?'

'That I've done well.'

'Come on,' said Henrik. 'We're in the middle of three major investigations. What do you want, a gold star sticker?'

'Liv clearly thinks I've got potential. You heard her the other day.'

'I did. She thinks you're a valued member of the team, just like I do.'

'Do you really?' said Mark, a blush creeping up his neck, nostrils flaring. 'I'm not sure. What I do know, though, is that you think the sun shines out of Funder's arse.'

So this was it. Mark was jealous. Henrik had suspected as much.

'It's not the first time you've done this either,' said Mark. 'Remember Lisbeth?'

Henrik did. Lisbeth Quist had been a member of his team until a year ago when she'd moved into a bigger role with the organised crime unit. Lisbeth was ambitious and smart, and, like Funder, she'd shown initiative.

He suspected Mark had been relieved when she left, hoping it would be his turn to shine, but this had never happened.

'If you mean that I have favourites, you're wrong,' said Henrik.

'But?'

'I believe that everyone must play a different role in order for the whole team to win. Stars and water carriers. You know the film?'

'What?'

'Giro D'Italia, 1973. But the principle is the same in any cycling race. The stars are the riders out in front, the water carriers are those who give up their own chances to help them, so the whole team wins. In this team, we win when we get justice for the dead and the walking wounded. I'll back anyone who has the right idea to achieve that.'

Mark laughed sarcastically. What had got into him? 'Like Funder, you mean? No one thinks she's got the right idea. Funder's a joke, and you're the only one who can't see it.'

'Mark, you're in danger of—'

'No,' said Mark. 'Don't shut me down. I'm sick of being overlooked. If you never give me a chance, how can you be sure I'm not a star?'

Oh, I know, Henrik thought to himself.

'I can see you're upset,' he began.

But Mark was already on his feet. 'I want you to know that I've asked Liv for a transfer. She said she'd discuss it with you first, but she wasn't opposed.'

He headed for the door, then hesitated at the sight of the sports bag on the couch. Henrik regretted not closing it. You could see his dirty work shirts inside, the bag with his shaver and shower gel. 'Wife's thrown you out again?' Mark said. 'Can't say I blame her. Has it ever occurred to you that maybe it's you who's wrong?'

He rushed out, bumping into Funder on the way.

'What's up with him?' she said to Henrik.

I really don't know, Henrik thought, but he didn't like it. Not one bit.

'Anyway, I've brought some news,' said Funder.

'Yes?'

'I promised to check a couple of things yesterday. I think you'll find this interesting,' she said, rather symbolically taking the seat Mark had just vacated. 'You know Mia Steen's baby? Well, Brix was the father.'

Henrik thought of Brix's initial denial that he and Mia had been lovers. He'd been so adamant. Was this down to a poor memory, or a talent for lying?

'What's the other thing?'

'Elise Berg's injuries. Jensen described scratches and red marks on her hands and forearms, and we were wondering if she could have got those through the jumper.'

'And?'

'They don't think so. In fact, they found a few of Elise Berg's hairs on the jumper but none of her blood or skin cells, which is odd in itself, don't you agree?'

I don't know, Henrik thought.

Clearly, they didn't have the whole story yet. The sooner they found Berg, the better.

59

Jensen welcomed the wind and rain as she rode her bike to the Potato Rows for what she hoped would be the last time. She and Brix had unfinished business: he wasn't her father, and he needed to know that.

She'd been in a daze since finding out what had happened to her mother. It explained so much. Marion had never dared attach herself to anyone. She'd built a life full of strangers, first in Copenhagen, then in remote North Jutland, where her circle had slowly shrunk.

Jensen felt guilty now for having thought she was hopeless, when in fact her mother had done everything to protect her, the only way she could.

A police officer got out of his car when she approached the house. She showed him her press card. '*Dagbladet*,' she said. 'I'm here to see Brix.'

The officer insisted on coming with her to the door.

'Jensen,' said Brix. 'What are you doing here?' He looked for a moment as if he wasn't going to let her in, but eventually he relented.

As soon as she was inside, she saw that they weren't alone.

Astrid, Brix's wife, had appeared at the end of the corridor with their toddler on her arm.

'Astrid, this is ... err ... the journalist I told you about,' said Brix, sending Jensen a meaningful look. 'She's the one whose baby was kidnapped.'

Jensen remembered Brix saying that he hadn't told his wife about her yet.

'I'm so glad to meet you,' said Astrid, coming towards her. 'You must have been so frightened when that mad woman took your daughter ... they were afraid at first that it was August she was after.' She hugged the boy, who tried to wriggle free. 'Valde says the woman saw you when you came to interview him, and assumed he was the father of your baby. How crazy is that?'

If only you knew, thought Jensen.

'I can't believe she got so close to you. It's like something out of a movie,' Astrid said.

'Me neither,' said Jensen. 'She was extremely convincing.'

'I just want them to lock her up.'

'They reckon she's waiting it out somewhere.'

'To do what?'

It was a good question. 'I'm not sure,' Jensen said.

'I'm glad you're here. There's something I want to ask you,' said Brix. 'Astrid, if you don't mind, I need a word with Jensen, in private.' He led the two of them into the living room and closed the door.

'Thanks for playing along,' he said in a low voice when they were alone. 'Astrid's rather nervous. I don't want to add to her stress.'

'I read the interview you gave. Seems you've done all right. Your secret's out, and the sky hasn't caved in.'

'Andreas is a formidable publicist,' said Brix. 'I'm sorry

you got caught up in it all. If I'd known she'd go after you, I would never have asked for your help.'

'Elise Berg.'

'Yes. I liked her. She was extremely pretty, knew her literature, had brains. There was a certain edge to her. It was exciting.'

'You thought she was called something starting with 'A'. She can't have made that much of an impression on you.'

'Never been good with names. Anyway, the first couple of times were fine. I'd really fallen for her. But then the third time . . .'

'You said it was a one-night stand.'

'One night, two, three, what matters is that it was extremely short-lived, because she began to talk about . . . you know, the future, and that had never been on the cards. I thought she understood, but clearly not.'

'You said the break was undramatic.'

'It was. I blocked her, and that was it. Or so I thought. I'd no idea she'd go to such extremes.'

'Murdering Vivian Sejer, you mean? Isn't she innocent until proven guilty?'

'The police seem pretty certain it was her.'

'And Mia Steen?'

'Search me,' said Brix.

Jensen felt anger bubbling up inside her again. Brix always had this effect on her. 'Why are you talking so quietly?' she said. 'Is it because you haven't told Astrid about Vivian and all the others yet?'

He nodded. 'Like I said, she has enough on her plate. But I will, soon.'

'All of it?'

'As much as necessary.'

'You're not afraid she'll leave you?'

'Jensen. When I met Astrid, I was with someone else. She can hardly plead ignorance of my ways. What was it someone said? When a man marries his mistress, he creates a vacancy.' He smiled. 'Now tell me, why are you here?'

'To tell you that Marion was right,' said Jensen.

'I beg your pardon?'

She took the letter out of her bag and passed it to him. 'See for yourself.'

'What?' he said, eyebrows shooting up as he stared at the piece of paper in his hands. 'I don't understand. There must have been a mistake.'

'No mistake.'

'Then who is it?'

'Marion has been saying all along that she doesn't know. It's probably time we believed her.'

'But she was in love with me. I was the one who cheated.'

I'm the bastard, Henrik had said.

Brix sounded like he was proud of the fact.

'Well,' she said. 'I'm living proof that Marion moved on.'

Brix looked crestfallen. 'So Ea . . .'

She finished the sentence for him. 'Isn't your granddaughter.'

'I see.' He sat for a while in silence as the news sank in. She saw no sadness on his face, just a kind of embarrassed wonderment turning slowly into relief. It seemed he was reaching the conclusion that his life would be all the simpler without her.

'What was it you wanted to ask me?' she said, suddenly yearning to get out of there.

'Oh, just a formality,' he said. 'The files I sent you, please go home and destroy them. If I see them again, in any context, I'm afraid I'm going to have to deny everything and send Brøgger after you with an injunction.'

He laughed but she could tell that it was no joke. Brix was threatening her to keep her mouth shut.

60

Henrik had been to Rigshospitalet, the national hospital (AKA Riget, 'The Kingdom') hundreds of times in his career, interviewing victims of crime, sometimes consoling grieving relatives, but it had never come to feel routine.

The sixteen-storey concrete building towered over Copenhagen in the area west of Sortedam Lake like a constant reminder of the cycle of life: you are born, you get sick, you die.

He held doctors and nurses in the highest esteem, and invariably conducted himself with greater decorum whenever he stepped onto the premises.

Funder was marching down the corridor ahead of him, and he followed, glancing left and right, occasionally spotting a patient through an open door. God forbid he should ever have to reside in one of those rooms himself. He'd asked Louise to quietly put a pillow over his face if he ended up a vegetable.

He supposed she wouldn't even do that for him now.

Funder stopped outside Jane Dahl-Thomsen's door. 'Brace yourself,' she said.

He was about to remind her that he'd put in his first shift before she was out of nappies when she went through. A young woman looked up from the bedside. 'They're here, Mum. You know Sarah Funder already.'

Jane turned her head. A week after the attack, there was still bruising around her eyes. One arm was in a sling, and her face was swollen. She squinted at them, mumbling something unintelligible.

'I didn't get that?' said Henrik, leaning closer.

'She said that she hasn't met you before,' said the young woman. 'Her jaw is broken so it's hard for her to talk. I'm Laura, by the way, her daughter.'

'I'm Detective Inspector Henrik Jungersen,' he said to Jane, as gently as he could, flicking open the warrant card on the leather strap around his neck.

'Why don't you sit?' Laura indicated two chairs on the other side of the bed.

'I'm glad you're better,' said Henrik as he and Funder sat down. 'You had us worried there for a minute.'

Jane Dahl-Thomsen wasn't quite smiling.

'It's best if you're quick,' Laura said. 'Mum gets so tired.'

'Of course,' said Funder. 'Jane, when I was here before, you said that you didn't remember anything before waking up in the park. Is that still the case?'

A nod.

'What's the last thing you remember?'

'The date wasn't good,' said Jane, very slowly. 'I went to the toilet. It was in the basement.'

'Yes,' said Funder. 'We've got you on CCTV going down the stairs.'

Jane said something else that Henrik couldn't decipher. He looked at Laura. 'Boxes,' she said. 'She saw all these boxes of empty beer bottles stacked high and had to go around them. When she did, she bumped into someone.'

'A man?' said Henrik.

'I think so,' Jane said. 'He was looking at his phone and hadn't seen me. He was leaning against the wall.'

'She didn't see his face because he had his back turned to her,' Laura said.

'Did he say anything?' said Funder.

Jane shook her head. 'I said sorry and walked past him. The toilet was around the corner.' She winced, closing her eyes.

'Let me, Mum,' said Laura, touching her hand. 'Mum stayed in the toilet for quite a while. She didn't want to go back to her date, so she was trying to drag out the time. She remembers looking at the mirror and putting on lipstick. But just as she was ready to head back upstairs, she began to feel really hot, like she had a temperature.'

'Is that right, Jane?' said Funder.

She nodded with her eyes tightly closed. 'I tried to find the way out, but it was dark, and there were so many doors. Then suddenly, I was outside.'

She began to weep quietly.

'It's OK, Mum. Shh . . .' said Laura. She turned to Henrik. 'Crying hurts her. I don't think she remembers any more.'

'Just one more question,' said Funder. 'Valde Brix, the author. You know him?'

'Doesn't everyone?' said Laura. 'And Mum does work for his publisher.'

Jane looked at her daughter meaningfully and a penny appeared to drop for the young woman. 'You mean it's him? The guy you've been going on about? Wait . . . isn't he married? I saw something online about him today.'

Jane looked at her daughter again, this time with a frown. Laura lifted her hands to her mouth.

'I'm tired now,' said Jane. 'Can we stop, please?'

When they'd said their goodbyes, Laura saw the two

of them out into the corridor, carefully closing the door behind her. She nodded at a passing nurse.

'About a year ago, Mum had this really intense affair. She spoke of him as though he was the love of her life, and as far as I could understand, it was mutual. She never said it was Valde Brix, I still can't believe it.' Her eyes widened. 'My God, does this have something to do with this stalker they're looking for?'

'We can't go into it,' said Funder.

'But tell us what happened,' Henrik said.

'Well, obviously it ended. Rather suddenly, and Mum was in a heap. She and my dad divorced seven years ago, and falling in love again, only to be rejected, just destroyed her confidence. It was me who persuaded her to create an online dating profile. I thought that was what she needed, to meet someone else and banish this so-called Big Love from her memory. That's why I just feel so guilty.'

'Guilty?' said Henrik.

'If I hadn't persuaded her to go out with that rubbish date last Wednesday, then she'd never have been raped, would she?'

She was wrong on that score, Henrik thought, though he didn't say anything. It was clearly knowing Brix that had made her mother a target.

And the perpetrator, whoever it was, had followed her very closely, preparing down to every little detail. Down to knowing where she'd planned to meet her date.

'I'm sorry, Laura, but I'm afraid we have to go now,' said Funder.

She tilted her phone towards him. On her screen, Henrik saw a message from Bagger.

Elise Berg just used her bank card.

61

When Jensen returned, she found Marion and Ea sound asleep in each other's arms. She made tea in her favourite London mug and tiptoed into her office.

That Brix had asked for the files he'd shared with her to be deleted was hardly a surprise. Still, he'd acted as if he thought he was in the clear.

He was wrong about that. It wasn't over for him. Not by a long shot.

She opened her laptop and copied his file onto an external drive, which she tucked away in her bag. As she did so, her fingers brushed against the letter with the result of the paternity test.

Negative.

Brix wasn't her father, so who was?

Who had raped her mother, and was he still out there somewhere?

She remembered the ancestry website and the possible first cousin or uncle she'd matched with, Erik Lange. With everything that had happened in the past week, she hadn't had a chance to check if he'd responded to her message.

When she'd logged on, she felt a little tug of excitement when she saw the red envelope icon.

Erik Lange was ecstatic to have heard from her.

> I'm trying to map a whole new branch of the family that I had no idea existed and you're the first connection I've found so far. What are your parents' names? Do you have any siblings? What are you called other than Jensen? So many questions!

He'd told her about his own parents and family and said that he was putting together a family tree and would be happy to share this when completed.

Her fingers trembled as she typed:

> My mother's name is Marion Jensen. She has no siblings and nor did her parents or grandparents. I don't know who my father is or was. Any information could be useful. Do share that family tree.

She typed in her first name, but deleted it again, explaining to Erik Lange that it had been a silly whim of her mother's, and that these days she referred to herself as Jensen only.

She drank her tea.

Then she picked up her phone and tapped Gustav's number.

'Tell me you've got news,' he said. 'If not, I'm busy.'

'All right, I've got news. Brix is not my dad.'

'What?'

'You shouldn't sound so surprised. Marion was right all along. I should have listened to her.'

'So who is he then?'

'Don't know yet. But I'm going to find out.'

She ended the call. When her phone immediately began to ring, she thought it was Gustav again. 'What?' she said.

'Jensen,' said a voice. 'It's me. Elise. Can we meet?'

62

The new red-brick housing estate in Albertslund, a mixture of flats and terraced houses, was arranged in a tight grid with parking around the perimeter, the newly planted beech hedges still fighting to take hold.

Funder and Henrik were sitting in the car, getting their bearings and waiting for the rain to stop hammering on the windscreen.

Number 102 was three doors up, as unremarkable as its neighbours. Each property had a black-painted bicycle shed placed at right angles to the façade, and a small patio at the back, crammed with swings, barbecues and parasols.

Similar estates were springing up all over Copenhagen now to cope with increasing demand, but not fast enough, leading to sky-rocketing house prices.

'I can't believe she'll be here,' said Funder. 'He was one of the first people we spoke to. Works in recruitment. Said he hasn't seen his sister in months.'

Elise Berg had used her bank card in the big Co-op in Brøndby down the road from her little brother's house in Albertslund.

'Maybe she's tired of hiding,' said Henrik. 'You go round the back, and I'll see if anyone's home.'

As he approached the entrance, he tried the door to the bike shed. It was unlocked and contained nothing but a few pieces of garden equipment and cardboard boxes.

Then he rang the bell. 'Daniel Berg?' he said to the tall, lean man who opened the door.

'Who's asking?' Berg took his time studying Henrik's warrant card.

He carried himself with a lot of swagger for a twenty-six-year-old. 'You're after Elise. I already told your colleagues that I don't know where she is.'

'You sure about that?' said Henrik.

Berg looked at him with hostility. He opened the door wide. 'Why don't you come in and have a good look around.'

The house was tidy, his and her shoes neatly lined up in the hallway, a wedding photo on the console table. It seemed Daniel Berg had done well for himself: good job, nice home, pretty wife. What was he trying to prove?

Meanwhile his sister Elise was in a bedsit in Emdrup, uncomfortable with authority and the trappings of success that her little brother had surrounded himself with.

The downstairs was open plan, except for a small office and a guest toilet. Henrik searched it in less than a minute. 'Stay here,' he said to Berg as he went upstairs. Again, he quickly concluded that Elise wasn't there.

'I thought you'd turn up eventually,' said Daniel when Henrik came back down. He was sitting on the sofa now, phone in hand. Had he warned Elise?

'Why is that?'

'Because I used her bank card at the Co-op a few hours ago.'

Henrik stared at him. 'It was you?'

'You didn't seriously think it would be her, did you?' said Daniel. 'She's just playing with you.'

'You mean she asked you to use it? I thought you said you hadn't seen her in months.'

'I haven't. She left a message in our post box, week before last, telling me that she was working on something and if everything went tits up and I saw her on the news, then I should use the card.'

'Why?'

'Throw you guys off the scent, I guess. You're here, so it worked. '

'I could have you for perverting the course of justice.'

'Not worth the paperwork, I'd have thought, but be my guest.' Daniel pointed to Funder, who was trying to hide unsuccessfully behind a parasol on the patio. 'You should tell your friend to join us. No point in her waiting outside.'

Henrik let her in. The rainwater ran off her and left a puddle on the floor.

'This is my colleague, Detective Sergeant Sarah Funder.' He pointed to Berg's phone. 'Can I take a look at that?'

Berg handed it over without question. 'Though you should know that Elise isn't stupid. That's why she left a note here, rather than call. I don't even have a number for her.'

'We'll need to borrow it for a while,' said Funder. 'Are you and your sister close?'

'I wouldn't say that. I mean we used to be. That tends to happen when your parents are useless, but we've coped in different ways. Elise lives life on her own terms. She's not the sort of person you invite around for dinner. Every now and again, she'll just suddenly make an appearance, though I always know she's looking out for me.'

'How do you mean?' said Henrik.

'She's my big sister. I can turn to her for anything. Elise is extremely bright, and she knows a lot of people. People she's done favours for.'

'How do you contact her?' said Funder, frowning. 'I mean if you don't have her number?'

'There's this Hotmail address we use, but before you get excited, I've already reached out to her there loads of times and she hasn't responded.'

'You're worried about her,' said Funder.

'Of course I'm bloody worried. Wouldn't you be if it was your sister being portrayed as some sort of master criminal all over the media?'

'She kidnapped a five-month-old baby for twelve hours, leaving her on the ground in a public park,' said Henrik. 'And we have reason to believe that she's been stalking the author Valde Brix for months, hacking into his email and trespassing on his property.'

'Ah, him,' said Berg.

'Did you ever hear your sister mention his name?' said Funder.

'You're kidding, aren't you?' said Berg. 'She's his number one fan.'

'But did she ever mention meeting him? Perhaps more than that?'

'I'm certain she'd have seen him at events and stuff, but she never mentioned anything else. Why? Are you saying there was something going on with him?'

'We can't go into detail, but obviously she must have developed some sort of obsession with him for her to have stalked him like she did,' said Henrik.

Berg looked at him strangely. 'She must have had a reason. Same with that baby she took,' he said.

'When did you last see your sister?' said Funder.

'I think it was around the time of my wife's birthday. That was in March.'

'How did she seem?'

'Angry,' said Berg. 'But then Elise is always angry about something. She gets really determined. But never aggressive. I know that you want to question her about that murder.'

'Vivian Sejer,' said Funder.

'Well, Elise would never kill anyone. I'm one hundred per cent certain she didn't do it. She wouldn't hurt a fly. She only ever hurt herself.'

'Do you believe him?' said Funder when they were back in the car.

'He clearly worships her. Doesn't exactly make him a reliable witness,' said Henrik.

Still, Elise hadn't sent them all the way to Albertslund purely to mislead them. She had wanted them to speak to her brother, knowing that he would advocate for her and perhaps sow doubt in their minds.

63

It was still raining when Jensen began the twenty-minute walk to Sankt Peders Stræde, so she put Ea in the pram. As usual, the rolling motion soothed her, and by the time they reached Liron's van, she was fast asleep.

It had stopped raining and the area smelled of wet asphalt and new green leaves.

Liron was wiping rain off the canopy above his van when he spotted her. 'Jensen, you look worried. What's up?'

'It's Elise Berg.'

'Ah, her. I see that idiot cop of yours still hasn't found her. Even though I literally pointed his nose in her direction.'

'She called me. She wants to meet, and I think I should.'

He stared at her for a while, then turned to his van, rummaging in the cupboard, before pulling out a small, battered saucepan and placing it on his camping stove.

'Sit down,' he said, measuring ground coffee into the pan and adding water.

She did as she was told. When he'd put the coffee on to brew, Liron turned his sandwich board around and wrote 'Closed' on it in large letters with white chalk.

'Now,' he said. 'Repeat what you just said, because I can't have heard you right. You think you should meet the woman who is wanted by the police for taking your baby?'

'I'm not sure she meant to do it.'

'Go on?'

'Gustav must have told you that she sent a message to Brix when he was arrested, warning him that she had his child, which turned out to be Ea.'

'Yes.'

'Well, she did that because she wanted him to confess to something. That bit hasn't been in the papers.'

'What?'

'Rape,' said Jensen.

Liron made a face, fanning one hand, as though he'd been burnt.

'You can't tell anyone,' she said. 'We don't know if it's true or who it is he's supposed to have raped.'

'OK.'

'But what if it was her? What if she was at home in my flat with Ea when she sent that message? It just said that she had her, not that she'd taken her somewhere.'

'Jensen, Jensen, Jensen, she's supposed to have bloody killed that woman . . . what was her name?'

'Vivian Sejer. But what if she didn't? What if she hasn't done anything at all, except for deceiving me? I think I need to hear her side of the story at least.'

'And where would this meeting be taking place?'

'I don't know yet. I'm supposed to be calling her back with my answer in an hour. What do you think?'

'I think you're crazy,' said Liron. He took the coffee off the stove, added a clear liquid from a small bottle, and poured it through a filter into a brass pot with a spout shaped like a half-moon. 'This dallah was my father's. He was Arab, did I ever tell you that?'

'But I thought you were—'

'Jewish? I am, after my mother. I'm both.'

He held the coffee pot high over a small cup without a handle and poured, then added half a spoonful of brown sugar. 'Qahwa. Arabic coffee,' he said, handing it to her.

She drank, tasting cardamon, cloves and rosewater, losing the sights, sounds and smells of the familiar street around her for somewhere far away.

When the last of the coffee was gone, she felt a new clarity of mind. It was as if her work brain had shuddered back to life. 'I've made up my mind. I'm going to say yes. I think Elise Berg holds the key to the whole thing, and I'm going to find out what it is.'

'You can't go by yourself. What if it's a trap?'

'Then help me, Liron.'

Liron cursed under his breath. 'You're bloody impossible,' he said. 'Give me that phone number and go home and wait. We'll do it my way.'

64

There was an odd atmosphere in the office when Henrik returned with Funder. As he walked down the corridor, people were busy at their desks, but superficially, not really looking at their screens or typing anything important.

News always travelled fast among the detectives. Maybe because they frequently saw each other in situations of extreme stress, which naturally brought them close. Or maybe because they were adrenaline junkies who got bored very quickly.

He'd no reason to suspect the gossip concerned him. Not until he spotted Mark staring so hard at his phone that it had to be an avoidance tactic.

The door at the end of the corridor opened and Liv came out, looking like someone in a film, with her light-blue silk blouse tucked into navy trousers. As she spoke you could have heard a pin drop. 'Ah, Henrik, you're back. Come in for a minute would you?'

She closed the door after him. Another bad sign. 'Sit down,' she said. 'Any news?'

'We spoke to Jane Dahl-Thomsen. Turns out she and

Brix didn't just work for the same publisher. They had a secret affair last year.'

'Doesn't make him guilty of anything.'

'No, as we discussed, it's just a strange coincidence, don't you think?'

Liv didn't say anything. He noticed that she wore a large gold ring on her right hand and that her nails were manicured.

'Oh, and we had a false alarm on Elise Berg. She'd used her card in the Co-op in Brøndby, or so we thought. Turns out it was her brother. Insists he hasn't seen her and doesn't know where she is, so . . .' Henrik trailed off, realising that Liv hadn't intended for him to go on this long.

Her question had merely been an ice breaker. 'What's going on?' he said.

'Henrik, something's been brought to my attention, which I find rather disappointing,' she said. 'Remember our conversation about Brix's daughter, Jensen?'

'She's not actually his daughter,' said Henrik. 'That was just something he thought. A paternity test proved him wrong.' He stopped, realising that he'd made a mistake.

'You see, that's exactly what's worrying me. You obviously know Jensen really well.'

'It would be strange if I didn't know her. Copenhagen is a small city, and we do work in the same field, albeit on opposite sides. There have been certain . . . investigations in the past where she's played a pivotal role. You can ask Mark, or Bagger, they'll tell you.'

Liv looked at him, at pains to put her point across in the right way. Perhaps she'd been on the same course as him: 'Respect at Work', or whatever it was called. He wasn't about to make it easy for her.

'When Jensen's baby was kidnapped on Monday, I

understand that she called you and that you drove straight out to see her in Nørrebro. Why?'

'She called me because she'd just seen me arrest Brix. She knew he had a stalker, and she'd just realised that it was the same woman who had taken her baby.'

Liv pressed her lips together. 'All right,' she said. 'But when her baby was returned to her, you seemed extraordinarily pleased. If I'm not mistaken you actually welled up.'

'I have three kids myself. I think any parent can imagine what she must have gone through. I'm not a robot.'

Now Liv looked irritated. She held up a hand. 'OK, Henrik. Let me say it as it is. I understand that you and Jensen have been intimate at some point in the past and may still be in a relationship.'

'Who told you that?' Bagger possibly suspected, and Goldschmidt had seen it with his own eyes, but neither of them would have shopped him.

It could only have been Mark.

'I can't tell you that, as you well know.'

'I think I have a right—'

'No you don't,' said Liv. 'We don't have rules about conflict of interest for fun. The people we serve are entitled to expect us to be unbiased. Do you or do you not know Jensen intimately?'

'I refuse to answer the question.'

'Then you give me no choice. I have to take you off all three cases in which Brix is implicated.'

'Even though Jensen isn't his daughter?'

'Her mother, Marion Jensen, is still a key witness,' said Liv. 'Henrik, I'm in charge here. If we're criticised in any way for our conduct in these investigations, it'll be on my head.'

Henrik began to get up. 'OK,' he said. 'Have it your way.

But I think you'll find that there's no one better placed than me to get to the bottom of what's been going on.'

'None of us is indispensable,' said Liv. 'Go and get some rest. Come back on Monday, andwe'll talk about where we can put your talents to best use. The past week has been hard on us all. And I understand that you're having some trouble at home as well.'

Now he knew for certain it was Mark. He'd seen his overnight bag in the office and commented on it.

'What?'

'Nothing,' said Liv. 'Forget I said anything. It's a private matter after all, but as long as you know that I'm here if you want to talk. You're clearly one of our strongest lead investigators, and I value you as part of the team.'

Part of the team my arse, thought Henrik.

As he walked out, via his office to collect the travel bag in which he carried his life around, he looked stiffly ahead.

Out of the corner of his eye, he sensed Mark coming towards him, suddenly keen to talk. He held up a hand to stop him.

Judas.

As far as Henrik was concerned, it would be preferable if they never talked again.

Day Ten

65

'This is very nice of you, Gustav,' said Jensen. 'But what's it in aid of?'

They were in a tiny Lebanese restaurant in Nørrebro. There were only two tables, and the other one was empty. Every few minutes, delivery drivers would come in, carrying away paper bags laden with boxes of hot, fragrant food.

There was a bowl of lemons on the counter, rows of jars with bright green and purple pickles on the shelves above it. You could see through to the kitchen where two men were busy working by a stove.

'It's to celebrate your birthday,' Gustav said.

'That was ages ago.'

'I couldn't afford it then. I just got paid for the first time.'

She frowned at him. 'You've worked at *Dagbladet* for at least three months.'

'Yeah, but the other times, I had to give it all to Margrethe to pay back what I owed her.' He took a massive bite of his *sfeeha*. 'So good,' he said, smiling with tomato sauce around his teeth.

Jensen could smell the ground lamb with cinnamon

and allspice from her own plate. The meat pie was pizza-shaped and dotted with parsley and golden pine nuts. She began to eat and had to close her eyes for a few seconds as the flavours danced around her mouth. 'So, let me get this right. You finally have some spare cash, and the first thing you do is invite me out for dinner?' she said, taking a sip of her lemonade.

'What's wrong with that?' said Gustav.

'When we spoke yesterday, you said you were busy.'

'Not any more. Nothing's happening, and the police aren't saying anything. Besides, I thought you deserved a treat after what happened with Ea on Monday. And now that the police are outside your flat and Marion's babysitting, I thought it was the perfect opportunity.'

'You never fail to surprise me,' said Jensen. Gustav was definitely being odd. Perhaps he needed a favour; that would make more sense.

'Bet you're glad Brix isn't your dad.'

'Ecstatic,' she said.

'You don't look it,' said Gustav, spiking a crispy falafel on his fork and biting into it.

My father raped my mother.

It was too shocking to think, let alone say. Despite his eighteen years, Gustav was still a relative innocent, impressionable and prone to overreaction.

Jensen knew that he was fond of her, and the truth could be difficult for him to deal with. Marion had handled it by shutting herself further and further away from anyone who wanted her to commit emotionally. Telling people, even Gustav, the secret Marion had carried for so many years would be a betrayal.

'What are you going to do now?' said Gustav. 'I mean how are you going to find your dad?'

'I sent my DNA to this ancestry site a while back. I found a relative and he can't be on my mother's side as they're all single children.'

She and Marion had discussed this when Ea was born, and Jensen had predicted that she, like her ancestors going back four generations, was going to be a single child.

'That's so cool,' said Gustav.

'He's creating this family tree and has promised to send it to me soon,' said Jensen. 'By the way, how's that big scoop of yours going?'

'Oh man, Jensen, if you knew. Keep it to yourself, but I might need to go abroad for a while.'

'When?'

'I'm just waiting for something to be confirmed, and then I'll know for sure, but remember, not a word to Margrethe, promise?'

'Promise.'

'Can I finish this?' said Gustav, pointing to the humous with his last wedge of flatbread.

'Be my guest. I'm stuffed,' she said, looking at her watch. It was after ten o'clock. The unusual lateness was as strange as Gustav's dinner invitation. 'I'd better get back to Ea,' she said.

'I thought you said you'd prepared a bottle for her?'

'I did.' She looked at him more closely. 'Gustav, are you sure you're all right? You seem a bit shifty.'

The two chefs in the kitchen spoke quietly to each other, drinking from bottles of water. It seemed like their shift was over. One of them began to wipe down the counter, the other went to the door and locked and bolted it.

Then he turned off the overhead lights, leaving on only a brass wall lamp next to their table. The pattern from the shade fell across Gustav's face.

'Stay,' the chef said to them. 'Finish your food, there's no problem.'

'I think we're done,' she said, looking at Gustav. 'So are you really picking up the tab or was this all just a ruse to make me take you out for dinner?'

'It's already paid for, don't think about it,' said the chef, continuing into the kitchen where he resumed the conversation with his colleague.

A blue-painted door next to the kitchen counter opened, revealing a third guest, a tall man with a baseball cap and strange grey eyes.

'Liron, what are you doing here?'

'I told you we'd do it my way. Now, give the boy your mobile phone.'

'I'm eighteen,' said Gustav angrily as he held out his hand to her.

She gave him her phone. Gustav walked over to the door and unbolted it to let himself out. 'Be seeing you, Jensen,' he said without looking back.

'Come with me,' said Liron.

She followed him into a dark, musty-smelling corridor. There was a brown sliding door with a brass toilet sign on her right, shelves with tins of olive oil and sacks of onions and flour on her left. In the back there was some kind of office, looking as if it was being used as a storage room for old cardboard boxes.

Then they were outside in the world's smallest dead-end street. Next to the wheelie bins, there was a silver car with tinted rear windows.

'Do you trust me?' said Liron.

'Yes,' said Jensen, but noticed that she was trembling. She assumed she was about to meet Elise Berg, the woman who had taken her baby, a possible murderer.

She tried to look inside the car, guessing that Elise would be in there waiting, but Liron shook his head. 'Not here,' he said. 'They were going to do it another way, but I refused.'

'They? Who are they?'

'The people who are protecting her. They were bloody going to kidnap you in the street, bundle you into the boot, so I said no, I'll take her. So this is how we're going to do it. Hands behind your back, Jensen.'

She put her hands around her back, and he joined them together with a cable tie.

'But why do I need them tied?'

'So that you don't pull this off on the way.' He lowered a black hood over her head and steered her towards the car and onto the rear seat, fastening her seat belt.

'Now sit back and try to relax.'

66

Henrik was getting stir crazy. On the first night, when Liv had sent him home, he'd slept like a baby after diving into the hotel bed.

This morning, he'd been to the gym, watched from a distance as his mother-in-law saw his children off to school, and eaten a decent breakfast.

But after this, the day had dragged on. He'd washed two white shirts with shampoo in the bathroom sink. He'd napped and surfed through the TV news, but everyone was talking about the cases.

His cases.

The room overlooked the hotel car park and a section of motorway. There was nothing going on out there, and it was only Friday night, with an eternity to go until Monday morning.

He missed his kids. Jensen had been right. He should just go home, tell his in-laws to leave.

His house, his rules. OK, so he'd only been alone with his kids a few times, no more than a few days, and his mother-in-law had come in to help, but he could work it all out, couldn't he? He wasn't stupid, and how hard could it be?

Still, he hadn't got up and packed his few belongings into a sports bag and left the soulless hotel. He didn't know why, but it felt impossible to do so.

He wasn't done yet.

Not that he blamed Liv. He didn't know what he'd been thinking, carrying on as normal after finding out that Jensen was mixed up in it all.

He'd been sailing close to the wind for years. Had it not been for his former boss's propensity not to see what was right in front of him, this might all have come crashing down around him a lot sooner.

His sense of unfinished business stemmed from something deeper: the vengefulness he felt on behalf of Mia Steen, Jane Dahl-Thomsen and Vivian Sejer.

And more tangibly, the unwise promise he'd made to Mia Steen's mother to find her killer.

How was he going to accomplish this now?

He lay back on his pillow and closed his eyes.

The knock on the door startled him.

'Who is it?' he said, thinking for one excited moment that it could be his wife or Jensen.

'Open the bloody door,' came a familiar voice.

'Funder, what are you doing here?' he said, as the excitement evaporated.

'Nice to see you too.'

She pushed past him, removed his clothes from the room's only chair and sat down. There was a brown paper bag and a rucksack in her hand. 'Do you have any idea how many hotels there are in Copenhagen?'

'No.'

'Me neither, but it took me at least two hundred phone calls to find you.'

'You abused your position as a law enforcement officer.'

'Only a bit,' she said, smiling broadly.

'How did you even know I'd be in a hotel?'

'Got it out of Mark, the little weasel. He said your wife threw you out.' She recounted this matter-of-factly as she looked around the room. 'I'm not surprised if you're this messy at home.'

'Funder, why are you here?'

'You left without saying goodbye.'

'I've had to declare a personal interest, which means I can no longer lead the investigations we're working on as they relate to Brix.'

'I know,' she said. 'Though they won't tell me what your personal interest is, the bastards.'

'Well, you won't be hearing it from me, so if that's why you're here . . .'

'Relax,' said Funder. 'I'm not interested. I'm here to tell you what I've discovered.'

'Didn't you hear what I said?'

'Yeah, yeah, you're not working on the cases any more. You said that already, but you'll want to hear this.'

Henrik sat down on the bed. 'I'm really not sure I do, but go on.'

'It's Brix. I found out that he knew one more of the eleven Polaris women, so two of them. With Mia Steen, Jane Dahl-Thomsen and Vivian Sejer, that makes five women he has known intimately who've been sexually assaulted. I mean, what are the chances?'

'Why are you telling me?'

'Who else am I going to tell? No one wants to hear it. They all think Brix is as pure as the driven snow.'

'You should be going back to the office. That's where you can be useful,' he said. 'By the way, who's taken over after me?'

'Lotte,' said Funder.

Detective Inspector Lotte Nielsen. A good choice, Henrik thought. She wouldn't mess things up, and she was an ally.

'But Liv told us all to take the weekend to rest, aside from a core few.'

'So why aren't you?'

'What?'

'Resting?'

'When there's a serial rapist out there? Fat chance.'

Oh God, Henrik thought.

Minutes ago his life had felt pretty grim. Now he was stuck with Funder as well. What did she have in mind that the two of them were going to do? Away from the office, without access to any of the relevant files?

'What's in the bag?' he said.

'A burger,' she said. 'I figured you might be hungry.'

'I am, as it happens.'

He watched her reach into the bag. She handed him the burger in a small box. 'Sorry I ate your chips.'

He opened the box. 'It's a cheeseburger. I don't like cheese.'

Quick as a flash, she reached out and grabbed the box. He watched as she lifted the top bun and scraped off the cheese with a napkin, before handing the burger back.

'There,' she said. 'Now eat. We've got work to do.'

67

Jensen quickly gave up following the direction of Liron's car on her internal map of Copenhagen. He'd thrown a blanket on top of her as well as the hood. To stop her from overheating he'd turned the air conditioning on full blast. The noise was disorientating.

Was she about to make a terrible mistake? What if something happened to her? She had faith in Liron, but even he had no clue what he was up against.

'Have you done this kind of thing before?' she shouted.

Liron laughed. 'Chill, you're safe with me.'

'Won't Elise mind you seeing where she's hiding?'

'We're not going there. An intermediary is bringing her to a meeting place, like I'm taking you. The deal is that neither of you know where.'

'Sounds like something out of a spy novel,' said Jensen. 'Is this your car? I didn't know you had one.'

'Stop asking so many questions. You worry too much,' said Liron.

'Of course I worry. I don't know where we're going.'

Liron cursed unintelligibly. 'Would you like to go back? I mean you bloody asked for this. It wasn't my idea.'

'No,' she said. 'Just drive. As long as you get me back in one piece before my mother and daughter wake up.'

They drove on a fast road for a while, then on smaller roads, before ending up on a bumpy track, the tyres crunching on gravel.

It was a relief when the car eventually came to a full stop and Liron turned off the engine. He kept the blanket over her when he helped her out. She could smell grass and wild garlic, and hear leaves rustling in the wind all around her, as they walked for a few minutes on a dirt path. Then she sensed that someone else had joined them.

'You stay outside with me, and if something happens to her, you're dead,' said Liron to the person as he pushed her gently forward.

No reply came.

Then she heard a door being opened; it rattled a little on its hinges. She guessed from the smell of creosote that she was in a shed. The ground under her feet felt like compacted soil.

She was pushed onto a chair, and the blanket and hood were removed by invisible hands, but not the cable ties. The door closed behind her. Then a naked lightbulb suspended from the ceiling came on, and it was so bright that she couldn't see for a moment.

Elise looked nothing like Karo. She wore a black wig in a short, blunt bob, and black-rimmed glasses, but her collarbone tattoo was just visible above the neck of her T-shirt.

'In case you're worried, my hands are bound too,' she said. 'Your friend insisted on it. It was this way or nothing.'

'He's less gullible than me.'

Elise smiled. 'I'm sorry, Jensen.'

'For lying to me or for taking my child?'

'All of it. I was so glad when you agreed to seeing me.'

'Doesn't mean I've forgiven you. What I want is for you to explain yourself. You'll still have to face the consequences of what you did.'

'Fair,' said Elise. 'I made a mistake, but I hope you can understand that it was always him I was after.'

'You'd seen me walking past his house?'

'Yes. A few times. And you had Ea with you. I put two and two together and got five,' she said.

'He thought I was his daughter, but I'm not.'

'Thank God.'

'He wanted me to help find you, his stalker.'

'I know that because I looked through your laptop.'

'I thought you probably had.'

'I was trying to do it that first time you left Ea with me, but then she woke up, and I took her down to the courtyard.'

'You did that deliberately to set me up.'

'You make me sound more cold-hearted than I am, but I understand. You're angry with me. I'd be exactly the same in your position.'

They looked at each other for a while. Jensen hadn't heard anything yet that she didn't already know. 'So tell me,' she said. 'Why did you do it?'

Elise sighed deeply. 'I need to start at the beginning.'

'I know you were a massive fan of Brix; can we skip your childhood and go to the bit when you first met him?'

'OK. It was exactly like I told you the time we walked along the lakes. We met in a bar. He couldn't take his eyes off me.'

'But everything you said after that was a lie.'

Elise ignored her comment and carried on. 'He was with his agent.'

'Andreas Lund?'

She nodded. 'Do you know him?'

'Brix calls him his fixer. Apparently he knows everything there is to know about him.'

Elise frowned as if something had just occurred to her. Then she shook her head. 'Well, anyway, they were having dinner, but Brix kept looking at me over the guy's shoulder. I'd recognised him instantly, of course.'

'You were alone?'

'Yes, I used to bring my laptop to that bar. I don't keep normal hours, so I'd do my work from there,' said Elise. 'Anyway, when they'd finished eating the agent left. I heard Brix saying goodbye to him. 'I just need to use the loo,' he said, but of course it was because he wanted to talk to me. I was so excited.'

'You knew he was married?'

'Yes. Do you think that's awful of me? Sisterhood and all that?'

Jensen remembered what Henrik had said whenever she'd felt guilty about their relationship: *I'm the bastard, not you.*

She was hardly in a position to judge Elise for choices she herself had made. 'No, but perhaps it should have made you realise that he wasn't being serious,' she said.

'He behaved as if he was. Love-bombed me. We went to a hotel that night, and again a few days later. He left in the early hours but paid for the room. Then the third time, I brought him back to this flat in Emdrup that I've been subletting. Maybe it was a mistake.'

'What do you mean?'

'I think maybe when he saw how many of his books I owned, he got scared and thought I was some sort of fanatic. We had sex, but after that he ghosted me. One minute, he'd never been more in love, the next he didn't know me. No explanation. Just, "The End".'

'So you began to harass him.'

'No, not at first. I wrote him a few messages, and I might have got a bit tetchy, but only because I was trying to understand what had happened. Anyway, I got nothing back, so I put it down to experience. Never meet your heroes, et cetera. That would have been the end if the other thing hadn't happened.'

'What other thing?'

'About four weeks after that night when I brought him home, someone broke into my flat and raped me. The first I knew about it was when I woke up, bruised and in pain. I felt sick, like I had the flu. I couldn't think straight. Then I saw that my door lock had been broken.'

'You went to the police?'

'No. Me and the police, let's just say that my experience with them hasn't been good. To say the least. But I did go to a sexual health clinic. They tested me for the usual VDs, and I got the morning-after pill. They asked if I could have had my drink spiked, but I hadn't even been out that night.'

'My God, that's terrible.'

'I was so angry. You see, I knew that it had to be him, Brix.'

'But if you were out of it, how can you be sure?'

'Because I'd just moved into the sublet. I'd rented it from a friend who was going travelling. And I hadn't told anyone else that I was living there. As you can appreciate, I'm extremely careful, given that I spend my life hacking into stuff and not everyone loves me for that. I thought I'd be safe with Brix. I mean with him being a famous author, what could possibly happen?'

'He was the only person who knew where you lived. But what if it was just a random attack?'

'How would they know I was living in the flat by myself?'

'They could have been watching you.'

'Not without me knowing. Experience has taught me to be hyper-vigilant.'

'So you're saying Brix returned to rape you?'

'I believe he did.'

'But you have no proof, and you didn't go to the police.'

'No. I wanted to make him confess. I know, stupid plan. Look at him now, you'd think he was some sort of martyr.'

'So you ramped things up a notch.'

'I couldn't let him get away with it. I saw you walking past his house with Ea and followed you home. The rest you know.'

Jensen felt hurt again to have been duped, not just for being lied to, but because she'd yearned so badly for a friend. Elise had understood this and used it to her advantage. 'How did you give yourself that black eye?'

'With a hammer. I knew you wouldn't be convinced unless I'd been seriously injured. It hurt like hell.'

'OK, enough,' said Jensen. There was no point in going over every little detail. 'A week ago when you knocked on my door in the middle of the night, pretending to have been beaten up by your boyfriend, you had scratches on your arms and hands. It was the night Vivian Sejer was killed in her Airbnb. Did you kill her?'

'No,' said Elise looking her straight in the eye. 'That's why I was glad you came, so I can tell you what really happened.'

'Go on?'

'I did write to Vivian Sejer pretending to be Brix. I

initially wanted to embarrass him. To show him that I could mess with his life any way I wanted.'

'How did you even know that he'd had an affair with her?'

'I was in his house a few times. I went through his laptop and phone. She was the affair after me, and he'd said all the same things to her. It made me sick.'

'You broke the law.'

'Yes, and I will take my punishment, but not for things I haven't done,' said Elise. 'Anyway, I decided to talk to Vivian, warn her, you know. So I went to the Airbnb. It didn't go well. I told her that it was me who'd invited her to Copenhagen and that Brix didn't know anything about it. This must have frightened her. Perhaps she didn't want to know, or she thought I was mad.'

'The two of you had a fight?'

'No, she slammed the door in my face. I stayed outside on the stairs, talked to her through the letterbox, but she wouldn't listen. She said she'd call the police if I didn't go away. So I went back down the stairs. That's when I saw this . . . this weird man.'

'What do you mean?'

'He was wearing a hi-vis vest and a hard hat. He was kneeling, unscrewing a wall socket in the entranceway. I rushed past him, not wanting to be recognised, though I was in disguise. But then I thought, it's the middle of the night, what's he doing fixing the electrics? So I turned back from the door and that's when he went for me. He just kept striking me, but I defended myself and somehow I managed to get back to the door and open it and get out.'

'Did you see his face?'

'No. It all happened so quickly, and I believe he was wearing a mask. It must have been Brix, though. If I hadn't made it out, he would have killed me, I'm sure of it.' She shook her head. 'I couldn't go back, he'd only come after me, so I went to yours. It seemed like the best place to hide with a person he was obviously close to.'

'You could have just left. You didn't have to take Ea with you. Was it you who wrote him that message, saying that you had his child?'

'Yes, but I wasn't going to do anything to her.'

'You took her away from me.'

'Because something happened. In your courtyard, I saw this guy in hi-vis snooping around. I thought Brix had found me.'

'I was with him at the time. He was being arrested,' said Jensen, trying and failing to grasp the fleeting thought that had popped up in her mind at the memory of that day.

'I didn't know that. I panicked. I couldn't leave Ea behind, so I grabbed her, and ran downstairs. We spent the day hiding. I fed her, changed her, made sure she was comfortable. Later I saw that Brix was being questioned by the police. I knew I couldn't go back to your place, so I did . . . what I did.'

'You left my daughter on the ground in a deserted park at night.'

'I waited until I saw that woman pick her up.'

'She could have been anybody.'

'I hung around long enough to see the police arrive.'

Elise had an answer for everything. But she'd lied before, extremely convincingly.

'How do I know you're not making all this up?' Jensen said.

'You don't. But I can tell that you have doubts.'

'About you, yes.'

'You wouldn't be here if you really thought I'd killed that

woman. And don't you find it odd that Brix didn't report me to the police until he absolutely had to?'

Elise was right, it was odd. Brix's reluctance to come forward had been counterproductive, to say the least. And something about her story had struck a chord, though Jensen couldn't put her finger on it.

'Even if I were to believe you, what do you expect me to do about it?' she said. 'My advice to you is to turn yourself in. Come clean about everything. The police are not the enemy.'

'You wouldn't say that if you'd seen what I have,' said Elise.

'Meaning?'

'Let's keep that for another time. I like you. I hope this isn't the last time we meet.'

Jensen didn't know about that. It was unlikely that she'd ever be able to trust Elise again.

She didn't know what kind of experience with the police Elise had alluded to, but if she'd only come clean from the beginning – if she'd not made all sorts of assumptions – then they could both have avoided a lot of pain.

As if she could read her thoughts, Elise lowered her head. 'Please just pass on what I've told you to the police, in whatever way you think best. Brix is pretending to be the victim, but there's another side to the story. Don't people deserve to know it?'

Jensen had heard enough. She would need to speak to Henrik, without dropping Liron in it. Hopefully, he'd be interested enough to ignore the fact that she'd met with a person who was at the centre of a nationwide manhunt.

'We're done here,' she shouted to Liron and whatever friend of Elise's was out there listening.

68

'Jensen, meet Detective Sergeant Sarah Funder. Funder, this is Jensen, *Dagbladet*'s chief crime reporter,' said Henrik, feeling as awkward as he ever had.

They were in his hotel room on the outskirts of Copenhagen, metres from his poorly made bed (he'd hung the do-not-disturb sign on the door), and he was introducing the woman he'd loved illicitly for many years to a colleague as though they were at some formal cocktail party.

But when Jensen had texted him, asking for a meeting, the hotel was the only place he'd been able to think of.

'I know you,' said Funder, pushing him to one side as she shook Jensen's hand. 'I saw you at Brix's house when we arrested him. I'm a big fan of your work.'

The two women were of about the same height and smiling at each other. 'That's very kind,' said Jensen. 'Though I'm actually still on maternity leave. That article I wrote the other day—'

'Which was epic by the way.'

'Thank you, but it was a one-off.'

'Enough of the mutual admiration society,' said Henrik. 'Can we get down to what you wanted to tell me?'

'Come in,' said Funder, pulling Jensen inside and making her sit down on the chair, while she sat on the bed next to Henrik. 'Coffee?' she said, pointing to the machine on the desk. 'We've at least two pouches left, though I'm afraid they're decaf.'

Henrik sighed. He could have predicted that Funder and Jensen would get on. As long as they were on the same side. God forbid they should ever quarrel.

'What's that?' said Jensen, pointing at the mess Funder had made of the wall between his bed and the window.

Using large paper sheets from a flip chart, along with pins and Sellotape, she'd transferred the photos of the eleven Polaris victims and recreated the display she'd made in the incident room at Teglholmen. Underneath she'd added the photos of Mia Steen, Jane Dahl-Thomsen and Vivian Sejer.

Funder looked at Henrik as if to ask for permission, which he grudgingly gave her. Jensen had seen it now; there was no going back.

'These eleven women were all raped, across more than three decades. The attacks were brutal, despite the fact that the women were drugged and therefore defenceless. In none of the cases was there any evidence, except one case where they got some partial DNA. However, the sample was poor, and no match was found,' said Funder. She pointed to the pictures of two women that she'd circled in red. 'Now these two women have something in common. They both had an affair with Brix.'

'I recognise their names,' said Jensen.

'How?' said Henrik. This was news to him.

'Brix gave me this list of women he'd bedded. I asked for

it as I thought it might help me find whoever was stalking him. The irony is that I'd already found her, of course. Or rather, she'd found me.'

'Can I have that list?' said Funder.

'He couldn't remember very many names. And he asked me to delete it.'

'I hope you didn't,' said Funder.

Jensen replied by pulling a memory stick from her bag. Excitedly, Funder plugged it into her laptop and opened the file. 'Let's see now. OK, that's one, two . . . no, three more of the women that he definitely slept with.'

'There's one more,' said Jensen.

Henrik and Funder both stared at her.

'My mother, Marion, told me that she was raped too, back in 1987. She doesn't remember how it happened. She'd been out drinking and the next morning she woke up in her bed with horrible injuries. It was only later she discovered that I was on the way.'

The room had fallen completely silent.

So this was what Marion hadn't wanted to discuss with him. 'But Brix isn't your father. You have proof of that now,' said Henrik.

'I know.'

'I'm very sorry to hear that,' said Funder, laying a hand on Jensen's shoulder. 'That must have been a horrible experience for your mother. But . . .'

'But?'

'I suppose we can't rule out that it could still have been Brix who raped her.'

'Who's my father then?'

'Someone else she'd met before maybe. Did you ask her if there were others?'

'I think she would have told me.'

Henrik could see Jensen's mind going into overdrive. 'Maybe it's a crazy coincidence,' he said. 'An unrelated case.'

Funder crossed over to the wall and circled three more portraits, adding 'Marion Jensen' followed by a question mark to the board, next to the Polaris eleven. 'So if we add Mia, Jane and Vivian, that's a total of nine women Brix has known who've been raped, murdered or both.'

'Hang on,' said Jensen. 'I don't think Jane is on Brix's list. Did he have an affair with her too?'

Henrik exchanged a glance with Funder. She consulted the laptop and pointed to the screen. 'She's here, but not by name, just "Woman in Aarhus".'

Jensen looked shocked. 'Jesus.'

'Yeah,' said Funder. 'In any case, I think we've gone beyond a coincidence.'

'I think you're right,' said Jensen.

Henrik cleared his throat. 'Before you both get carried away, may I remind you of what you said a moment ago, Funder. There was no evidence in any of the eleven Polaris cases and, so far, none in the more recent three cases connected to Brix. Jensen, why don't you tell us why you're here?'

'Before I do, can I ask for immunity?'

He stared at her. The situation was moving beyond bad. Had Jensen broken the law as well? 'What have you done?'

'Promise me I won't get into trouble.'

'I can't. If you have something to say, you just have to take the risk. Not normally a challenge for you.'

Funder was looking at them like a spectator at a tennis match. She was smiling. It was obvious that she had worked out his conflict of interest, the very last thing he needed. 'Are you two . . .?' she said.

'No,' said Jensen and Henrik in unison.

‘Forget I said anything,’ said Funder, holding up her hands.

‘I met Elise Berg,’ said Jensen.

‘What?’ said Henrik. ‘You met the most wanted woman in Denmark? Where is she?’

‘I don’t know,’ Jensen said. ‘We were brought together. I was blindfolded on the journey, so I couldn’t tell you where it was.’

‘This gets better and better,’ said Henrik under his breath. ‘Who blindfolded you?’

‘I . . . can’t tell you that. Do you want to know what she said or what?’

‘We do,’ said Funder. ‘Carry on.’

‘She believes that Brix raped her. They had an affair. The third time they met, she took him back to a flat she’s been staying at in Emdrup.’

‘We know the place,’ said Henrik. ‘We searched it. It’s like a shrine to Brix.’

‘Well afterwards he blanked her. Then four weeks later, she said she was drugged and raped while she slept in her own bed. Brix was the only person who knew that she was living in the flat.’

Funder folded her hands as if in prayer. ‘Please tell me she reported it.’

Jensen shook her head. ‘That’s the whole point. She doesn’t trust the police. That’s why she stalked Brix instead of telling you.’

Funder went back to the wall and wrote ‘Elise Berg’ with a question mark. ‘That takes it up to ten victims with links to Brix.’

Henrik held up his hands. ‘Wait,’ he said. ‘Elise Berg lied. We have evidence that she was in Vivian Sejer’s flat.’

‘Must have been planted,’ said Jensen. ‘Elise admits that

she wrote to Vivian, even that she went to the Airbnb. She said she tried to warn Vivian about Brix, but left when Vivian refused to let her in. On her way out she saw a man in the stairwell. At first she walked past him, but then she turned to confront him and that's when he hit her. She thinks that might have been Brix on the way in.'

'She didn't see his face?' said Funder.

'No. She says he was wearing some kind of mask.'

Henrik couldn't believe that Jensen had been taken in a second time. 'It wasn't me, officer, it was this mystery guy in a black mask.' Just how stupid did Elise Berg think they were? 'She lied to you again,' he said.

'You can't prove it didn't happen that way,' said Funder.

'Nor that it did,' said Henrik. 'We're no further on than we were.'

'It was really strange,' said Jensen. 'The man Elise saw wore a hi-vis vest and a hard hat. He was pretending to fix a socket, which she thought was odd, given how late it was at the time.'

Henrik's palms began to tingle. Funder looked at him. 'Hi-vis. Now do you think Elise lied?'

'What's going on?' Jensen said.

'Some of the Polaris victims reported seeing someone in hi-vis prior to their attack,' said Funder.

'Then it's got to be the same man. It could have been Brix,' said Jensen.

She was right, Henrik thought, but it wasn't exactly evidence. They needed more if they were going to persuade Liv to listen.

'What do we do now?' said Funder.

Jensen looked animated all of a sudden. 'I have an idea. Elise said that Andreas Lund was having dinner with Brix on the night they met. What does he know about Brix's relationship with her? And all the other women? Perhaps he's seen or overheard something without appreciating its significance?'

'Almost certainly,' said Funder.

'So what if I spoke to him?'

'Ah, I don't know,' Henrik said. 'It should be done officially, by us. Besides, Brix is Lund's meal ticket. He's hardly going to grass him up.'

'Inadvertently he might,' said Jensen. 'I'll probably get more out of him than you. After all, he knew my mother. I'll record the conversation, so you can listen to it afterwards.'

'He should still be staying at D'Angleterre, though I believe he's due to move back to the apartment shortly,' said Funder. She turned to Henrik. 'If he does tell Jensen something, then we can use that to try to persuade Liv to change her mind. Meanwhile, you and I can go over everything again, make sure there's nothing we've missed?'

Henrik looked past her at the motorway where the Saturday traffic was moving sluggishly. Mikkel, his eldest, would be at football practice, and his two youngest, Karla and Oliver, at swimming – only a few kilometres away but it felt like another universe.

Ten days ago, he'd welcomed the chance to do better. Instead he'd managed to land in the biggest mess ever.

'Go on then,' he said.

Things couldn't get any worse, could they?

Day Eleven

69

Jensen hesitated in front of the opulent pink and purple flower arrangement towering over her in the gilded dome lobby of Hotel D'Angleterre. Already, she felt the eyes of the security guard on her back.

She was wearing her smartest clothes, a silky blue dress with a short black jacket, but her old trainers and shoulder bag gave her away as someone who couldn't afford to be there.

The champagne bar around the back of the hotel was a favourite haunt of her friend, the politician Esben Nørregaard, but no one questioned you when you were with Esben, who behaved as if he owned the place.

Thankfully, she saw a hand waving at her from the lobby bar. Andreas Lund was early. If someone had asked her to conjure up the image of a literary agent, he would be it. He was shorter and less charismatic than Brix, interesting-looking but not enough to steal his client's thunder. Dressed in khaki chinos, a white shirt and brown-leather sailing shoes, he stood up and shook her hand as she entered. 'Jensen, I've heard so much about you,' he said.

Lund had responded quickly when she'd asked to meet him, suggesting coffee at his hotel on Sunday morning. She'd told him that she needed closure following the dramatic events of the past few days, and that Brix was pre-occupied with the ongoing search for the stalker.

She'd spent last night reading up on him from the press cuttings in the old filing cabinet in her office, though there were hardly any compared to the thick file on Brix.

A waiter came over, and Lund ordered coffee and ice water for them both. 'I'm glad you wanted to meet,' he said. 'I'd like to thank you for everything you've done for Valde, despite . . . well, now we know that . . .'

'He's not my father?' she said.

'Yes. He was so excited to think that he was. Especially to have a granddaughter. He had always assumed that he was the love of Marion's life. I must say, your mother rather took us both by surprise there.'

Jensen stayed quiet. Lund was saying things that it would have been nice to hear from Brix himself. She guessed that Lund had spoken so often on his client's behalf that he regarded them as one unit.

'I should also tell you how genuinely mortified he was that you got caught up in the business with the stalker. We simply had no idea that woman had befriended you.'

'Elise Berg.'

'Yes,' said Lund. 'It's such a relief that they know who she is. Now they just need to find her.'

Something about Lund made it hard for her to take her eyes off him. She wondered if they'd met before. Perhaps she'd seen him in the background in the many videos she'd watched of Brix.

'Anyway, I'm glad your daughter is safe,' he said. 'Where is she now?'

'My mother's looking after her.'

'Ah yes, Marion. You have her eyes, but I'm sure you know that. I haven't seen her since that time all those years ago.'

'When Mia Steen was killed and someone put her behind the wall in your apartment,' she said.

Lund fell silent as the waiter arrived with a tray and got busy arranging cups and glasses on the table between them. When he spoke again, he had lowered his voice though the American couple on the table next to them were locked in an absorbing conversation of their own. 'It's such a terrible tragedy, I'm still struggling to believe it. I'm actually moving back in today to begin to clear up the mess. Mia's remains have gone, of course, but I'm still not sure how I feel about living there now.'

'You knew her.'

'We all did. She was a wonderful young woman, hard-working and interested in everything.'

'Interested in Brix, it seemed.'

'So I gather. I didn't know that the two of them had been together, but I suppose I shouldn't be surprised,' said Andreas. 'You'll know from what Valde has shared with you in confidence that he's fond of women. Mia was pregnant with his child when she was murdered. Did you know that?'

Jensen was astonished. No one had told her, and it hadn't been in the papers. Had Brix known all along?

'Valde was shocked, absolutely devastated when the police told him,' said Lund. 'You know, sometimes I wonder if your mother had an inkling there was going to be a baby, even back then. She was furious with him when she left, raging. Of course, now we know why.'

'Did you tell the police that?'

'Didn't want to cast aspersions, so I just said that the

two of them broke up. She was always very intense, your mother. Brix is the same. I guess that's artistic temperament for you.'

Jensen frowned. 'Surely, you don't find it odd that she was upset? Given the man she loved had slept with someone else?'

'Not at all,' said Lund, sipping from his coffee. 'I can well understand if she was very angry. Maybe she . . . no, she can't have.'

'Maybe she killed Mia. Is that what you were about to say? I refuse to believe that. I mean, it wasn't Mia's fault that Brix couldn't keep his hands to himself. Why take it out on her?'

'Absolutely right,' said Lund. 'Mia was devout. She wouldn't have flaunted herself in any way. Valde could, and still can, talk the pants off a saint. Well, you've seen his list.'

'I have,' said Jensen.

'And destroyed it, I hope.'

She shrugged. 'He asked me to.' She poured milk into her coffee and drank. It was lukewarm. 'Brix was infatuated with Mia and Jane and Vivian. And many others besides.'

'You're right. He loves being in love.'

'You make it sound so innocent. I wonder if it is,' Jensen said.

'What do you mean?'

'I believe you were there on the night that he met Elise Berg?'

'Was I? I don't recall.'

'Yes. I think Brix told me that,' she said, blushing now. Lund could not find out that she had met Elise, and that she was working with the police.

'If I'd seen what was going on, I would have reminded him discreetly that he's married.'

'You don't approve of his affairs?'

Lund shook his head. 'No. But Valde is an adult. I can't stop him doing what he wants. Just gives me more work, that's all. It's a headache.'

'How so?'

'Keeping stories out of the press, dealing with the women when he doesn't call them back. I'd rather he left off, to be honest.'

'How well do you know him?'

'Extremely well. I don't think you'll find anyone who knows him better.'

'In your view, is he capable of rape and murder?'

Lund put his coffee cup down and sat up straight. 'Jensen, that's some accusation.'

'You made one yourself when you suggested that my mother could be culpable.'

'I know, but Valde, I mean come on . . .'

'Did you ever see him angry or violent?'

'Many times. Like I said, he has that artistic temperament, which he shares with your mother. But I never saw him physically hurt anyone.' He paused. 'I mean there was this one allegation against him when we were in high school, but it was later dropped.'

'An allegation?'

'A girl said he'd forced her to have sex with him in the school toilets during a ball.'

'She alleged he raped her?'

'Well, yes, but I think everyone found it a bit hard to believe. I mean Valde didn't usually have to force women if you know what I mean. They tended to throw themselves at his feet. Anyway, there was this big brouhaha. His and the girl's parents were called into the headmaster's office, but then it all went away again.'

Now they were getting somewhere, Jensen thought. If the school still had a record of the incident, it might be useful for Henrik and Funder.

She guessed that these days Brix had Lund to make stuff go away. He'd said himself that he spent a lot of his time keeping stories out of the press. Had he been covering for Brix?

He smiled at her. 'I hope I haven't given you the wrong idea about Valde. I wouldn't want you to use that tale from more than forty years ago against him. Anyway, we now know that it was Elise Berg who killed Vivian Sejer. To think that she'd do such a thing, just to set up a man who'd turned her down.'

'I agree,' said Jensen. 'I find it unbelievable too. But then she hasn't been convicted, and besides, there's still a question mark over who killed Mia Steen, not to mention who raped Jane Dahl-Thomsen.'

And the rest, she thought.

The bar was filling up and getting louder. She wondered how much of their conversation had been picked up by her mobile phone. She was going to take the recording back to Henrik and Funder in the hotel room. Then it would be up to them to see what they could do with it.

The past half-hour hadn't exactly persuaded her of Brix's innocence. She got up. 'I'd better get back to my daughter.'

'Of course. I hope this was helpful in some way?'

'Oh yes,' she said. 'Very.'

He shook her hand again, smiled. 'Do remember me to Marion.'

Day Twelve

70

'Henrik and Sarah, what are you doing here?' Liv said. She was standing behind Mark, pointing at something on his screen. 'You're not due back until tomorrow.'

There was a despondent mood in the office, and not just because it was a Sunday and only a handful of people were in. Elise Berg remained at large and, judging by the look on everyone's face, no imminent breakthrough was on the cards. Mark looked wrecked; there were three empty bottles of Coke on his desk, along with a blister pack of paracetamol and empty sweet wrappers.

'Can we have a word?' Henrik said to Liv. He glanced at Mark. 'In private.'

They followed Liv into her room, and she shut the door behind them. You couldn't tell from the way she was dressed – in a pink shirt, smart trousers and high-heeled boots – that it was the weekend. In contrast to Chief Superintendent Monsen, who never worked a minute longer than he needed to, Liv was always in. She couldn't have much of a private life with those hours, Henrik thought.

He and Funder took a seat at the small meeting table, but Liv remained standing. 'What is it?' she said, clearly irritated at having her day interrupted, but nevertheless maintaining a professional tone.

Henrik thought back to his former boss's frequent angry outbursts, grateful that the unit finally had a grown-up at the helm. 'Remember Sarah's project? Operation Polaris? You should have the report in your inbox.'

'I remember,' said Liv. 'But I haven't got around to reading it yet. Is that what this is about? If so, you two really could have picked a better time.'

'May I?' said Funder. 'Henrik will have covered the bases when he briefed you, so I'll skip to the pertinent points. As you know, we've linked Brix to Mia Steen, Jane Dahl-Thomsen and Vivian Sejer. These three cases all have certain features in common with Polaris. So I went back through the files, and I've discovered that at least five of the Polaris victims also knew Brix personally: as in, they'd been in a relationship with him before they were assaulted.'

Now Liv was looking interested.

'Brix also slept with Elise Berg, and we know that she threatened to report him for rape,' said Henrik.

'Yes, a rape we believe she set up in order to frame him for it,' said Liv.

'But maybe we got that wrong,' said Henrik. 'Andreas Lund has remembered something of potential importance, which he'd forgotten to tell us about.'

'Which is?'

'According to Lund, who went to high school with Brix, he was accused of raping a fellow student back then,' said Henrik. 'We won't be able to confirm this with the school until tomorrow, but we can do that first thing.'

'Was it a police matter?'

'No. It got dropped before it reached that stage,' said Funder.

'In that case, do you really think there'll still be a record of it?'

'We don't see why there wouldn't be. And we should be able to get it in time for Brix's custody hearing,' said Funder.

'I really think we need to haul Brix in again,' said Henrik. 'We need to put him under pressure. Meanwhile we should search his house more thoroughly. Especially in light of what Sarah has discovered about his links to the Polaris victims. It's been my impression all along that he's hiding something, and it wouldn't surprise me if his agent has been covering for him. The man has as much to lose as Brix if his career goes down the toilet.'

'You said that Lund had forgotten to tell us about the rape allegation. So how did you find out?'

Henrik exchanged a quick glance with Funder before replying. 'Jensen, the *Dagbladet* journalist, interviewed him this morning and sent us the recording. You can listen to it if you like,' said Funder, deftly avoiding any reference to the fact that the three of them had conspired in Henrik's messy hotel room.

At the mention of Jensen, Liv sent Henrik a sharp glance. He returned it with a shrug. He hadn't formally admitted to them being in a relationship, and he wasn't going to do so now. In any case, Liv wouldn't be reinstating him as investigations leader, and, as the conflict of interest was real, nor would he want her to.

Lotte Nielsen was in charge now.

As if on cue, Lotte burst into the room, looking suspiciously at the three of them. 'What's going on here?'

'You'd better take a seat. Henrik and Funder have

something to tell you,' Liv said. 'I really hope I'm not going to regret this.'

Brix had been brought in. He was furious. His wife and son had been taken to a local police station until an arrangement could be made for them. With Elise Berg still on the loose, no one was willing to take chances with their safety.

Lotte and Funder had gone with the team to search Brix's house in the Potato Rows. Henrik was back in the office with Liv, praying for a jackpot against the odds.

Last time Brix had been arrested, they'd gone through his devices without finding anything, aside from the email exchange with Vivian Sejer, which had since been called into question.

The hope was that somewhere inside the house there would be something, anything, to link Brix to the crime scenes: clothing, a letter, a receipt, a trophy or memento, whatever.

It was, as Brøgger had been quick to point out, a fishing expedition. They were, in essence, looking for something that they wouldn't necessarily recognise when they saw it.

Now, they were over four hours into the search, and still nothing. Henrik was watching proceedings on Funder's camera. He could tell that she was getting tired after trawling through Brix's office, including his dozens of meticulously organised notebooks.

'I think we're getting to the point where we have to acknowledge that there's nothing in the surface layer of the house,' said Funder.

He sensed her wavering. After all, she only had her instinct on Brix to go by. A deeper search of the house would involve splitting cushions and taking apart wall panels. It would take days they didn't have.

Once Henrik had found the components of a gun hidden in a U-bend in a dirty toilet.

Mia Steen had been hidden behind a brick wall, so well that it had taken nearly forty years for her body to be discovered.

It didn't make sense for them to have to go to such extremes in Brix's house, not yet.

If the author had hidden anything, it would have been from his wife. Where could he have concealed something to make her extremely unlikely to find it?

Louise never went in their attic, a freezing, dusty dump of old baby stuff, match programmes and discarded bits and bobs that she was always on at him to go through.

'Is there a loft space?' he said to Funder.

'Let me see.' He waited as she moved up the stairs to the top floor. She cursed as she yanked open the blinds. 'Can't see a bloody thing up here.'

Sunlight flooded in through Velux windows cut into the sloping ceiling. The room was bare, aside from a small double bed and a bedside table with a lamp.

'A guest bedroom, by the looks of things, and there's a loo and a small shower,' she said, opening the door to a tiny windowless bathroom. 'There's got to be more though. This can't be the entire attic space.'

The camera panned across the wall opposite the windows. 'What's that low door?' said Henrik.

'Looks like some sort of cupboard,' said Funder. 'Wait.' She opened the door and got on her knees. 'It's a storage space.' She turned on her torch and pointed it into the long narrow room: old suitcases, a set of golf clubs, cardboard boxes, a foot for a Christmas tree. 'I'm going in,' she said and began to move forward, ducking her head.

If Funder, who was tiny, had to duck, then Brix would

have to crawl to get in and out of the space. Most of the stuff in there looked ancient. He noticed a cardboard box with 'Mum and Dad' written on it.

'It's more organised than it first looked,' said Funder. 'Everything is stacked up neatly so you can pass through the middle. I think I'm at the end now. I suppose we'll have to empty it all out and have a good look?'

'Go back a little,' said Henrik. 'What was that just there?'

'Just an old vacuum cleaner,' she said.

'Why keep it in there?'

'Maybe it's broken?'

'Open it.'

'What?'

'My parents had one of those. Unclasp it and lift the top off as if you were emptying the bag.'

'What the hell?' said Funder, shining her torch inside. 'There's a plastic bag in here. It's . . . it looks like . . .'

Henrik could already see the yellow and orange colours, and the light-reflecting grey bands that ran across the hi-vis vest. Funder had also pulled some black clothing from the bag.

The camera images went shaky as Funder retraced her steps out of the storage space and began to shout for Lotte. She ran down the stairs, at one point almost stumbling over her own feet. 'I found something,' she shouted. 'A disguise. It was hidden inside an old vacuum cleaner in the attic.'

Lotte was under the stairs, in a small cloakroom where she'd removed a shelf above the concealed cistern. 'I found something too.' She held out her hand, revealing a slim, rectangular silver box in her palm. 'This, I believe, is a hard drive.'

*

The wait was unbearable. Henrik had been out three times for coffee and had now taken to biting his nails. He, Funder, Lotte, Liv and Bagger were all crowded around Fie Pedersen's screen.

It had taken Fie a while to deal with the encryption, but she'd told them it wouldn't be long now.

Bagger was looking at her with an almost fatherly pride. He wasn't easily impressed, but Fie's ability to navigate the digital universe was clearly leaving him awe-struck. Understanding almost nothing of these things, Henrik was equally amazed. Especially that someone as timid in real life as Fie could be so bold armed with a mouse and a keyboard.

'I'm in,' she said. 'Looks like we have a large number of video files.'

Everyone leaned in closer.

'They seem to be ordered by letters. Some sort of code?'

'That's not a code,' said Funder. 'Those are initials. Try that one,' she said, pointing to a file named AB.

Fie opened the file and hit play.

Everyone took a step back.

Liv covered her mouth. 'Bloody hell.'

'That's Agnes Beck,' said Funder.

The video was of poor quality, but the woman was clearly recognisable from her photo, lying naked on a bed, bleeding from her nose. She was sobbing and pleading in an incoherent and slurred voice, holding up a hand towards the camera.

It was horrific. Henrik felt an overwhelming urge to reach into the picture and stop what was happening.

'Wasn't this the case where some DNA was identified that was thought to have come from the perpetrator?' he said.

Funder nodded. 'A spot of blood. We'll check if it came from Brix.'

'I think we've seen enough,' Henrik said. 'Go back to the files again.'

There were nineteen in total. Nineteen initials. Nineteen victims. His eyes ran over them. 'There's no MS, no Mia Steen,' he said.

'Like I said before, perhaps she was the first. The one it all began with,' said Funder. 'Maybe if we understand what happened to her, we'll understand the others. A Rosetta stone, if you like. He got Mia pregnant, that's significant; she was different from the others.'

Henrik wasn't sure he wanted to understand. To his horror, he saw a file named MJ for Marion Jensen. Jensen had told them that her mother believed she'd been raped; the video confirmed it.

'Open the one that says JDT,' he said.

The video of Jane Dahl-Thomsen was even worse than the one of Agnes Beck. You could just about make out her pale, confused face in the poor light between the bushes and shrubs in Frederiksberg Gardens.

This time Fie stopped the video without being asked. Lotte, Funder and Liv looked horrified.

Only Bagger, a man who'd seen some of the worst things human beings could do to each other, had retained his composure. 'Judging by those clips, he never filmed himself with the victims,' he said. 'Recording their faces and their suffering seemed to have been more important. I wonder why.'

'We haven't seen very much yet,' said Liv. 'He could be in there somewhere.'

Henrik thought of the poor sod who now had to watch and catalogue it all. He hoped it wouldn't be Fie, who had turned white as a sheet.

'We'll go through everything methodically, of course,' said Bagger.

'Those videos are souvenirs,' said Funder. 'A record of sorts. Notches on a bedpost.'

'It's very strange,' said Bagger.

'Seems Elise Berg was telling the truth,' said Fie. Everyone turned to look at her. Henrik remembered Fie telling them that she knew Berg from the hacker community. She double-clicked on the file named EB.

They didn't have to watch for long to see that it was her. 'My God. She was telling the truth. He raped her,' said Funder.

'If only she'd come to us,' said Liv.

Funder shook her head. 'Without evidence, we wouldn't have been able to do very much.'

There was a look of grim determination on Liv's face. 'Well, we have evidence now. Lotte, you'll take the interview with Brix. I want to watch.'

Day Thirteen

71

Jensen was at home with her mother watching the late evening news. Sitting side by side with mugs of tea and a plate of cookies felt so good that she had to remind herself how unusual it was: Marion in Copenhagen, the two of them close.

Even Wolfgang, the cat, appeared to like it. After days of hiding, he was now rubbing his head and body against Marion's leg.

Jensen reached out and took her mother's hand, ran her fingers over her hard silver rings. 'We can turn the TV off if it's too much?' she said, conscious that Brix's face was filling the screen.

Her mother shook her head. 'No. I'm delighted he's been arrested again. It must mean they've found something. I hope that what I told them about his character helped in some small way.'

All day it had been almost impossible to open a news channel without seeing Brix's face. Most of the outlets were using the same clip of him taken at a red-carpet event: wearing a dinner jacket, he had his hand on Astrid's backless silk dress in a gesture coming across as lecherous in the context.

Jensen suspected the coverage would go on for weeks. It wasn't every day that a famous author was remanded in custody, suspected of having raped multiple women.

It was far from over yet. Henrik had told her, in strictest confidence, that the police were working through a vast number of distressing videos of the victims found at Brix's house. However, none of the videos connected Brix to the murder of Mia Steen, which remained unsolved.

'I need to know: was there a video of my mother?'

'Yes,' he'd said solemnly. 'I'm so sorry, Jensen.'

She hadn't told her mother about this yet. It was too confusing. If it was Brix who had raped her, but not made her pregnant, then who had?

Jensen, feeling Marion's hand squeezing hers, sensed that her mother wasn't ready for that conversation.

After her shocking – yet somehow also expected – revelation four days ago, it was as though she'd become lighter and freer, and Jensen had even heard her laugh once or twice.

What a terrible burden the rape must have been for her to carry over the years, watching her daughter grow up, and all the time wondering what was in there of *him*, never able to forget how her life had been torn apart.

Marion had chosen to carry the burden alone, afraid that Jensen would feel unloved, but finally letting go had obviously been a relief. As far as Marion was concerned it seemed that was the end of the story.

'What are you going to do now?' Jensen said. 'Will you be going back to North Jutland?'

'Do you want me to?'

'No. I'd like you to live here with me and Ea, like a proper family. There's plenty of room for a studio.'

'I don't know, the light here is different, and the sky is smaller, although . . . maybe it's time to move on from the landscapes.'

Jensen knew that Marion had dozens of paintings in her cottage. They were everywhere, leaning against the walls in every room. No one was buying them any more. 'That sounds like a good idea. Maybe we could organise an exhibition?'

They watched the news for a bit longer, while Jensen checked her emails, wondering if Erik Lange had sent her the promised family tree yet. She'd been checking diligently, but today she'd been so absorbed by developments that she'd forgotten.

To her surprise, she saw that the email had arrived hours ago. She jumped up. 'Sorry,' she said to her mother. 'There's something I have to do in my office, back in a tic.'

The family tree was a colour-coded spreadsheet. At first it was overwhelming, but then she got a handle on it. There was one set of great-great-grandparents who'd had six children: four girls and two boys, followed by three further generations. Erik had left some of the family branches blank.

Following the line up from Erik's name, she saw that his father was Ove Lange, who'd had one sister, Kirsten Lange, who'd married a man named Axel Lund. Following the line down, she could see that Kirsten had given birth to a son in 1964.

The hairs on the back of her neck stood up when she saw the name.

Andreas Lund.

Next to Andreas, Erik had added Marion's name in red, and one line down, Jensen saw her own name followed by a question mark.

Trembling, she opened Erik's message. 'Could I be your uncle, rather than cousin?' he wrote. 'I'm not one hundred per cent sure, but I can't fit you in anywhere else. It's a headscratcher.' He'd added a sweaty-smiley emoji.

Jensen wasn't smiling.

She dialled Henrik's number. No reply. Dialled it again with the same result.

Then she ran into the living room. 'Marion,' she said. 'I need to ask you something. It's important.'

Marion looked wary. 'I don't like the sound of that,' she said.

'Please just answer,' said Jensen. 'Could Andreas Lund be my father?'

'Andreas?' she laughed a little, then abruptly stopped. 'What are you saying?'

'Did you sleep with him?'

'No, never.'

'Then could it have been him who raped you?'

'I'd long left his apartment when it happened. I don't think he even knew where I lived.'

'He could have found out. How hard would it have been? I mean, you had friends in common, didn't you?' Jensen said.

'But it's ridiculous,' said Marion. 'Brix's little whipping boy? He wasn't even into girls.'

'You said he liked Mia.'

'Mia, yes, he did like her. They used to talk after she'd finished cleaning. But that was very unusual in itself. I'd never seen him with any other woman, and he certainly never showed the remotest interest in me. I'd have rebuffed him if he had.'

'You were already taken,' said Jensen. 'But what if he really, really liked Mia and then Brix snatched her away from him? Maybe raping you was his revenge?'

'No, it's too weird,' said Marion.

We've long gone past weird, thought Jensen.

Maybe there was more than one Andreas Lund born around the time of Brix's agent. She didn't know if he'd been born in 1964 after all. Erik Lange could also have muddled up his charts in some way.

Henrik would say it could all still be a coincidence.

The only way to find out would be to ask Lund himself. She could just see him now, sitting in the bar at D'Angleterre, friendly and affable, saying that she had her mother's eyes. He'd seemed so familiar; she'd tried to work out why.

Suddenly, she felt angry. It couldn't wait.

'I need you to babysit for me,' she said.

'What, now?' said Marion.

'Right now.'

72

Henrik let himself into his house in Frederiksberg and dropped his keys in the bowl on the hallway table. The irony of this wasn't lost on him. His wife had tried for years to make him put the keys there. Now that she was gone, he did it automatically.

He was dog tired, and the familiar smells of the house made him yearn for his own bed. Eight nights he'd spent away from home. Eight nights Louise had spent away from him.

Now he was back. The investigations were far from over, but that was to be Lotte Nielsen's headache. He'd asked Liv for permission to take a few days off. Tomorrow morning he would thank Jytte and Knud, his in-laws, then politely ask them to pack their bags and go home; he would be taking it from here.

Running everything on his own would be a steep learning curve, but he was actually starting to look forward to it.

He'd removed his boots and was about to tiptoe upstairs to check on the kids, before turning in himself, when the door to the living room opened, casting a shaft of light into the hallway.

'Henrik, is that you?' said Jytte. She turned on the overhead lights, momentarily blinding him. 'You must be done in with everything that's happened. Valde Brix. Who'd have thought it?'

'It's been a tough few days for sure,' he said.

'Can I get you something to eat? There's plenty left over from dinner.'

'No thank you,' he said, still tasting the onions from the sub-par burgers and chips that had been brought into the office for everyone to help themselves.

'I was just reading my novel,' said Jytte. 'I couldn't bear watching the news. I'm afraid Knud has already gone to bed.'

Henrik was delighted to hear it. Knud was the last person he wanted to see. For all her kindness, small-talk with Jytte was trying enough after the day he'd had.

'Kids OK?' he said, though he already knew the answer from the updates Jytte had been kind enough to send him during the day.

'They're wonderful children,' Jytte said. 'Such a credit to you and Louise.'

Just Louise, he corrected her silently. Aside from genetics, and the family tradition of supporting Brøndby FC, his input had been severely limited. He was ashamed of this now and swore to put it right.

Starting tomorrow.

'Sorry,' he said, waving his phone at Jytte. 'There's something I need to . . .'

'Of course. Well, goodnight.'

He went through to the kitchen. It was spotless and smelled faintly of *frikadeller*, the Danish meatballs that were his youngest son's favourite.

God bless you, Jytte.

Scrolling through his phone as he poured himself a glass of water, he saw a few missed calls and a voicemail from Jensen.

But what interested him more was an email from the head teacher at the high school in Copenhagen that Brix had attended between the ages of fifteen and eighteen.

Henrik had spoken to the man first thing, and he'd promised to have a look through the archives, though he'd cautioned that there might not be anything to find.

Henrik had forgotten all about it till now.

His heart began to race as he read the first line: *Found something to my great surprise.*

One of the head teacher's predecessors had made a note of the incident, which was alleged to have occurred in the spring of 1982. A female third-year student had been found drunk, and with her clothing torn, in a disabled toilet after a school ball. A few days later, the girl's mother had made a formal complaint to the school accusing a classmate of forcing himself on her. However, the boy's parents had made such a passionate plea for their son that the girl's parents had eventually agreed to withdraw the allegation. The girl had subsequently been moved to a different class.

This seemed extremely unfair to Henrik. After all, it wasn't the girl who'd done anything wrong.

He read to the end of the email and stopped.

What?

The odd thing is that the incident was exactly as you described, but the boy in question wasn't Valdemar Brix, the head teacher wrote. *It was someone named Andreas Lund.*

My God.

Lund must have placed the hard drive and hi-vis clothing at Brix's house, sensing that time was up and deciding to sacrifice his cash cow. He'd probably held a spare set of keys to Brix's place, gaining access just after the author had been arrested.

Henrik should have known; they'd found the planted items all too easily.

Was that what Jensen had called him about? Had she worked it out? He was running back into the hallway, about to listen to her message when he saw a call coming in from Funder.

He thought she'd gone home like the rest of them. She sounded downbeat. 'The drop of blood in the Agnes Beck case, it wasn't from Brix.'

'I know,' he said, jumping on one foot, as he tried to put his boots back on while grabbing his keys from the bowl. 'It's Lund. Lund is Polaris. I don't have time to explain, just get to the apartment in Bredgade. I'll meet you there.'

73

Jensen locked her bike against the railing outside the art gallery next to Andreas Lund's building. It was late on a Monday night, and the traffic in Bredgade was reduced to buses and taxis.

The dome of the Marble Church loomed against the deep-blue sky, as gloomy and foreboding by night as it was majestic by day. The air was sharp and cold, and she shivered in her thin jacket as she walked out of the golden light from the gallery window and into the shadows.

Her anger had subsided a little on the ten-minute bike ride, yet her feet kept carrying her forward. She had to know the truth, and she was so close now.

Someone had left the door to the building wedged open with a piece of folded cardboard. She guessed there would be work going on to make good on the water damage.

Thanks to the video Gustav had shot for *Dagbladet*, she knew she was in the right place.

The stairwell smelled strongly of damp. On the second floor, some wall panels and sacks of plaster had been left on the landing, along with a pallet of bricks wrapped in plastic.

The higher she went, the less confident she felt. Andreas Lund was a respected literary agent, kind to everyone, according to her mother.

Why would he have sought Marion out weeks after she'd left his apartment? Even as an act of revenge against Brix for stealing Mia from him, it felt implausible.

Brix was the bastard. He was the rapist. Wasn't he?

On the top floor, the street noises had faded into the background. All she could hear was her own laboured breathing.

She realised that coming here had been a mistake. She'd been impulsive, taken off without thinking, after studying a complete stranger's stupid family tree for all of a couple of minutes. Even her mother had found the idea of Andreas raping her ludicrous.

But what if it wasn't? Suddenly she was aware how alone she was, in an empty building where no one would hear her scream. In the past, she would have forged ahead regardless, oblivious to the risk, but she was a mother now, and Ea depended on her.

She turned around, intending to head back down the stairs as quickly as she could, when her phone began to ring, startling her.

Henrik sounded like he was in the car. She could hear the sound of the engine revving over his anxious voice. 'I heard your message,' he shouted. 'You're right, it was Lund. It was all Lund.'

'What do you mean, it was all Lund?' she said, her voice sounding slow and strange in the empty stairwell.

'Polaris. Mia. Your mother. Everything,' Henrik said.

Of course.

Now it was coming back to her, the connection she'd failed to grasp a week ago. Lund had sounded breathless and strange on the phone when she'd called to tell him that Brix had been arrested. It had to have been him Elise had seen in the courtyard wearing hi-vis before she'd fled with Ea.

Elise had been right all along, only she'd suspected the wrong person.

'Don't go there Jensen. Don't go to the apartment,' Henrik shouted.

'Too late,' she said.

The door in front of her opened. Lund stood in the dark hallway, smiling. 'Too late for what?'

'Fuck!' Henrik slammed his hands on the steering wheel and floored the accelerator. The streets of Copenhagen roared past him in a blur.

Jensen had got herself into danger. Again. Because she couldn't leave things alone. One day, she wouldn't make it – he would arrive to find her dead, her tiny daughter virtually an orphan, seeing as her father would never be let out of prison.

Was that day this one?

The sound of Lund's voice in the background as he'd opened the door to her had chilled him to the bone.

He knew now why Lund had looked so familiar. Jensen might have her eyes from her mother, but she definitely had her mouth and gappy teeth from Lund.

Awkward and inexperienced with the opposite sex, a young man who had already shown violent tendencies, Lund had been desperately in love with Mia Steen. And Brix, the one all the women wanted, had taken her from him like sweets from a baby.

Henrik guessed that Lund had lured Mia back under some pretence, then murdered her and bricked her up inside the wall of his apartment as a reminder never to let himself be humiliated again. Then he'd gone after Brix's other conquests, picking the more serious ones off one by one, starting with Marion. It had made him feel powerful and in control.

In his egotistical quest to get at Brix, he'd left behind a string of entirely innocent victims; he'd shown nothing but contempt for women, regarding them as objects to do with as he wanted.

Henrik arrived in Bredgade with screeching brakes. Funder had got there just a few seconds before him and was already at the entrance, reaching for her gun.

'Back-up's coming,' she shouted, and Henrik could hear distant sirens as he followed her inside.

Then they both stopped, looking at the panel above the lift; it was ascending.

Someone else had got here before them.

74

Lund was strong. Jensen fought with everything she had, kicking and screaming as he dragged her down the corridor by her arms, but his sheer force and speed prevented her from getting back on her feet.

When finally he stopped, she saw that they were in a kitchen. She was looking into a wall with a gaping hole in it.

Mia Steen's grave, she guessed.

'I wasn't going to kill her, not at first. But then she told me about the baby. Of course, Valde didn't want it. He didn't even really love her.' Lund spat out the words. 'She woke up after I'd put her in there, but I just kept going. Brick after brick after brick, till I couldn't hear or see her any more.'

Jensen sat up slowly, rubbing her arms and trying to work out if anything was broken. Her ankles and coccyx were throbbing in agony. 'Why hurt Mia?' she said weakly. 'It wasn't her fault that Brix couldn't keep his hands to himself.'

The slap came out of nowhere. It knocked her to the ground, face first. Her nose began to bleed; the pain took her breath away.

'Shut up,' he screamed. 'Valde knew I liked her, but he just took what he wanted. He ruined everything.'

So Mia had to die because Lund was angry with Brix? Because she was his prize, and now Brix had spoiled it? Jensen pressed the sleeve of her jumper to her nose to stop the bleeding. There was a metallic taste in her mouth.

She had to keep Lund talking; it was her only hope of getting out of here.

'And the other women, what had they done that they deserved to be punished?' she said.

The kick to her stomach was hard and quick, winding her. 'I told you to shut up.' He kneeled down, pulled her hair back and shouted into her face. 'Valde would be nothing without me. What's his is mine.'

Of course, Lund would have had full access to Brix's emails and contacts as he dealt with much of his correspondence. Perhaps he'd even cloned Brix's phone.

He could have followed Elise and Brix to her flat, returning later to drug and attack her in her own bed.

For years, Lund had operated undisturbed, trusted by Brix and attacking the women in his wake. Until Elise had got in the way, pointing the finger at Brix and messing things up. But somehow Lund had tracked her down to Jensen's flat. That's why Elise had run off with Ea.

Jensen felt cold all over at the thought of what might have happened if she hadn't done that.

Her ribs ached when, slowly, she managed to get up on all fours, spitting blood. 'That was the police I was speaking to just now,' she stammered. 'They know everything. It's over.'

'Not yet it's not,' he said, yanking hard at her hair again. 'They don't have any proof.'

'They have me. I'm proof of what you did to Marion.'

'It'll be her word against mine.'

'They also have a drop of blood with your DNA.'

He looked thrown for a moment. Then scrunched his face up in rage as he reached for her.

'Don't hurt me,' she cried. 'Please don't. My baby's only five months old. I'm all she's got.'

She flattened herself to the ground, tried to crawl away on her belly, but already she could feel him pulling her back by her ankles. 'I told Valde not to get you involved, but he knew best. Of course, you were so useless, you couldn't even see what was right in front of your eyes. I had to find her myself.'

'But she got away from you,' she said, managing to twist onto her back. 'You've no idea where she is now.'

He leaned over her.

'I'm your daughter,' she shouted, as she felt his strong hands closing around her throat. 'Don't you even care?'

'You're nothing. I should have killed your mother while she was pregnant. I should have put her in that wall with Mia.'

She tried to pull his hands away, tried to wriggle, but he held her fast, and she knew this would be the end. All she could do was hope it came quickly.

Not all truths are worth knowing.

Her vision began to fade, a shadow slowly creeping upwards.

'Let her go!'

The voice was a roar.

Female.

Elise?

Through the encroaching darkness, Jensen saw Elise raise both hands in the air. She was holding a brick. Lund looked up in surprise, his grip on Jensen's throat loosening.

Then Elise brought the brick down and there was a sharp cracking sound as it connected with Andreas's skull.

Jensen felt his body landing heavily on top of her, a fountain of blood springing from his broken head as Elise raised the brick and brought it down on him a second time.

Again and again and again, she brought the brick down until what had been Lund's head was reduced to a crimson pulp, and Jensen was drenched in his blood and gasping for air.

All sound had disappeared when she saw Henrik and Funder come running into the kitchen. As if in slow motion, Funder wrapped her arms around Elise and pulled her away.

The last thing Jensen saw before her vision went completely was Henrik, leaning over her with his eyes full of terror.

August

75

The garden was a mess, but Henrik didn't care as he let himself flop onto the sun lounger in the tall, weedy grass, cold beer in hand.

At the start of the summer break, he'd longed for it to be over, but the sight of his three children bouncing on the trampoline made him nostalgic that it was coming to an end.

Not that it had been easy. In the early days after his in-laws had moved out, he'd been almost overwhelmed with the amount of work it took to keep three children fed, watered and clothed. The house had quickly descended into squalor, but somehow he'd muddled through.

The kids had taken advantage of his inexperience, bartering for takeaways and late bedtimes in exchange for doing chores.

Mikkel, the eldest, had questioned his right to call the shots. 'I hate you,' he'd shouted as he slammed the door to his bedroom, though eventually they'd called a truce.

Watching the boy now, forgetting that he was a cool teenager as he laughed on the trampoline with his younger siblings, made Henrik intensely happy.

Their school bags were inside, lined up in the hallway with new water bottles and pencil cases, ready for tomorrow.

Henrik knew he still had a lot of work to do to catch up as a parent. Trust took years to build and just a few ill-advised moments to destroy, he thought wistfully as he sipped from his beer.

Would his wife ever trust him again? At this point, he didn't even know if she would be coming back.

Mark Søndergreen had blown his trust when he shopped him to Liv for concealing a personal relationship with Jensen. It didn't matter who was in the wrong. You always closed ranks in a team. Mistrust was corrosive and, in their line of work, could lead to errors on a life-and-death scale.

Mark had been profusely apologetic, admitting that he'd been jealous of Funder, but the damage had been done. It was a few weeks now since he'd moved into Lotte's team.

Meanwhile Funder had been justifiably lauded for her tenacity on the Polaris investigation. Liv had now formally established a cold-case unit for sex crimes under Funder's supervision, though most of the work would be carried out by retired officers.

It had initially angered Funder that Lund had escaped justice and his victims been denied their day in court. Elise Berg was now facing a long sentence for manslaughter on top of everything else. Lund wasn't worth that, Funder thought, though Elise herself disagreed.

'I'm not sorry,' she'd said, over and over, as they'd led her away from the bloodied corpse.

Henrik couldn't say he was sorry either.

No one who had watched the videos of Lund's suffering victims would ever be able to forget. The survivors would have to live with the knowledge of what he had done; it would never be over for them.

According to Elise Berg, it was her clandestine meeting with Jensen that had made her realise who the real perpetrator was. She fled from Jensen's flat after seeing a man in hi-vis outside; it couldn't have been Brix, who'd been in the process of being arrested at the time. Lund knew all about Brix's affairs; he'd had both the means and the opportunity to find out where Elise lived.

At last Jensen now knew who her father was. 'I'm glad he's dead,' she told Henrik when he visited her in hospital.

'I'm glad you're not,' he said.

He'd thought she was, lying on the floor underneath Lund's body, covered in his blood.

He suspected it would take years for her to process what had happened. She was haunted by guilt that she only existed because of what Lund had done to Marion, she said.

He pointed out that actually she existed because her mother had wanted her despite what had happened. 'Like you wanted Ea.'

Jensen became pensive then, turning her bruised face towards the light from the window.

We could be together now, he thought, taking her hand.

As he looked at her, he imagined how it would be, living in her huge flat, his kids coming to stay every other week. Daydreaming in this way used to lift him, but now that a life with Jensen was within reach, it worried him.

Not all truths are worth knowing, she'd told him earlier. She'd been talking about Lund, but the phrase had taken on a wider meaning.

As if she could hear his thoughts, Jensen smiled at him. 'Sometimes I think you and I had a lucky escape,' she said.

'What?'

'I mean, can you really see us shopping in the Co-op together on a Saturday, arguing over whose turn it is to take the bins down?'

'Yeah, you'd be an absolute nightmare.' He laughed, but she didn't join in.

'Let's not find out,' she said, squeezing his hand. 'If we never try, we'll never fail.'

Now he looked up, realising that the garden had fallen quiet. His kids had stopped jumping on the trampoline and were staring silently at a point behind him.

Turning around, he saw that Louise had walked in through the garden gate and was standing in front of the house with her two suitcases. He barely recognised her. She'd cut her hair short and looked tall and tanned in a floaty white dress.

The kids began to scream and run towards her, and the four of them tumbled laughing into the grass.

'Hello, Henrik,' Louise said when she'd caught her breath.

She was beautiful. There was something fundamentally different about her face. Her gaze was soft, her brow smooth; he realised that she looked happy for the first time in ages.

'You've come home,' he said.

'Back at work from tomorrow,' she said.

It wasn't an answer.

'Home to stay?'

She looked at him for the longest time, and what he saw in her face made him nervous. It was something new; it was uncertainty.

'I haven't decided yet.'

76

Jensen had butterflies as she entered *Dagbladet*'s reception wearing her staff pass. It had only been eight months, but she was a different person. She'd grown up.

Ea was changing too. She'd begun to shuffle across the living-room floor and developed her first tooth. In just a few months she would be walking.

Jensen was glad that her mother had decided to stay, and not just because this meant she could return to work sooner than anticipated.

Her mother was smart, irreverent and surprisingly funny. Despite never showing an interest in food, she was also an imaginative cook, putting tasty meals on the table each night. Jensen had bought canvases and materials for her, and she'd begun to paint again.

It was Marion who insisted on being Ea's childminder, at least for the time being. 'It'll be a chance for me to make up for a few things,' she said.

'There's nothing to make up for,' Jensen told her. Any self-pity she might have felt in the past over her unconventional childhood had been misguided, she realised. Her mother's sacrifice had been far greater than her own.

None of them had wanted to talk any more about Andreas Lund, determined that he should have no further place in their lives.

Jensen smiled and waved at a couple of colleagues she recognised as she walked across to Gustav's desk in the corner of the room. He was travelling now, having finally had the breakthrough he'd been waiting for on his big exposé. No one knew what the story was about, or where he'd gone off to. His desk was swept clean; only his bucket hat remained, sitting on top of the monitor.

Jensen opened her laptop. Later this morning, she would be interviewing Sarah Funder about her new cold-case unit. It was an interesting story and she looked forward to seeing Sarah again. The two of them had exchanged a few messages over the summer. They were planning on going out for a drink soon.

'Welcome back.' She looked up to find Margrethe striding towards her. 'Am I glad to see you, at long last. Did you read the news?'

'What news?'

'Brix's wife is divorcing him.'

Jensen wasn't surprised. Brix's euphoria at being exonerated had been short-lived. He was innocent, but his womanising – which had been revealed along with the coverage of Andreas Lund's horrific crimes – hadn't gone down well with the public.

His big Hollywood movie project was the latest in a long line of casualties, and his book sales had gone off a cliff. He'd been afraid of being cancelled and now it had happened anyway.

'Fans. They make you and they break you,' Margrethe shrugged. 'Anyway, have you heard from my nephew lately?'

Come to think of it, Jensen hadn't heard from Gustav in a while. 'He's not been in touch with you either?' she said.

'Not for ten days or so. He refused to tell me what he was working on.'

'He's keen to impress you.'

'That's what I'm worried about. Alas, he lacks your experience,' said Margrethe and walked away.

Experience was all very well, but it hadn't helped her much recently, Jensen thought.

The older she got, the more doubt she felt about most things. When it came to investigative journalism, there was something to be said for youthful self-confidence.

'Is this desk free?' said a voice.

The man standing next to her was tall and thin with dark hair and strange pale-blue eyes that seemed to look right inside her. 'Sorry,' he said. 'Only this is my first day.'

'That makes two of us.'

They shook hands.

'I'm Malte, by the way. Malte Storm.'

He smiled at her and she sensed that this was the beginning of something. As she returned his smile, she decided it was time. She was going to say it without caveat or shame or explanation.

It was what it was.

'My name is Jensen. Fortuna Jensen.'

Acknowledgements

While many of the locations in *The Woman in the Wall* exist – such as Frederiksberg Gardens and the beautiful and atmospheric Frederik's Church, better known as the Marble Church – this book is a work of fiction, and any resemblance to real characters and events coincidental.

I would like to thank forensic pathologist Hans Petter Hougen, former homicide investigator Bent Isager-Nielsen and chief consultant in the Danish police Lars Jung for sharing of their knowledge and experience. Any mistake I may have made is entirely my own. Thanks to Kate and Sarah Beal of Muswell Press, and Lena Stjernström and Elisabet Brännström of Grand Agency, for their belief in me – and to Laura McFarlane and Catherine Best for their astute editing.

Long before this book reached you, I shared an early draft with my friend and fellow author Helen Pike, who has for years been one the first people to see my manuscripts. This book is dedicated to Helen and all the first readers who see narratives at their most tender and flawed and spur them on. Where would we be without you?

Finally, my thanks to the readers of this series for taking Jensen to heart.